The Witch of the Wood

The Witch of the Wood

Michael Aronovitz

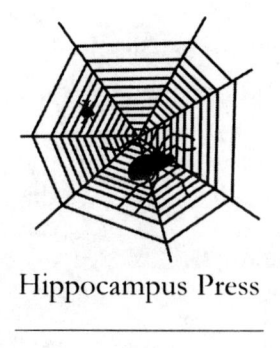

Hippocampus Press
New York

Copyright © 2014 by Michael Aronovitz

Published by Hippocampus Press
P.O. Box 641, New York, NY 10156.
http://www.hippocampuspress.com
All rights reserved.
No part of this work may be reproduced in any form or by any means without the written permission of the publisher.

Cover art by Lyndsay Harper.
Cover design by Barbara Briggs Silbert.
Hippocampus Press logo designed by Anastasia Damianakos.

First Edition
1 3 5 7 9 8 6 4 2
ISBN13: 978-1-61498-066-7

Contents

1. Witch 7

2. Warlock 47

3. Wolf 133

4. Wanderer 229

Chapter 1

Witch

Professor Rudy Barnes was like an assassin, if only for the fact that he could easily be lost in a crowd. He was in his mid-forties, divorced, tall, a bit gangly. He was balding, but didn't have any of those awful age-veins spidering his nostrils. He had black-rimmed glasses and close-set eyes, yet wore an honest countenance about him that set his students at ease when they came for help on their papers during his office hours. His coeds viewed him with sober trust, often slipping into little narratives about their overbooked schedules, their boyfriends, their families. Shana Porter, for example, was a lovely brunette, all cheekbones and lashes, a bit too skinny for her own good but unable to deny the points of those glamorous hips you could make out even through the nondescript bagginess of her oversized sweatpants. She had actually burst into tears when Rudy was carefully explaining to her the way to fix her issue with those overly dramatic pop-up words like "very" and "so."

Her wet sob surprised him, even cut him inside just a bit, but Rudy's face was a mask, well practiced. He leaned back, hands webbed across his stomach. He didn't have any tissues, and she used her fingers, wounded gaze flitting up at the ceiling.

"I'm so sorry, Professor," she said. "It's just that I can't sleep. There are these guys living right above my dorm room who get drunk until after midnight and then start wrestling and banging and knocking stuff over." She looked down and shrugged tragically. "And I miss my mother."

The back of her knuckles went up under her nose, and for the billionth time Professor Rudy Barnes marveled at the ironies life brought. Decades ago, when he was a freshman himself, a looker like Shana Porter wouldn't have even acknowledged his existence, let alone opened her world to him. She was out of his league even dressed down in her sweats and Ugg boots. When she'd first worn shorts last semester in Comp 101, he'd glanced twice, the second time a bit too long over the rim of his glasses. Definite athlete at least through her high school years, cheerleader or field hockey, pick your skirt, feed your fetish. But here he was, the nerd with an advantage, the stoic nerd who had gained enough life experience to finally enter the arena.

Passively, of course. Always passively.

"Shana," he said. "I understand what you're going through, really. Still, I want you to consider something for a moment. I don't mind telling you that the relationship between my own mother and me has been strained for years. Often, I want to tell her of my accomplishments, but I still feel she would condescend. Last year, in fact, I published an article in the *Winstrom Academic Journal*, and I kept this from her. Even at my age, I wanted her approval, and the pride in me kept it locked up like a secret." He crossed one knee carefully over the other. "You, on the other hand, have a mother to miss. You should consider yourself fortunate. As for the wrestlers, get a broom and bang the business end of it against the ceiling until they shut the hell up."

She forfeited a short laugh and looked up at him through those long, dusty lashes.

"How could anyone not love you, Professor?"

"Hell if I know." He hunched back in toward the desk. "Now look at this sentence and read it aloud for me. Then tell me which synonyms we could use to up the level of your discourse."

Shana would get an "A." Rudy would work the rest of his Thursday in a state of vague emptiness and disconnectedness, eventually leaving Widener to go to Rutherford University late that afternoon for a mandatory staff development session. He wasn't even a full-time professor there, just an adjunct, playing the game, splitting his time between Widener University, Cabrini College, and Rutherford in their continuing ed. program. Good old, dependable Rudy. The ghost in the eaves. The shadow-daddy.

He stopped at McDonald's for a Big Mac, skipping the fries so he could keep at least a shred of dignity, and ate it in his car in the parking lot. After this in-service (God, he hated these boring things) he had his apartment to look forward to. A bit dark. Fairly neat. A half bottle of Mondavi up on the sink, stains on the label. He drove up Route 7 missing his ex a bit, but he knew this was fraudulent. He missed having someone there to fill in the other side of the couch, that was all. In reality, it had gotten old, a job, a bad debt. When he'd quit public schools to ragtag around the university circuit the relationship went visibly sour, and when he'd defended himself with a rare defiance she told him in that tired kind of wheeze that his dreams were too expensive. Oh, she was the dream-killer all right, had been since their first year of marriage way back in the stone age, but now she was fifty pounds heavier with a case of old-lady face. They split last year, not really because of said argument, but because of a million other little failures and idiot-patterns they'd invented and stood by until they were just thanking God they could keep it civil.

He pressed the buttons on the radio and finally found the new one by Seether, shouting down from the rooftops, baby. He liked rock and roll, almost felt himself foolish for allowing this blemish of immaturity to continually surface, but he'd come to the conclusion that adults were all really fourteen-year-olds inside, amazing themselves every day that with the proper language and mannerisms they could pass through the world as absolute counterfeits.

It had gone dark by the time Rudy made the light at the Winfield Business Center, and when he turned right off the highway straight into the boonies, a light snow began filtering down. Back here there was a double yellow line, but the twists and jogs were tricky as the road narrowed and threaded its way into the wood. There was the Nut Brown Ale House, a light at Rock Ridge Road with a church on one corner and a train depot on the other, and from there it was all forest rising up at the moon on both sides. A former student had told Rudy that the dorms facing Rutherford's South Pasture were small, quaint, and smelled faintly of cow shit. You got used to it after awhile, got to like it even. It was sweet, like coming into a house where they were baking cookies and cinnamon sticks. Rudy had never smelled the cow shit. He taught adult education classes on the opposite side of campus in the ROTC building, a dark wetland in the background, but no cow pastures. He had about as much to do with campus life at Rutherford as the contractors re-facing the brick on Anderson Hall. In and out. Faceless. His usual.

He pulled in to the long drive leading to the Knickerbocker Quadrangle, where the third building in housed the Continuing Ed. offices and a huge first floor foyer they always used for faculty meetings. There were balloons tied to a stone entrance pillar and a sign that said, "Welcome Adjuncts." Yeah, hoorah. Rudy hoped this would be short and sweet, maybe some lukewarm theoretical garbage, like a presentation on formative assessment, or maybe just a PowerPoint on the latest computer advancements: tutorials for using the virtual library, techniques for troubleshooting the new gmail system so you didn't have to bother the tech support staff. As long as they got through the roundtable bullshit without too many questions prolonging it. Rudy hated "question-guys," those silver-haired, soft-talking bastards who always thought they looked oh-so bright and inquisitive, while everyone else in the room really wanted to yank their tongues out with a pair of hot pliers.

On the way up the steps, Rudy happened to glance down and see that he had sesame seeds on his black coat. He brushed them off, absently wondering if he was wearing more of his dinner than the dull arch lights were revealing, maybe a gob of special sauce on the zipper guard, a tiny strand of lettuce stuck at the bottom of his chin. He opened the door and looked for the bathroom. None to either side, and the presentation had started. There was a reception table, a buffet of appetizers and wine across from it, and rows of chairs facing away, most of them already occupied at the far end of the room in front of a podium.

"Hello," someone whispered. "And you are?"

"Rudy Barnes," he murmured, setting down his stuff. He unzipped his coat, absently feeling around his chest pocket for a pen and simultaneously reaching for one of those silly nametags they had there on the table in a glass dish. The man at the pulpit was doing some sort of long introduction for the head of Human Resources, all yuck-yuck and campy and smug, as if the adjuncts would do best to envy and appreciate the camaraderie of the office staff.

"Well, hello, Rudy!" she said, still a whisper, soft and professional. "It's so nice to finally meet you!"

He glanced down at the woman sitting at the other side of the table taking names, and suddenly wished he had detoured to a bathroom to check his coat, his face, and his tie to make sure it was centered. She was stunning, black hair cut in a shoulder-length soft-feathered bob, her face a sketch of daring edges and lines, thin along the jaw, sharp at the nose and chin. And there was a sparkle about her, like Champagne, like diamonds. She had soft brown eyes, but they were mischievous. She had a wide smile, but her teeth were white and even. Rudy let his glance fall, just for the barest flicker down south a bit, and he almost forfeited an audible groan. Her collar was open and there was cleavage nice and deep. And sun freckles. Rudy Barnes was a sucker for texture, and he was feeling it below the belt now. He looked up quickly, and her smiling eyes widened at him for a bare second as if to say, *"Shame on you!"* then blended right back into an expression of warm and personable courtesy.

The Witch of the Wood

"I'm April Orr," she said. "Materials and Support. We've e-mailed a number of times."

Rudy offered his hand. "Glad to see you," he said.

"Hmm," she said, taking his hand, still smiling, but looking at him a bit sideways. Did she just made a chiding yet welcoming reference to his "Glad to *"see"* you" . . . teasing him about the way he'd just been caught looking at her tits? Her fingers were smooth and long and he was fully aroused and suddenly sure she would see it. But she never looked down. Yes, women really were stronger than men, and here was the empirical proof. Oh, there was a paper in this for sure.

Someone came into the periphery to Rudy's left and hissed his name, the cold coming off him, forcing Rudy to move a step to the side. April addressed the guy politely, all confidence, leaning forward and flashing that wide, welcoming smile, and Rudy just stared on for a second, arms dangling down. That was a smile meant for *him*, and no matter how irrational that feeling was, he felt it right down to his tailbone just the same. His mouth was ajar. The newcomer was reaching for a nametag and April's eyes slid back over. She'd caught him staring again! Would his social blunders never cease? But she crinkled up her nose, shoulders shrugging all cutesy and personal, as if they had just shared a joke, or a third-grade Valentine, or one of those middle school message clovers that revealed they were meant for each other. Then she was back to her newcomer, talking about some science workbook that was in the module, yet only available through the department website.

Rudy shuffled off and took a seat in the back row next to a woman with a screaming tight ponytail, a pants suit, and a briefcase. He had the aisle chair, so there was room on his left for his book bag and small thermal lunch bag with the yogurt in it, just in case his stomach started growling in the middle of one of those quiet moments where the "dynamic" speaker was playing one of his dramatic pauses. Of course, if he opened it after an offense, the rip of the Teflon would key everyone in on the fact that he was a guy in his mid-forties controlling an "issue," so he opened it up as a precaution and got out a Yoplait.

He ate spoonfuls of banana-strawberry miserably. He was a middle-aged man with a gurgling stomach and strategies to handle it just long enough so he could go back to a dark, sparsely furnished apartment. He had female students who idolized him and shared nothing with him in common. He had a broad circle of acquaintances more settled in the world, who had all made the better choices far earlier. All the women he knew had married doctors or lawyers or plumbers who had their own businesses or dentists or financial wizards or professors who had actually gone on and *earned* their Ph.D.s so after getting tenure they could afford a trip to the Caymans or a summer place in Cape May. And what did Rudy have to offer? His dry wit? His stoic ability to correct rambling sentences? A shitty apartment, a cheap car, and a health plan that didn't even have reasonable co-pays?

Rudy crossed his legs the other way and took another spoonful of this foul, nasty, oversweet lady-paste. He swallowed silently, barely focusing on the dean behind the podium, talking about this new requirement from the state that made the university responsible for more out-of-class assignments to represent added seat time. The instructors had to come up with measurable proof in their syllabi, yes, and Rudy had to have some kind of meaningful companionship soon or he was going to just burst, or die, or more likely wither and finally blow off to some unnoticed corner like a curl of black ash.

"And now, to talk about updates and materials, I'll sacrifice the stage here for Helen and April."

There was a scatter of applause, and Rudy sat a bit straighter in his chair. Free look. Wouldn't even have to cock his head. And she just *couldn't* be as perfect as she'd seemed sitting behind the table. That would make all this absolutely unbearable. No. She had to have cankles or a severe case of bubble-ass or doughy flesh rolls sagging over her elbows, or maybe a big black mole on the back of her neck with a coarse hair growing out of it like the leg of a spider.

Movement to his left, and he kept his glance forward, letting her naturally enter his field of vision.

"Oh, my God," he muttered. It was faint, barely a whisper, but the pants suit next to him shifted her position. She'd heard! The secret was out! Rudy Barnes had the hots for the materials lady! Call the papers, put it on Google!

She had a dancer's body, lean and strong, and personality just bursting from all angles: the supple neck, the black feathery shawl across her shoulders, the hourglass waist, the yellow silk skirt with frays dangling just above the knee. It took all Rudy's willpower to keep his mouth closed. She had strong-looking, shapely calves snugly covered by black leggings and finished off at the ends with high-heeled lace-up witch's boots, clicking smartly up to the podium.

The other lady talked first. She was tall and spindly with odd, frizzy hair and a bit of a New York accent that she played up a bit, keeping it "real." Something about mandatory attendance and snow cancellations. Rudy stared at April Orr, drowning himself in this bonus one-way face-time, studying every curve and hollow. He wanted to kiss her throat. He wanted to touch her and make her groan, make submission flash through those gorgeous, sparkling eyes.

April Orr approached the podium with shy confidence and spoke carefully, clearly, each word a fragile little portrait dancing on the air. By the time she was finished talking about the move the department had made between scholastic publishers because of delivery and bonus compu-lab materials, Rudy was almost in pain. She concluded to the spatter of applause and walked back down the aisle, eyes straight forward, measuring her steps, manufactured smile.

Speaking in front of crowds made her nervous—oh, Rudy was dying!

The rest of the presentation was standard fare: a dean talking about a move toward more universal syllabi, one of the department chiefs gently chiding professors who were rumored to have lately succumbed to brash students asking for their four-hour class sessions to be cut shorter, a techie showing the newest icons leading to the latest files and fields that were going to make course layouts more expeditious (that is, if we didn't all die of old age trying to remember all the passcodes and pathways), the usual. By the end of it all, Rudy was glazed and dull and deadened like everyone else in the room, and he just wanted to get the hell home. When the initial speaker suggested they all stick around and read one another's nametags, Rudy gathered his effects and made a bee-line for the door.

Of course, the sign-in table had been long folded up and removed, so any chance of seeing April Orr again was gone. She'd probably left right after her speech, scooting back to a big house with cushy furniture, a roaring fireplace, two pedigree Labradors, and a kitchen with an island in the middle of it. If her husband wasn't home, he'd certainly text a number of times through the evening, in the short break he was taking from performing a delicate heart surgery, or the multi-million-dollar merger he was burning the midnight oil to save, or the old, dusty law books he'd found that would crack the case of the century. No, Rudy hadn't looked at her left hand, but there was no way on God's green earth that a looker like April Orr could possibly have anything less than a boulder on her ring finger.

He got to the archway and looked out the window. The snow had turned to sleet coming down in a driving slant, so he put his stuff on the floor and dug in his bag for his umbrella. It was one of those short black four-dollar jobs, with one of the skeleton ribs busted under the hood.

"Super Fresh or Giant?" she said.

For a moment, it didn't compute.

"Hmm?" Rudy said, still struggling with the stubborn spring locking clip. An arm linked with his and he stopped, caught a hint of perfume. He looked down and April Orr was right here, close up, touching him, and even though it was just a polite and perfunctory gesture, like shaking hands or waving hello, she was, in fact, *touching him.* She looked at the broken fixture.

"I'd say Super Fresh, the umbrella stand by the flowers and watermelons. Classy." She looked at him directly then. "Walk me to my car? I left my umbrella in the trunk."

Rudy paused for a moment, and someone who had just brushed past them opened the bay door. A sharp wind cut across the foyer, and April linked both of her hands around Rudy's elbow now, snuggling in closer, stamping her pretty little black boots.

"Pretty please?"

"Yes. Of course," Rudy said. He looked forward and nodded a bit, hating himself for the puritanical manner he'd adopted, but also knowing it was the best he had in the wardrobe. He was poor and book-smart, socially challenged and practiced in patriarchal politeness. Of course, chance favored his coming away from this empty-handed in reference to his instinctive fantasies, but at least he was going to walk her to her car properly.

Their footsteps made echoes on the stone floor, and out in the night the wind brought darts of sleet from the left, April's side.

"Jesus Lord!" she said. Her fingers closed over Rudy's, and he forfeited the umbrella. His arm went around her shoulder then, and she drew into him. Just like that.

"Smooth," she said wryly, her step quickening with his.

"It was innocent, I assure you."

"Then you used me as a wind-buffer, Rudy?"

He looked down into her face, the wind whipping her hair around, her smile still genuine.

"Never."

She glanced off and nodded a bit to the right.

"I'm the black Volvo over there."

They adjusted course, and it brought more of the icy wind to her back. She squealed a bit, snuggling in harder, her free hand going around his back now, and suddenly Rudy had the feeling he was being had. It was just too perfect, too easy. And it wasn't only her lack of an umbrella, or the timing in the archway, or the goddamned direction of the wind. It was the way he had just been thinking about all he lacked in terms of clever wordplay and social maneuvering, and she'd somehow managed to make him look witty and suave. What was she feeding here, and the better question was why? Was there some kind of office pool going down, odds stacked upon how much of a fool she could make out of him? The wind changed, blasting in from the front for a second, and they bent into it. He fell then to internal argumentation, weighing the improbability of April Orr choosing him because of some credible need or attraction against the idea that she would actually profile him for a prank. And neither made sense. None of this did. Hell, maybe she really did just want a companion in the sleet, and this, coupled with the crinkling of her nose, the clever conversation, and the fact that she was the most beautiful woman he'd ever seen made Rudy feel horribly lonely.

"This is me," she said, releasing the umbrella that Rudy did his best to shield her with as she opened the door and tossed her purse on the seat. When she bent in and sat, her skirt rode up showing off an inch or two of thigh, and then there was a sudden "whap-whup" sound as Rudy's umbrella pulled right out of his hand, a wounded bat flapping off on the knifing wind to the darkness of the lot.

"Shit," he said, the sleet blasting him like wet shot. April got hit too, the open door a poor shield. She gave a short screech and shut it, but before Rudy could give a little wave and run off the other way with his free hand in his pocket, he heard the engine give nothing more than an audible "click." The headlights flashed, then deadened. The door opened slowly.

"My battery is dead, Rudy. Can you drive me home? I don't live far, just off campus."

Her hand was saluted across her forehead, eyes batting, and the cold rain made lovely, running beads down her cheeks. Her dress was damp-darkened now, that beautiful leg offering its long shape all the way up to the hip.

"Of course," he said.

She somehow made it seem graceful, getting back out of her car and pushing her wet skirt between her knees as the wind threatened to blow it up over her head. When she took her place again beneath Rudy's arm, both were soaked, his coat shiny with it, strands of her black hair plastered to her cheeks. They hunched together then into the wind of the storm and hurried to Rudy's Toyota. Once inside, soaked to the bone, April Orr scooched on over and cuddled up next to him, and by this time Rudy had stopped questioning this about her. She was cold, that was all. He was a body. Available. She was simply charming enough to be able to borrow these moments for her own comforts, no questions asked, no string attached. Some people just "had it." April Orr was one of them, and it was almost ungentlemanly to suspect there was more to it than that.

Rudy concentrated on his driving, peering through the smear the wipers left on the windshield and navigating the dark road unfolding before them. Sleet swarmed in from the left and made odd rainbows in the dull blare of the headlights. April was wet and warm and close and she smelled good. She guided him to the right off the main road, and two lefts back in toward the thickest part of the wood. There, in a culvert, was a white house with a river running to the side of it and a walking bridge. Rudy pulled up into the drive, put it in park, and turned toward her. She brought her palms to his face.

"Thank you, Rudy," she said. Then she bent in and pressed her lips to his. It wasn't long enough to be considered what the kids called "first base" when he was growing up, but it was no peck either. There was audible suction on the release, and they looked at each other.

"April . . ." he managed.

"Do you want to come in for a minute," she said. "To get warm?"

"Are you kidding?"

"No."

"I was being rhetorical."

She put her palm on the chest of his wet coat.

"Then come in just for a minute. I'll make you a cup of hot chocolate."

"But you hardly know me," he said, wanting immediately to kick himself for the gentle scolding, the fatherly tone he'd adopted, the role he just couldn't help but fall into time and again.

She looked at him with big, serious eyes.

"Then you won't come in?"

"I didn't say that."

"Good," she said, brightening, reaching for the door. "It's the gentlemanly thing to do."

Rudy paused. Hadn't he just thought that, or something like it, something with similar wording just a minute or so before? What on earth was going on here? As if chiding him for pausing, she wasn't even waiting for him to be her weather-guard at this point, and he got out quickly, awkwardly, following her silhouette to the front door, the surrounding trees covering the sky in scattered patterns thick enough to fend off the sleet to relative intermittence. April opened the door and pushed into the foyer, then bending up an ankle to the back of her thigh to remove her boot. Of course, she was a bit off-balance and used Rudy's shoulder for support; he got there with perfect timing, his or hers, undeterminable. Oh, they were in rhythm, to be sure, and Rudy played the mimic, kicking off his wet shoes, removing his coat, and putting it on the hook next to hers, his scarf right there by her shawl. There was a towel on a hook, and she used it first, brusque and brisk. When she was done, she gave a little pout and pose, funny, because her hair had frizzed a bit. Then, the nose crinkle and shrug Rudy had fallen in love with back at the sign in table, and she handed over the damp towel.

"Dry off and come on in, Rudy. I'll put on the hot chocolate."

She flicked a light and walked off toward the back kitchen area, and Rudy took a step or two into the living room, rubbing the towel across the top of his head, then his face, drawing in a breath, smelling her. He was actually tempted to pocket the towel, and while on one level this bothered him because it was so akin to stealing underwear out of a drawer, it more deeply disturbed him that even considering this symbolic action confirmed his assuredness that he wasn't going to get to experience her fragrance close up in a more personal way. It was an admission of failure before failure, and while he despised himself for it, he was always the fundamental realist. April Orr was friendly, kind, maybe some kind of weird philanthropist when it came to wallflowers like Rudy Barnes, drawing them out by the hand and making them feel some kind of worth. But she wasn't going to fuck him, not now, not tomorrow, and Rudy knew better than to think that by some strange bend of fortune this plot was going to twist. He'd just been around too long to believe in miracles.

He stepped into the living room and remained standing at the edge of it. The place was welcoming but strangely unfurnished, an easy chair that seemed a bit too low to the ground, a lamp beside it, a fireplace without irons, a sofa that dipped down a bit toward the wall as if one of the leg supports were broken or bent in.

There was a noise from behind, an audible creak from the stairs.

And right here and now, Rudy was dead-positive that April Orr's husband had woken from the second-floor bedroom, shock of graying hair sticking up on one side, jammy-bottoms stuffed in his sweat socks, bathrobe floating behind him like a cape. And he'd grabbed the Smith and Wesson double-barrel from the top shelf in the closet, shoved in two humongous rounds, and snapped it closed with that deadly, masculine click of hook, clasp, and cold oiled steel. He'd never actually fired it before, didn't really know its range, but this towel-sniffing, cleavage-watching son of a bitch was going to be the guinea pig, taking advantage of a poor girl just trying to get shielded from the sleet.

Rudy turned hard.

There was a boy on the stair, two at the eldest, dressed in red pajamas that had the feet sewn onto them. He had crystal-blue eyes beneath arching brows and blond hair that lay on his forehead like corn silk. He had his mother's jawline, and he had a hold of the banister with one hand, the other playing with his bottom lip, hooking it, keeping it wet and ajar. Then, slowly . . . *slowly*, he turned his head toward the kitchen, keeping his steady gaze fixed on Rudy, pivoting the eyes in the skull to give the illusion of remaining stationary within the swiveling base, and it was a deliberate move that made it appear the kid was measuring him from the corner of his eye, and the eyes were suddenly crystalline doll's eyes, and Rudy was overcome with an irrational flood of childlike fear one would associate with clowns, or monkey toys that bashed little cymbals together, or eighteenth-century marionettes that had squared off mouths that slowly dropped open.

The feeling of dread was crippling, and Rudy sat right there on the floor, his long knees angling out at odd points. Normally, Rudy Barnes was the cold analyst, practical, sensible, breaking things down to their working parts and deducing flat truths, and he fought this irrational burst of melodramatic foreboding with everything he had. There was nothing about this rather handsome toddler that was actually frightening, nothing the little boy could do that would harm him, but Rudy felt absolute terror in places he wasn't used to focusing on: his shoulders, the back of his neck, his throat, his spine. He forced himself to break glance, looking off toward the part of the house April had run off to, trying to scrape forward the rational adult at the rear of his mind who was mouthing, *"Where's the babysitter?"* And when Rudy turned back to the stairs, the boy was no longer standing on them.

He was right there at Rudy's knee.

He was wobbling a bit now, rocking back and forth, and Rudy couldn't breathe. This was impossible, yet not, an optical illusion as if the boy had jumped camera frames, but he was right here before him just the same.

The boy crawled into his lap, and suddenly the fear vanished, as if it were sucked right out of Rudy's stomach, replaced now by an overwhelming desire to protect this child, to hold him, to kill for him if necessary, and Rudy understood this wave of fierce sentiment as little as he'd been able to fathom his feelings of horror. The boy smelled like baby and April Orr, and he reached up to play with Rudy's sideburn.

"Are you going to ride Mommie now?" he said. "Like a horsie?"

Fingers slipped under the boy's armpits, and April straightened, hauling him up to her chest where he buried his face in the hollow of her neck and collarbone, his legs dangling down. She kissed the side of his temple long and deep, and whispered into his hair, "You got out of your crib again, honey." The boy lifted an arm and slung it around her, and she glanced down at Rudy. "I see you've met little Wolfie. He's a quick one, isn't he? Don't worry, it just takes a little getting used to. He moves when you blink."

She padded off and up the stairs, sing-songing softly over her shoulder, "Be right down."

"O.K.," Rudy whispered back, still sitting cross-legged on the floor.

Are you going to ride Mommie now?

Did he hear that correctly?

Like a horsie?

It hit a deep chord, the image that boy had put in his head, the way it was voiced as if this was the natural way things should go, as if it was not only acceptable, but expected that he mount this woman and pump her until he burst.

She was back on the stair now, and Rudy stood heavily. His breath was thick and, as he moved toward her, she came to the landing to meet him.

Something snapped.

It was red and high and urgent and savage, and it was him and it was not, as if he stood like a silent, hulking shape in the corner watching himself go through the motions of coming undone, taking her by the shoulders, turning her, pulling her dress sleeves and bra straps down, ripping the clothing, feeling at her breasts.

"Grab the banister," he growled, "Do it!"

"Oh!" she said, as if to say, *So it's gone to this level? You brute! I didn't realize it was such an emergency!* and there was such sarcasm in it because she'd *caused* the "emergency," and Rudy reached down and pulled the bottom of her damp dress over her hips. She arched up onto her toes for him and Rudy saw in slants and flashes it seemed, her long legs, the black stockings going nearly to the crotch, the black silk underwear that had slipped deep between her buttocks on one side, and he squatted a bit to have one good stroking of her thighs, then went impatiently back north to rip away that undergarment as if it were an enemy.

"Oh!" she said again, and this time there was a short laugh in it, like, *Is that the best you've got?* and Rudy went into what felt like a frenzy. His pants were at his ankles, and when she tried to shift he jerked her hips back in place where he wanted them. When he entered her it was not slow, and when she turned her head back to him, mouth dropped wide open, indignant eyes accusing him as if to say, *Really?* he thrust in her so hard and so fast that she actually did have to hold the banister for dear life, palms for buffers, arms as shock absorbers, knuckles bone white.

Rudy pistoned his hips furiously, making hard, flat sounds against her, finishing in a series of rough, panting bursts. When he was done he rested on her back for a bare second, and when he pulled out of her he fell off to the side, almost stumbling over the lasso his pants had made around his ankles. He drew them up, clumsy and drained, breathless. He turned to her sheepishly, and she was on the first stair now, face wet with tears that had made their way down to the crevices of her nostrils. Her hand was up at her mouth and she shook her head slowly. Then she ran up the stairs, holding the hem of her dress above her knees with one hand, the torn bodice up to her chest with the other.

Rudy didn't follow.

He went to the foyer and numbly got on his coat, never more ashamed and embarrassed in his entire life. He hadn't given her one bit of consideration, offering her nothing for her own pleasure. He'd fucked her like a whore and she despised him now; that was made clear by her reaction on the stairs.

He walked into the wind, got in his car, and backed out of the driveway, hating himself, hating the world.

But by the time he'd made it to Route 7, his emotions had twisted down to a sick and cold spreading fear. He'd ripped her clothes, hadn't he? She'd moved and he'd yanked her back in place. She'd said "Oh!" a couple of times, but did he hear it wrong? Had she really said, "No"?

Did he just . . .

He thought of her standing on the first stair, her hand up at her mouth in pure shame and disgrace.

Did he just rape April Orr? He stopped at the light at Hunter

Hill Pike and suddenly expected flashers in his rearview. But wait. Did he not have a case? Did she not initiate this whole thing? Kiss him on the lips? Put her hand on his chest? Ask him in for hot cocoa, for Christ's sake?

She said "no" twice.

But that was "Oh!," that clever little game where the female played innocent, as if she didn't know that this was exactly what was on both your minds, right?

You pulled her in place and held her there.

Was she really trying to escape? She'd just posed for him, making that perfect angle of legs, ass, and arched back like some perfect piece of geometry. She'd *wanted* him to pull her back into place so he could feel more in control, more manly, the wallflower becoming Paul fucking Bunyan.

She looked back over her shoulder at you in open-mouthed indignation.

But wasn't that more of the "Go Daddy" pouty thing, playing the role of the bad girl, the spoiled brat getting a lesson?

You made her cry, put her hand to her mouth, and shake her head slowly back and forth. If that's not a clear reflection of the word "NO," then what is?

Rudy drove on, suddenly aware of other discomforts besides his probable guilt in what was unfolding as some horrific sexually based legal offense. He was cold, first of all, frozen to the bone, and now that the car began to warm around him, he noticed that he was wet, more so than what the sleet should have been able to accomplish on his treks to and from the car. He was actually soaked through in strange areas like the seat of his pants and all over his torso, his shirt a cold snakeskin, his toes frozen and numb. He felt freezer-burned. And his loin area stung as if someone had taken sandpaper to his pelvis, then down in the folds made by his upper inner thighs.

Streets and the vague shapes of buildings flashed by outside in blurs through the side windows, and the closer Rudy came to his apartment the more uncomfortable he felt physically, as if he had frostbite. And by the time he pulled into his usual spot in the lot by the dumpster and Goodwill clothing bin, his whole body was throbbing, his crotch area raging.

He pushed the car door open and pulled himself up off the seat using the roof. The wind plastered his clothes to him, harshly reminding him of the fact that somehow, some way, his clothes were soaking wet, as if he'd fallen in the creek by the walking bridge and forgotten about it in his haste to exit the premises. When he bent in to get his bag, he saw the water stain he'd left on the seat.

Oh yes.

He'd soaked it in a dark oval, the line of his ass smack in the center of it.

He shut the door, and the wind came up so fiercely he almost screamed breathlessly into it. He clapped across the pavement, free arm across his face, limping, thoughts jumbled in fear and discomfort.

Inside, the shadows were thick like the feeling in his throat. There was a newspaper on the sofa, a throw-blanket on the chair. Rudy dropped his bag and peeled off his clothes, leaving them there on the living room floor. He needed to think about this, to figure out exactly what he had just done, what the consequences might be, and what on earth he would say if asked, for God's sake. He also wanted a look at himself, and he stumbled into the bathroom. Cold he could handle; frostbite, manageable. But what was going on in the creases between his genitals and legs and slightly above in his pubic area? He almost laughed. Here was another paper to be written, concerning which you focused on first, your possible moral undoing or an immediate physical vexation. Yes. As his ex would have said, "It's all about you, isn't it?" Of course. Pain first. Ethics later.

Rudy Barnes turned on the bathroom light.

He looked down.

And almost fainted.

* * *

The hot bath had steamed the mirror, and Rudy kept draining an inch or two from the top and capping it back off with the hottest water he could stand, the emergency bottle of Johnny Walker in hand, a third of it gone, mother's milk for men measuring the tainted virtue in their souls.

And making battle plans.

First stop tomorrow would be the hospital if the rash didn't go down. He didn't know what it was . . . had never seen anything quite like it, but April Orr had given him something. He had swelling in a rough arch around his privates, like a horseshoe branded across his pubic area and down along his upper inner thighs. And there were dark tiny dots in the reddened skin, sensitive to the touch, burning and smarting. At first, Rudy thought they were crabs, but they were not moving. They were embedded, like blackheads, part of the skin, raised up in high irritation. As for the rest of him, his extremities were fine, now soothed and supple in the hot soapy bathwater.

He took a long pull from the bottle and then raised his forearm, coughing hard into it.

His situation was anything but "supple" or sublime. In terms of the scale of justice he'd made in his head, plates on each side, a Greek goddess in the middle, he'd long forced himself to decide it was a stone draw, rape or no rape; there was simply too much evidence on either side to go one way or the other. And while the tears formed in the curves of her nostrils and running over her lips really tipped the balance toward the dark side, the intellectual in him calmly and rationally focused on the linking of arms, the kiss in the car, and especially that small gesture of going up on the toes at the banister, as if presenting herself in willing sacrifice. Oh, rationalization wasn't difficult at all when you did deconstructive analysis against the contrary viewpoint. Theories, even those built on shifty platforms, could come off like fact; it was an old game, one Rudy had perfected through years of teaching students to dismantle oppositions and work around their own annoying logical fallacies.

It was the gritty realistic side of him that kept him drinking, the paranoid realist that made him consider what he would actually say or do if there was, in fact, an accusation. He was no legal expert, but didn't they do rape kits as on Law and Order, going into her vaginal canal looking for abrasions, the rest of her body for contusions? He'd fucked her hard enough to make ripples travel up through her buttocks like whitecaps in a hurricane, thrusting and pitching his hips violently enough to bruise her palms on the banister, gripping her up and holding her in place with enough squeeze and press to leave marks. It wouldn't look like sensitive lovemaking, that was for sure.

Suddenly, Rudy stopped drinking mid-draught, the backlash burning his nose, his eyes watering up.

Oh God. Oh shit.

He took the bottle from his lips and almost dropped it in the water, his jaw slack, face ashen and pale.

He'd suddenly figured out the riddle of the child and how April could have left a two-year-old toddler alone in the house. Of course, the boy hadn't been alone. There must have been, in fact, a babysitter upstairs all along, probably some fifteen-year-old girl who wore braces and horn-rimmed glasses, sitting in the soft lamplight by the sleeping child, twisting a lock of hair behind her ear, doing her math homework.

And she'd seen it all, most likely from the shadows at the top of the stairs, scarred now for life. Oh, Rudy was going to jail, certainly. If there was a husband up there, he would have stopped it. No, it was a teenage girl, watching in mute horror, a bona fide witness. The two of them were talking about it right now, comforting each other, gathering the strength to dial 911 if they hadn't already.

At any time now there would be a hard knock on the door, men in the hallway asking for entry, a badge and a few in plainclothes, all with short, slicked-back hair, square jaws, and stony eyes, asking their questions, curling their noses ever so slightly as if the room smelled like garbage, not wanting to touch him except with their fists and the bone-hard points of their boots and dress shoes.

There would be a scandal. He didn't know if this actually warranted a "perp walk" with flashbulbs popping and reporters sticking microphones in his face, but it would make the papers for sure. "Professor Rapes Office Assistant." His mother would be mortified, his ex disgraced. He'd do time, grow old in prison, never work in higher education again, come out of lock-up a broken man, helpless and homeless.

He stumbled out of the tub, drained it, dried off gingerly, and eventually crawled under the covers, drunk and shivering, waiting for the crisp pocket to warm to his body temperature. The horseshoe rash was killing him, inflamed and smarting and underscored by a deep itching he knew he couldn't get to without something medieval, or at least some sort of sharp gardening tool. He'd treated it with Vaseline, and it did nothing but make him feel greasy, as if he wasn't dirty enough already. Normally he slept naked because clothes made him sweat, but tonight he had on wool jammie bottoms and his thick St. Joseph's University sweatshirt. Either way it was going to be a damp night, and Rudy clasped his hands together while lying there on his back in the semi-darkness.

Dear Lord, I've never been a praying man, but I ask your forgiveness tonight. Please don't take away what little I have, please let me be all right. I . . . I may have hurt someone. Please let me know what to do.

He was met with silence.

All night he lay awake, running the incident through his mind, terrified of the banging on the door that was sure to come any second. He tossed and turned himself sober, making multiple trips to the bathroom, and by the time morning light crept under the shades he knew at least a couple of things.

The Witch of the Wood

First, the horseshoe rash had gone purple at its edges, infected and raised up like a relief map. He needed professional medical attention. Now.

Second, he was going to go to the police and confess to the sexual assault of April Orr. If there was going to be one last thing he'd have control of, it was his own sense of personal justice. Considering even the possibility that he could have hurt that beautiful, delicate woman, it was simply the right thing to do.

But he didn't go to the police.

He didn't even make it to the hospital.

They were quills, or stingers, or splinters of some kind. The next morning Rudy had showered, focusing on the "sensitive area" with a wash towel, then a plastic back-scrubber, and finally a fucking soapstone, razing the skin raw, drawing blood. He'd gone all night letting it work its maddening itch deeper and deeper until it actually felt as if it was in the base of his balls, and this was payback. He was going to the hospital anyway, right?

Of course, it felt like heaven for the moment, then fell right back into that deep-seated itching, now seasoned with a fresh stinging, and when Rudy shoved his pelvis forward into the shower spray, blood running off in little threads, he saw a few of the dark "dots" poking up out of the skin. He dropped the soapstone behind him and picked at one of the offenders, thumb and index in an O.K. sign. It pulled the skin a bit with it, but came right out, a cork from a bottle, and though there were about a hundred of these little bastards, Rudy actually felt relief from this solo evacuation.

He held it up close to the eye. What was this? Did April have some kind of vindictive, stinging parasite infesting her privates? He was no doctor, but he simply found it hard to believe that she could have this multitude of vermin nested in her crotch area without climbing the walls and constantly going at it with a hairbrush or something.

Rudy reached out around the curtain and set the sliver down on the sink, where it swam in a diluted red droplet. Down low, the bleeding was petering off, and Rudy soaped and rinsed one more time, gingerly, gingerly. After drying off, he went to the kitchen and got a monkey dish, a short drinking glass, and a bottle of alcohol. Of course, he had seriously considered going to get this looked at professionally, the original plan, since it was possibly some new strain of African swarming mite, dormant and incubating in the loins of its female human host, immediately curling up its hindquarters and stinging out in case of contact from the human male. And maybe these barbs had poison in them?

But he wasn't poisoned, just infected a bit by the penetration of the stingers themselves.

And there was nothing "alive" down there between *his* legs. Rudy was no entomologist, but he had enough common sense to know that bugs didn't just sting and curl back into the home fold. With contact like this there would have been live ones transferred, eggs. And he would have been able to see them, since the "stingers" were big enough to draw out with his fingernails. No, he wasn't going to go to some emergency room, explaining first to the receptionist, then the nurse practitioner, next the "fellow" organizing the charts, and finally the doctor, with his female graduate assistant taking notes because they were a "learning facility," that he got quills, or barbs, or stingers, or splinters from a woman they'd advise he contact at his earliest convenience.

He got his beard trimmer and shaved off the entire triangle of hair, put the toilet seat down and a set a towel over it, poured the rubbing alcohol in the drinking glass and got out his tweezers, the sharp ones with the needle points. An hour and twenty minutes later, he had seventy-nine bloody barbs in a dish. The bathroom stank of sweat and pain and intensive finite exertion, his T-shirt soaked through under the arms and down the back of the neck.

He'd gotten them all.

Time to confess.

But he didn't confess, and this decision finally came from the same place inside him that had campaigned for home surgery. He was in the parking lot of South Detectives in the Visitors Section with the engine running, next to the handicapped slot and a sandwich board advertising both the hours for license photo I.D.'s, and a raffle that would make one eligible for a membership this summer at the Bala Swim Club, and he just couldn't make himself go in and say it.

And it wasn't the rash, his own self-loathing, nor even a fear of actual incarceration, at least he didn't want to think so. It was the possibility that it was not rape at all that stayed his hand here. What if the crying was part of the game for her, a release after the bait and catch? What if she had a husband who was away on a business trip? What if the babysitter upstairs had petered herself out on quadratic equations and fallen asleep in the lamplight? Yes indeed, what if this was all that it had seemed from the beginning, a fantasy played out, now sealed tight with the unspoken expectation that Rudy would keep his mouth shut and be an adult about it as they both went back about their lives? Would April Orr really want to admit to some detective, a reporter, a jury, her family, the *world* that she fucked some guy doggie style against the banister in the living room with her kid awake in the crib just upstairs?

And if she really wanted to make a federal case out of this, he'd have gotten that knock on the door by now, flashers in his rearview. Right?

Rudy's crotch area had gone from pinpricks and fire to a gnawing kind of ache that ebbed and pulsed, and his responsibilities became suddenly clear. He didn't look forward to it, but medicine didn't always taste like cherries. He was a bit hesitant in terms of possible inappropriate workplace suspicion, but the guise of casual vocation was fairly solid armor here. He backed out of his parking spot and wondered if Bravo Pizza was open yet. He wanted an Italian hoagie, no cheese, extra hot peppers and oregano. Then he had to make a stop at the drugstore for some gum, and back home to iron a set of dress clothes. Though he'd lucked out with the scheduling this semester leaving his Fridays free and clear, Rutherford University was open for business, all rattle and hum.

Uncomfortable, yes, but federal case, no.

Time to visit the Continuing Education Offices.

He had a couple of questions for the Materials and Support specialist.

Rudy Barnes had been nervous at different key points in his life, sure: coming to bat as a nine-year-old in a pressure cooker against the South Marple Little League Red Sox . . . playing a junior high school Battle of the Bands in the gymnasium in front of a crowd of a thousand . . . asking Lisa McFee to the senior prom in front of her friends in the lunchroom by the steam table and rack rollers.

But when you struck out looking, botched the high note in "Can You See the Real Me" in front of the student body, and got laughed at by the strawberry blonde who would later land first runner-up to the prom queen, they all just moved on. Forgot you. Focused on more interesting material promptly and assuredly.

The cold fact remained, however, that April Orr wasn't going to forget the events of last night *ever*, and that thought was absolutely crippling. Rudy sat there in the Rutherford parking area, acting as if he was searching for the right hanging tag for the rearview, stalling. Change of heart? Possibly. Nervous? How about terrified? What if she did translate the event as "forced," but had been too embarrassed to come forward in some official way? What if she just wanted to let it go, move on, and let the wound heal privately?

The Witch of the Wood

But the idea of never knowing the truth was unfathomable, living week to week in muted fear, always wondering if there would come a day when April Orr's therapist finally convinced her to face her demons. Then, that hard knock at the door.

Rudy made himself get out of the car. Like the moment he'd had the night before when he'd been somehow displaced as a dark, hulking figure in the corner watching himself tear at April Orr's dress, this also felt like an out-of-body experience. He was a witness to Rudy Barnes's walk to the gallows, the electric chair, the firing squad, across the parking lot. Students crisscrossed in front of him, hurrying to make their 10 o'clock classes, laughing, talking, looking in their cell phones, and he made his way between them, numb and awkward. What was he going to do when April looked up from her papers and the shame and the hatred, yes the pure and unadulterated *hatred* registered there in her eyes? What would he say to her?

Uhh . . . about last night . . . I was a little rough on ya, wasn't I, sweetie? Well, sorry about that. By the way, I might recommend for you a certain prescription pubicide, yeah, Houston, we have a bit of a problem.

He entered the building and walked through the carpeted hall to the office complex located to the right after the conference room and the men's lavatory. He'd only been here once before, when signing all his entrance papers and tax forms, and had wondered in the back of his mind where the girl's room was. Probably on the other side of these offices . . . I mean, how many places were you going to run pipes anyway . . . ?

He was here. Glass doors, curved reception counter, elderly secretary sitting behind it. She glanced up and now Rudy had to go in, no choice, no tomorrow. He pushed through and approached. She had dull white hair that was thinning up top, sprayed for position and cover, so a sour mood seemed rather expected. Rudy tried his best not to stutter and failed miserably.

"Could I . . . excuse me, could I see April Orr, please?"

She took her glasses off and let them dangle there at her chest on their chains. She folded her hands and leaned forward.

"Who's asking?"

Ordinarily, Rudy would have said something witty. In social situations he was a dead zero, but he had always been good with the old cronies behind desks in the workplace. Still, he wasn't ready for this, for any of it, and he faltered, regressed back to elementary school in the principal's office, or worse, in front of Ma, trying to explain why he'd set off an M-80 in the school toilet, or shot a beebee gun on the back porch, or lit a fire in a trash can out back.

"Uhh . . . yes . . . Rudy Barnes. I'm sorry. I'm an adjunct here and I have a question about . . ."

What? Think! Something of relevance, please!

"Materials," he managed. The woman pursed her thin, bluish lips. Stared at him. For a moment he actually thought she was going to tell him that his plea wasn't good enough. Instead, she reached for the phone, dialed an extension, and murmured into it, eyes still on him with what he read as wary disdain.

"She'll be out in a minute," she said, returning to her work. Rudy stared at her dumbly, and she glanced back up.

"Mr. Barnes, you can sit over there." She was pointing with her pencil, and Rudy looked behind him. Of course. A pair of waiting chairs. So you didn't stand at the counter like a dunce watching the secretary answer phones and file papers. He backed off and sat, wishing there were magazines to look at. He hadn't even brought his bag with him so he could fake grading papers.

Steps were coming from the hall to his right. His positioning had the arch acting as a shield, a torturous blind spot, and he fixed his stare at the carpet between his feet. Then she was there, dark flat-heeled shoes, charcoal slacks, dress shirt with a high white collar and black bead buttons, a vest. And long red hair, bobby pins, split ends. She had wide set eyes and fat ruddy cheeks; absolute "boy-face," and homely as hell.

A stranger.

"Rudy," she said, offering her hand for a good masculine shake. "Nice to see you again. Sorry, I had to run after my little speech last night. I had to get my brother from the airport, just back from Afghanistan. What can I do for you?"

Rudy sat where he was, looking up at her and blinking.

"I . . . uh . . . I was in the neighborhood and just wanted to make sure you got me signed in. I was late and I didn't want the powers that be to think I was ducking."

She crossed over to the counter and the old bat had a sheaf of papers waiting. "April" took it and gave a brief study.

"No, I marked you in." She returned it to be filed once again and came back over, arms folded now.

"How's the 122 class going? APA updated the manual last week, and I have a virtual copy online. The shelf text comes in next Wednesday—should I mail it to you?"

"That would be fine," Rudy said faintly. He was still sitting, looking up at her rather helplessly, twisting his fingers in his lap, embarrassed, but he had to say it. "April Orr, right?" She pushed out her lower lip and actually did that thing where she blew upwards to fluff her bangs.

"The one and only. Gosh, Rudy, you're as forgetful as I am!" She gave a hearty laugh and patted him on the shoulder. "Well, we all love a good conversation around here, but the pile on my desk isn't getting any smaller. Unless you'd like to help me alphabetize freshman plagiarism forms . . ."

"No!" Rudy laughed, palms out, finally playing it as it was presented before him, then pushing to his feet. "Thanks again, April, for everything."

The second he made the outer hallway, the plastic smile vanished. What on earth was going on here?

He walked across the parking lot and got in his car.

To go to her house and ask her.

Except there was no house. Rudy reforged the same path that he'd driven last night in the sleet, the right off the main road and then the two lefts, but when he came to the culvert there was no driveway, no residence. Rudy pulled in as far as he could off the road where there were old wear-lanes made in the dirt and wild grass, his tires crunching over morning crystal and frozen mire. He stopped. The exhaust rose from the back left and blew gently over the hood, falling in with this weird staging, this creepy scene unit unfolding all around him like dream theater.

Here in the culvert was a glen of sorts, to the side a river, and crossing it, a walking bridge, the same as last night yet different altogether. Rudy had only caught a glimpse of it in the semi-darkness through the driving sleet, but his impression had been "decorator bridge," made of the finest woods, newly installed. This ruin was years old, possibly hundreds, all stone, much of the base by the near bank chipped and eroded with lime deposits darkening the curve of the underside.

Rudy got out of his car, breath making little plumes on the air. There were footprints in the newly hardened mud, all his, going up and back into and out of the glen. He put his shoe in one of them and it was a dead match, and then he followed the prints, his breath-plumes getting shorter and harsher.

Like the odd, displaced familiarity of the bridge, the glen was a haunt of memory as well, except the easy chair that had seemed a bit too low to the ground was actually a tree trunk, cut at its base and petrified, the lamp beside it—a small spruce sapling with branches frozen over and cracked, the fireplace—a part of an old fieldstone wall half buried in brambles and overgrowth, and the sofa dipping down on one side—a huge uprooted oak covered in ivy and frozen yellowed moss.

There was a sound, something faint on the cold wind, so slight it was almost lost, to the left where the stairway would have been. It was a suckling sound. Rudy looked over with wide eyes to where the banister had stood and saw a humongous maple, broken at waist height from some past storm and angling up and off into the forest where it had fallen and come to rest on the buttress of other surrounding foliage.

There at the apex of the crack, between stubborn bark on both sides that had stretched and held, Rudy saw something move.

He stumbled away and ran for his car, his foot catching sideways in one of his frozen prints giving one of those twists and yanks he'd feel more tomorrow. He thought suddenly that his car door would be locked, and while he pulled uselessly and bloodlessly on the handle, some spotted arm would come from under the fender, sneaking up his trouser leg, something with nodules and tentacles gliding over the roof, snapping for purchase around his shoulders and throat.

The door creaked open, and there on the wind he heard a moaning sound from behind him. It sounded like *"Rudy..."*

He bent into the car, dragged his legs after him, and slammed shut the door, all the sounds of the forest cutting off to the quick.

"Rudy," she said from the back seat.

The car seemed to jerk forward, zero to ninety or more, all G-forces pressing Rudy into the cushions and hard against the headrest. His gritted teeth were exposed, lips curdling around them, eyes wide and tearing. In front of him, the forest remained absolutely stationary, but for all intents and purposes he was being hurtled through space at hundreds of miles per hour. There was movement in the rearview, and though he strained to focus on it, he couldn't quite get the angle.

"This is an exercise in empathy, Rudy," she said. "This is a percentage or two of what I'm going through. You can only take a minute or so of the treatment before you hemorrhage, so I'd pay attention."

"I'm so sorry for what I did!" Rudy managed.

"Quiet," she said softly. "I was the one who took you by force, at least in a sense, not the other way around. That's why I wept at the foot of the stairs. Please don't interrupt me again or you'll die."

Rudy tried to will his eyes over just one millimeter further to the right, just to get one good hard glimpse in the rearview, but all he got was a blur, a flicker of bone white, streaks of black. Now she was close, right up in his ear.

"I know it's rude to lecture you, Rudy, but time is too much of a factor. I'll do my best to be brief, but I must pause here to ask. May I continue? I need permission."

"Yes," Rudy strained. "Please, go on."

"And I may be blunt?"

"Yes, of course, please."

Rudy's eyes felt as if they were going to explode. And when she sat back and went on as if the content of her discourse wasn't forced and outrageous, he welcomed it. Anything to distract him, take his mind off the motion, the vertigo, the free fall. It sounded like music from the back of his Toyota Corolla, deep and rich and poetic and dark.

"I'm a witch," she said, "one of millions who were created thousands of years ago for one purpose and one purpose only. To be companions to men, our rougher counterparts. For centuries we lived in harmony, both immortal, the males hunters and conquerors, the witches their sensuous shape-shifters, always adjusting to their ever-evolving sexual need. We didn't just fulfill fantasies,

The Witch of the Wood

Rudy; we created them. Tell me, did you ever have a picture of the one you called 'April Orr' in your consciousness? Or was it her newness, her subtleties that drew you to her, she who tapped into emotions and attractions you didn't even know existed? Man's happiness was always our special art, our tailored craft. I happen to know, Rudy Barnes, that a single year and fifty-two days into the given hypothetical relationship you would tire of April Orr, her newness becoming routine, her spark dulled in your sexual perception. Were I your mate, I would change for you then. I would become the twenty-nine-year-old physical therapist you'd meet after straining a muscle in the arch of your foot. She would still wear a ribbon in her long auburn hair in fond remembrance of her days as an undergraduate varsity gymnast at LSU, and she would be interested in you because of your ability to help her with term papers coming up in the new nursing research classes she signed on for at night so she could eventually become an RN. She would have small firm breasts and legs with beautiful lines, and she would wear eye makeup heavy on the rust and greens, yet no lipstick ever, her mouth so strong, her jaw so defined, her cheekbones so high. She'd be willful and intelligent, knowing just when to praise, to tease, to submit, and when you tired of her, I'd become the porcelain Asian beauty with the stunning waist and velvety voice working behind the desk at the insurance agency, or the bad-girl you'd discover at Repo Records with the nose bud, long black hair, clever eyes, and spectacular ass if you felt like slumming, don't you see? We were perfect for you, absolute equals, and you betrayed us."

"How?" Rudy managed, but barely. The G-forces were overwhelming him, making him dizzy, and consciousness seemed dreamlike at this point. At the same time, he was well aware of the interest he'd maintained from the moment she had described the physical therapist. And just as she'd claimed, he'd never had a "picture" of this woman in his mind specifically, but even the verbal outline had him half in love with her already. "Why?" he continued, neck straining. "Why the betrayal? We had it made."

"Power," she said. "Man's true love. You didn't want equals in the end, you wanted dominance, even at the sacrifice of your own sexual happiness."

There was a sound then, a croaking, and Rudy realized that the entity in the back seat was crying. He strained with everything he had to turn, but a bonelike hand rested upon his shoulder.

"It's all right," she said. "I'm all right. I'll have to be. This is hard for me, Rudy, not only emotionally. As I said before, I am under incredible physical duress right now, and projecting my image around is an unbelievable burden."

Rudy made himself relax as best he could, the pressure on his head making everything tinge at the edges with a creeping blackness.

"They lied to us," she continued. "They claimed to have discovered, through the art of science and medicine, a flaw in the continuum, a fissure in the chain of female existence, and with their smooth equations and black politics they convinced us to spawn. They gave us wombs, impregnated us, had us birth a new race for them."

Now she was crying, choking and weeping, her words staggered and stuttered as if ripped straight from her soul.

"The beings you call 'women' are the descendants of this heinous experiment. They were our daughters! Sensitive, beautiful, vulnerable, born and bred to be slaves, and taken from us before we could teach and engage their magic. And the result? The real fissure, the introduction of the eighty-year life span on both sides, confusion, horrible inequalities our daughter-race still attempts to rectify, pregnancies lasting nine months rather than a pure-breed's nine moments, and the whole idea of intimacy redefined to be something fleeting, memories inside those who tire of each other long before they can bring themselves to admit it. You introduced the

THE WITCH OF THE WOOD

institution of marriage to safeguard the species, and look where it has gotten you; look at the numbers. Are you happier? Has the power been worth all this pain?"

The pressure suddenly stopped, and Rudy felt he needed to catch hold of his breath. She was next to him now, and he didn't look; he'd changed his mind, too scary, too strange. And while the little boy inside him kept his eyes down, the long-seasoned teacher held his voice even.

"What happened to the witches?" he said. "Was it some sort of massive, universal holocaust?"

"Worse, Rudy. Prison. Forever."

"Where? How?"

She paused, then said the words with disgust.

"The trees, Rudy. Your world is not all it seems, and there is atrocity just beneath its surface. Each tree is a jail cell, its stalk above ground mere decoration. The buried roots in reality are hideous arms and gnarled, clutching fingers, each set holding a witch there in her living grave, under the dirt in disgrace."

"But . . ."

"I know. How about the ones cut down? Well, we are immortal, Rudy, but not indestructible. Any cut or uprooted tree brings about the automatic passing of a witch, no evidence, no trace, at least in any form you would associate with death. You see, we are human, yet not, God's wondrous mixture of beauty, flesh, spirit, and shadow. We color your world, and when we leave it as a living entity we rejoin it as hue. Every tree houses an imprisoned witch, Rudy, and every shadow is a dead sister. You pass through us every day, wear us on your faces, let us slide down your backs, shade the paths before your feet."

"And the ones still 'living' can never escape?"

She laughed there next to Rudy, and it was a hoarse, bitter sound.

"Oh, we have tried! But wood is our enemy, and we don't pass through it easily. So many suicides, so many long journeys through the grain, out through the branches and leaves in the formless shapes of poor lonely shadows, only to be projected across the landscape, giving proportion to what is no more than miles and miles of graveyard and prison-city. Why do you think most of your race gets uncomfortable when lost in the woods, Rudy? Because it is there that you feel us the most, wailing and begging from underground. For centuries we have been searching for a way to break the spell that has kept us prisoners of the dirt, Rudy Barnes, and I was the one to finally solve the riddle. You see, it makes sense the way poetry 'makes sense,' or anti-poetry, all with a dark universal symmetry, depending on how depraved a vision you are willing to accept."

Rudy wanted to look at her, but still couldn't summon the courage. Instead, he stared at his hands, somehow looking old and clawlike there in his lap.

"How do you break free then?" he said. "What's the formula?"

"The sin of the womb. A revisitation to the pattern of the original crime. An escape from the grip of the root is not an escape after all. It is a rebirth, and it has got to be breech."

She started breathing heavily, as if talking about it brought on nausea.

"But going through feet first is torture to us. We are not bats! If we have one innate weakness, it is that we are terrified of being upside down. And an exit backward through the grain is long and laborious. It's like fighting one's deepest phobia, and prolonging the battle for what would feel like eternity. Picture someone afraid of water, heights, and darkness being hung from a rope out of a helicopter by the feet and flown over a stormy sea at midnight. Then imagine asking that person to write scholarly prose or do calculus during the process. That is what this is like, Rudy. I tried to go through backward, tried to stand on my head and push with my palms, but I lost my nerve and balked. Just after breaking ground-surface I brought my feet back down, just to feel the bottom, just for a moment for reassurance, and then came the snow from three nights ago. A heavy ice formed in the top of my maple prison and weighed it down, splitting it right at the base. I am both trapped and exposed now, spell partially broken, touching my toes and touching your world, able for a brief moment to work the old magic as I did with you last evening. But I'm dying, Rudy, and the April Orr projection took everything in my power to maintain." She pleaded then. "I'm upside down, tied by my feet to the helicopter, and trying to do calculus."

"What can I do?"

"You have a choice. You can drive away and leave me to die, or you can approach me in my prison-house, as you did last evening. You can have me again, Rudy, but for my life to have meaning, for my revenge to be realized, it has to be of your own free will."

"My . . . what? I don't understand."

"Look at me, Rudy. See what I really am."

He looked.

What he saw was not of this world. She was a skeleton with bright white skin stretched across like Saran Wrap, eyes black and bulbous, lips blood red. She was beautiful in a most alien fashion and horrific, and while part of his mind was that child writhing and screaming, the intellectual in him was raising his fountain pen above his head in victory. Of course. She was a shape-shifter, and he was viewing the blank slate.

Then she changed, merged, shifted, and transformed into April Orr. She leaned toward him and lifted her hand to stroke his cheek, the pain and wanting set deep in her eyes.

"Make love to me again, Rudy, and I'll give you the world. And when you question what you believe forms the foundation of your ethics, please remember two important issues. First, think of your world as the mass graveyard it already is, the prison-labyrinth with the decorative cover, highlighted by the shadows of all my sisters who have affixed their dark ghosts to the structures of your thoroughfares. And second, just consider this simple idea. Were you happy, Rudy? Ever?"

She was gone.

Rudy was still in his car, all dizziness ceased. He opened the door, got out, and made his way across the glen to the broken tree, and there at the crack, between stretched barking connecting the two halves, he saw it.

There in the wood was April Orr's pussy, waist level where he'd had her last night, except she hadn't been holding any banister. Inside the trunk she must have been touching her toes, mostly buried in there, just her vertex exposed to this part of the world. Trembling, Rudy reached forward with his fingers, touching her.

There was a moaning that came from the earth and she materialized, walls forming around them, and a roaring fire in the hearth keeping them warm. She was beautiful and she was naked, arched the way he liked her, looking back at him over her shoulder with an expression of slight indignation.

And right before Rudy entered her, she whispered,

"Do you know what a male of my species would be, Rudy? A beautiful, terrifying demon. A destroyer of men, faithful only to the ones who created him. You saw his 'preview' last night as the boy on the stairs. Do you have the courage to make him real?"

Rudy fit himself into her, pumped hard, and exploded. When he pulled out, the cold wind blasted all around him, and he fell backward, cutting his bare ass on the hard ice formed on the dirt beneath him. A yard or so above him, the vagina in the tree trunk then bloomed and swelled, bloody feet working their way from between the bloated folds. Rudy stood and drew up his pants. He then grabbed the small feet as gently as he could and helped ease the child out into the world, accompanied by a symphony of sucking sounds, a masterpiece of blood, bone, flesh, and gelatin.

The boy cried out into the wind, and he had the face of the child Rudy had seen last night, crystalline eyes, like a doll or marionette ready to steal the world's breath and blacken the remains.

A destroyer of men.

Faithful to his creator.

Are you happy, Rudy?

Are you ready to be the king of the earth?

There was a last cry from inside the wood, and a shadow burst from the opening, rising fast, catching on the wind, flitting and filtering between the branches and flying off in the direction of the sun.

Rudy Barnes cuddled the wailing child.

He considered his ethics and weighed them against his relative happiness.

Then he made his way quickly out of the forest, this new bloody treasure nestled safe in his arms.

Chapter 2

Warlock

Wolfie aged quickly. Even straight out of the womb, he had the strength of a toddler, lying wet and warm in the folds of the black coat zipped around him, tiny hands and arms wrapped around his father's neck, feet digging and pushing against Rudy's stomach if he began to lose purchase.

Sunlight stabbed through the windshield and Rudy forced himself to drive slow as molasses, afraid of being pulled over with no car seat, no towels, no baby bag, no blankets. Looked like a kidnapping right out of the birthing room, and the fluids were smeared all over him, past the collar and neck area. When they'd first got in the car and situated, Wolfie had reached up and felt Rudy's face, like a blind child getting to know the contours. Rudy had told him in a flat, informative tone that this was inappropriate, and the child had immediately stopped. As if he'd understood. At first, Rudy thought it was a coincidence, but when he tested the theory, gently commanding the boy to put his arms around his neck so he wouldn't slide down into the jacket-papoose where he couldn't see him, Wolfie did it.

Super-being. Strong as all hell. Wired for language in a manner that clearly defied all we knew about cognitive growth or psychology. A destroyer of men.

But really?

Rudy look down for a moment, straining his eyes, forcing a reddish tinge at the rim of his vision. Wolfie was looking straight up at him, round face, crystalline eyes. The lids lowered in a slow blink, a doll's trick, and then came back open. Cold gems, but there was trust in them.

The Witch of the Wood

He's beautiful, Rudy thought, immediately feeling weird about it, looking back to the road, making a turn onto Lovell Avenue. The words that had just flashed into his mind didn't fit him, not even a little bit. Though he'd always believed in love fundamentally . . . almost like one adopting some religious faith for the sake of insurance, he'd only really felt it in flashes. In reality, he'd spent most of his adult life alone, at least metaphorically, stumbling for years through a passionless marriage, concluding that what we all shared most was the *dream* of some idealized concept and the denial of our collective isolation. Then, of course, what was not real, we'd invent, and that's where Rudy checked out of this particular hotel. He'd always been uncomfortable with sentiment and sensitivity, finding them constructed and overplayed in the media not only through the more obvious, formulaic Oprah episodes and reality television shows, but in what was considered "real news," the given reporter asking a victim how he or she "felt" at the moment (as if the one interviewed wasn't aware of the microphone, the viewing audience, the YouTube possibilities, or potential book deal) or worse, asking another reporter what the "public perception" was concerning some hotbed issue that stirred the emotions (as if a poll were taken and they had actually come to Rudy's house to cap off the vote). Feelings had become too easy to "study," and Rudy despised the mass production of it all, as if the world was supposed to masturbate all together on three or something.

It angered Rudy, actually, and he turned left on King Avenue, screeching the tires a bit. It wasn't just the fabrication of the melodramatic that bothered him so, but more the misplacement of it. We paid attention in class because the teacher was hot, we liked someone's music because of the tattoo, we voted for a candidate because of his honey voice. And the words that had floated through his mind, *He's beautiful,* were not his words but those of his mother, he suddenly realized. They had invited her over for one of the championship games between the Sixers and Lakers back in 2001, and she had busied herself sewing a hem throughout the affair, blue lips pursed as if they'd been tightened by drawstrings, sitting on the most comfortable chair they'd angled for her so she'd get the best view of the TV she wasn't watching. There had been a steal and a run the wrong way down the hardwood, and Rudy had wanted the room to join him in his bitter Philadelphian's disappointment as another one went down the toilet. Mother had looked up, fixed her watery gaze on the curly-haired Laker who'd just burned us (Rick Fox it was), and said, "My . . . he's beautiful."

Rudy had just turned thirty-seven, but it somehow triggered a teenager's rage he'd bit back down and promptly and conveniently forgotten.

Until now. And the question was, why had his mother's words suddenly resurfaced, laying themselves delicately over his own, like a soft molestation?

He looked down at Wolfie, he who was staring back with those shock-blue eyes. Rudy laughed, and it sounded creepy and awkward. An "ah-ha" moment. A cold one.

Of course. Wolfie could manipulate your sentiment or lack of it, pick your poison.

The world didn't have a chance.

Rudy backed into his parking space and sat there for a moment, slightly hunched down. He had to be careful, especially on the short trip across the lot to stairway. It should have been isolated back here, like a ghost town mid-morning on a Friday, everyone at work where they belonged, but Rudy had picked this rental for the view beyond the cross street like everyone else in the building; walking trail, peaceful reservoir, rising stand of dark pines in the background. And the parking lot was a sudden flurry of activity, almost like one of those bad thrillers where all the clichés passed by all at once, minding their business while the serial killer watched them through his tinted windows and the eyeholes cut from the burlap he'd stretched over his head and tied around his neck with a cord. Every time Rudy thought the coast might be clear, there was another pop-in from the side or across the way—three ladies powerwalking by with their ear buds, visors, and designer shades, a stocky college kid in a blue Alaskan parka heading to the bus stop with his backpack and laptop, an elderly couple shuffling past with sneakers big as clown shoes, the perky stay-at-home dad with the balloon-tire baby carriage he jogged behind, the black body spandex making him look like a faggot no matter how liberal you thought you'd become.

Someone knocked on the passenger side window, hard.

Rudy jumped and banged his knees on the bottom of the steering wheel.

"Jesus!" he said out loud.

It was a head on an angle, Sam Finkelstein, his neighbor from 2B. Sam was a strange guy, sort of gently intrusive: when it snowed he walked the parking lot putting everyone's windshield wipers up. He had an oblong "Munster" head and eyes that sagged at the edges, giving the impression that he was a bit slow, but Rudy knew that he wasn't. Just odd, different standards, like one of those ladies with a hundred cats, or the kind of guy who thought it was a big score when the elementary school threw out their old computers and he got to scour the dumpster.

"What you got there?" Sam said, all muffled and displaced outside the closed window. He tilted his head the other way and squinted. "That a baby there?" He was pointing now, tapping the pad of his index finger on the glass.

Rudy felt Wolfie twist a bit, turning his head so he could look at the man in the window. When their eyes met there was a jolt, and the three of them were suddenly connected in some odd psychic triangle that only Sam was utterly unaware of. And for a moment

Rudy knew things, private things about his neighbor he never would have guessed in a million years.

Sam shaved his legs because he had itch compulsion, and the hair against the inside of his trousers could literally incapacitate him for hours. He'd had bloody noses since he was in junior high school, and the Vaseline'd Q-tips and Swiss humidifiers only helped marginally. He'd never been married, but he'd been engaged, he'd tried for a doctorate in psychology but couldn't finish the dissertation, he was presently unemployed but remained hopeful.

He was also addicted to Internet pornography, and every day that he swore he would stop became another instance where he rationalized that his hard drive was so loaded with smut that one more surf wasn't going to make too much difference.

He liked costumes: French maids, Indian squaws, cowgirls in jean shorts, schoolgirls in plaid skirts.

And nurses.

Old school nurses. He was in love with the image emotionally and sexually, hopelessly drawn to the mother-sister type seemingly unaware of her own severe beauty and playing you with the contradiction. There was another jolt, this one zinging Rudy right through the bottom of the scrotum, and the image delivered here was an older one, black-and-white film run too fast all jumpy with age lines and little burn bubbles running through it: Sam's deep, dark past, visiting his Cleveland cousins as a boy of twelve and meeting his second Aunt Esther who told them stories about Israel, all of them sitting cross-legged on the floor before the sofa, the one with the odd flower patterns and ancient vinyl slipcovers, and she sat there above them—an exotic jangle of earrings and bracelets and dark glass-bead necklaces, with her tight black skirt riding up over those pretty bare knees, and when she re-crossed her legs there was that sweet red mark left on one of them, and she'd seen Sammy looking and straightened uncomfortably. She'd tucked her hair behind her ear, pinched her long nose between her thumb and index finger for a moment, and then gone upstairs, returning soon with a bit of an alteration in her attire, her legs now covered in white panty hose. And even though the supple skin was no longer catching the glow of the overhead light, the sculpted form of those calves was undeniable, and she was his *relative,* far from perfect with her hawklike features and the mole under her left eye, her skinny smile and nervous laugh, but those *legs* . . . and he knew he was naughty, and little Sammy wanted to rub his penis so badly that he thought he was going to die.

It wasn't difficult math. The Aunt was the forbidden mother-figure Sam had reconfigured into the safer fantasy. He even got to transpose the white stockings, for God's sake.

Sam wasn't looking in the car window anymore. He was looking away toward the reservoir, and when Rudy followed his sightline he didn't see any bus stop or walking trail. It was a long hallway, and at the end of it was a sofa with flower patterns and vinyl slipcovers, and sitting on it was Aunt Esther. She had her Seventies perm, but it was bobby-pinned back behind her ears and topped off by a starched white cap. She was wearing a belted white pinafore over a short-sleeved blue blouse with a white collar, and she'd just kicked off her padded white shoes.

She pivoted a bit to the side and drew her knees in, one leg arching up and out, toe pointing, and she slowly began to remove those white panty hose.

Sam started walking toward her, head cocked a bit in dumb disbelief. By the time the panty hose lay in a feathery pile on the floor, Sam was halfway to her, walking faster now, and by the time he reached her, she was rubbing the back of her ankle as if she required as potent a physical soothing as the mental comforts she'd just supplied to her patients.

Sam reached to touch those legs, and she let him.

Rudy felt them too; she had goosebumps.

As if back to the grainy black-and-white film stock, she jumped camera frames then, making Sam move ten feet laterally to get to her, lying on her back on the kitchen table, knees up, ankles together. He approached and palmed those knees, spreading them slowly, her heels making rubbing sounds on the tablecloth, letting the shadows disappear up her thighs, and Sam saw her dark pussy, one of the lips sticking just for a moment, then coming off the other in a sweet unfolding, and Sam bent in to tongue it, his back cracking softly, and he and Rudy smelled her deep musk.

But right at the very moment he made to slide his tongue into her, she jumped frames again, now twelve feet deeper into the house in the baby's playroom, naked on all fours and sunken down in front with her elbows and forearms flat to the carpet, ass pointed ceiling-high in a lovely heart shape, waiting there, just for him.

Sam was desperate now, bright purple in his passion, eyes rolling, and he stumbled to her, unbuttoning his pants, wading and waddling as they fell to his ankles, voices in his head pleading, "Oh my God," and "No, please . . ." and that made it better somehow as he fell to his knees to ram his second aunt from behind, and he was amazed in a distracted sort of way by the roughness of the carpet.

Then the playroom vanished, and so did his second aunt.

"Oh," Sam said, voice small. Initially, he hadn't been running his fingers along goosebumped flesh, but the pitted bumper of the old Chevy illegally parked and booted with three old tickets fluttering from under the windshield wipers. He hadn't been palming knees and spreading a pair of bare legs, but rather, he'd moved down the sidewalk to the bike rack and strategically pushed apart the tires on a couple of old ten-speeds that had been abandoned, and now he was in the street with his pants down, knees scraped, bus braking desperately because it had been doing fifty-seven with "Express" flashing across its automated route identification board.

"Wait," Sam said, just before the bus hit him dead on.

The Witch of the Wood

The kid in the Alaskan parka, the one who had actually said, "Oh my God," was still digging to try to get a bit of this on his cell phone. The woman next to him who had said, "No, please . . ." was looking away, face screwed in like a prune.

The front of the bus plowed into Sam and kicked him backward, his head slapping down to the street, blood bursting behind in an egg-shaped spray. The tires screeched and smoked over him, the back end of the bus fishtailing, Sam's body puppet-jumping as it was caught up and mangled by the under carriage.

Rudy got out of the car and moved toward the apartment's rear entrance.

"Thanks for the subtle diversion," he muttered numbly. Before taking hold of the doorknob, he looked down at his son.

Wolfie was smiling.

Rudy brought his child in, put him on a blanket on the living room floor, drew a bath, went through the motions. Every three seconds or so he looked back over his shoulder from the bathroom to check, and Wolfie basically stayed put like a good little baby, reaching his fingers playfully into the red ambulance lights washing across him through the picture window facing the reservoir. It gave the illusion of movement, a lunatic carousel.

"You've got to kill him before it's too late," Rudy whispered under his breath. Then he said back to himself, "Yeah, right."

So did Wolfie, and he was right in the doorway, wobbly, but standing there naked and bloody. Rudy's heels kicked out from under him and he sat hard, right on the spot where two of the tiles had come loose, and his ass hit an edge. He winced, bit it back. Yes, he'd forgotten about this particular foreshadowing. Wolfie moved when you blinked. He'd also learned to talk through this psychic sort of connection they had going, and even though it was a mimic, Rudy was pretty sure it wouldn't be too long before the kid was making speeches.

"Safe," Wolfie said, and then he waddled straight into Rudy's lap. The professor drew him in, held him, lost himself for a moment in the warmth of it. He loved this boy suddenly, deeply; he felt it in his neck, his back, high in the temples, and this was no media-driven piece of hyperbole.

"Of course you're safe," he murmured.

"I meant you," the boy responded.

Rudy started a bit, and then it was all game face, lifting Wolfie into the tub, washing him, making sure to hit all the tucks and creases. Of course Rudy Barnes was safe, and the math was staggering. Wolfie could read minds, at least to some degree. He somehow knew even at this early juncture that his father was a moral figure and would struggle with the bloodshed. He also knew that at the end of the long cycle . . . with the returning arc of the pendulum . . . when the roller coaster finally slowed at the exit gate, pick your metaphor, love and loyalty would be Rudy's landing point. Flat and fundamental. Personal, not publicized.

And Wolfie was aware of this psychological roundabout at the age of an hour. Rudy dried him off and kissed his forehead mechanically, searching for something cushy to wrap him in. It was mind-boggling, the puzzles Wolfie would be able to solve in a matter of weeks, days, hours, that would leave his own father behind in a state of absolute ignorance.

Rudy got the Eagles floor cushion with the couch-arms, two pillows from his bed, and a quilt from the linen closet. He arranged them in the middle of the floor the best he could with Wolfie in the crook of one arm, and then set the boy there and wrapped him. He stayed there for a second, above him on one knee.

Blind faith. No choice here.

His son worked his tiny hands above the top edge of the quilt covering, and for a moment they played at the air spasmodically, like the hands of any infant painting his formless colors into the world. Then he gained a level of motor function right there before Rudy's eyes, turning his palms in, staring at them with the interest of a much older boy looking at his butterfly collection. He flexed his fingers, then closed them, making slow fists. Stopped. Looked at Rudy directly.

"There will be gifts," he said.

And Rudy believed him.

The Super Fresh was crowded, and Rudy felt ridiculous, pushing his big cart around like some "Main Line Mom" gone haywire. Usually, he was in and out with a handbasket scattered at the bottom with the stuff he needed for a day or two: a rib-eye steak, a purple onion, a pack of double-A batteries, a stick of Gillette Cool Wave gel. But here, he was blocking the aisles at weird angles, pausing, reading labels, loading up on diapers, wet naps, formula, paper towels, Band-Aids, cotton balls, ammonia, the works. Next would be the "Baby Store," and he wondered how much of this shit he could fit in the car. He needed a Diaper Genie, a playpen, a chest of drawers, clothes, and about fifty thousand other things he couldn't think of right now. At least he'd pretty much decided to nix the crib. They'd sleep together in the big bed no matter what the psychologists had to say about it. In fact, Rudy looked forward to it.

A woman wearing a beret and those popular tight black leggings she was really too fat for cut Rudy off in front of an end cap stacked with cases of sale water and Coke Zero. Her little one was in the built-on baby seat facing her, slapping at the plastic shapes on the arched wire-mount, spinning them. The kid smacked the blue elephant straight on and it whirred around to a blur.

"Whoa! *Awe*some!" Mom said.

Yeah, bravo kid, Rudy thought. You're destined for participation trophies and accommodations, loopholes and parent advocates. You'll learn to play the system and we'll call it delicate genius.

A voice slipped into his mind.

Rudolph Christopher Barnes, come in please.

Rudy shuddered, palmed his ears hard. Felt like a spider web floating along the regions of his mind, sticking to the ridges.

"That you, Wolfie?"

Beret Lady glanced over casually and noticed he had no ear-to-phone hookup. She pushed her cart away hard then, actually nipping the corner of his, her sneakers squeaking on the smooth shiny floor. Her fat ass looked no better in retreat then it had from the side.

"The same," Wolfie said, voice itching, teasing, all sticky silk. *"I'm getting bored here all by myself."*

"Right. Got it," Rudy said sort of into his collar. His face had gone scarlet, and it wasn't because it looked as if he were talking to himself like a mental patient. Just how many literal and ethical laws had he broken, leaving that child by himself in the house? And worse, had he really a choice?

He navigated his way to the self-checkout lanes, jumped in front of an old guy rolling his dentures around in his mouth, and started beeping barcodes as quickly as he could. He swallowed hard, tasting copper.

What he going to come home to, anyway?

He bagged up quick and shoddy, pondering these last three questions and trying to discern which of the answers scared him the most.

Rudy reached to the passenger seat to make what would be the first of multiple trips inside with the plastic bags of groceries and everything else. He hoped that when he finally lugged up the boxes containing the particle board for the baby bureau in the big oblong crates no one would question why he'd bought particle boards for a baby bureau, or the two cases that made up the changing station, or the glider, or the new lamp with stars and moons on the shade.

The Witch of the Wood

The mess out on Maple Grove Avenue had been cleaned up already, and the only reminder was an arc of residue on the asphalt where Sam's head had struck down. From the car just now it had looked shadowed, still damp on the glistening street, and from the puddles in the gutter, Rudy had figured the EMTs or the police had had some kind of portable pressure washer.

Gorge rose up in the back of Rudy's throat, and he almost threw up right there in the car. He couldn't do this. A man had died. And what had been a distracted sort of passing fear in the grocery store was now coming back to him in glorious Technicolor; Rudy had left a baby all by himself in a dark apartment where there were about a thousand and one things that could hurt him. Just how advanced was this kid, and in how many subject areas? Just because he could talk and "promise gifts" didn't mean his other facets of intelligence had fully developed.

For God's sake, Rudy hadn't locked up his poisons, and they were waiting there for Wolfie under the kitchen sink, all skulls and crossbones and danger flags and other various icons and logos that any kid would find nifty just for the colors. If the kid could speak he could probably read warning labels, but would he? For sure? And the iron, oh God, the iron—no more than a heavy steel arrowhead right there in the living room closet, lurking at the edge of the top shelf, cord possibly dangling down just waiting for a good pull. There were electrical outlets all over the place, sharp edges and corners, knives in the drawers, medicines on the shelves, and the toolbox was out.

Rudy got out and slammed the car door a bit too hard, bringing the bags around with the momentum and clacking some of the Gerber jars loud enough to indicate he might have cracked them. The wind came across and made his eyes tear up. He folded himself into it, head down, and once inside, his shoes made gritty echoes on the stair grids.

Wolfie would be curled up dead on the floor by the radiator, face blackened, lips blue, throat mottled and stretched to the shape of the bottle of White-Out he'd tried to swallow. That, or he'd be face down in the toilet, arms limp on each side of the bowl because he'd thought he'd found a neat little tunnel to try and dive down, or worse, he'd be this smiling, skeletal cinder because he was advanced enough to walk, he moved when you blinked, and he'd evolved to the point that he could jump up on the stove, monkey-squat there because the perspective was new, then lean over the front and turn on the knobs.

At his door, bags thrust up one forearm, Rudy struggled with the key and heard some kind of moan from inside. He stopped. Silence. And the noise was hard to identify now in retrospect because of the relative racket he'd been making, mistaking his Widener office key (as he so often did) for the one that fit the apartment lock because the two copper stamps looked so much alike.

Something fell inside the apartment, something distant, as in the back by the bathroom, and Rudy fumbled the proper key in the hole, thrusting the door open.

Semi-dark. Vacated, it seemed.

"Wolfie?" he said, voice dead and close.

Something came from around the corner of the bedroom, the shaft of sunlight from the picture window cutting across on an angle. It was the silhouette of a little girl, hair tousled and frayed, shoes clicking on the hard wood floor. She stopped, head tilted.

"Daddy?"

There was a sudden shriek, and she burst through the shaft of window-light.

Rudy recoiled, dropping the bags on the floor.

What came through the light and the dust rising in it was a child-monster, face bruised purple and blue, mouth torn open and smeared bright red.

She crashed into him, and he crumpled to the floor with her, heart pounding, and she looked up at him there in his lap.

Her face wasn't bruised or smeared; she'd been playing "makeup" with someone's Revlon and Maybelline. He breathed a sigh of relief and she squeezed shut her eyes, as if Rudy's image was too beautiful to bear.

"She loves you unconditionally," Wolfie said from the archway, "and I didn't find her by accident." He was a boy of six or seven now, at least physically, standing there under the hall arch wearing Rudy's old black and gray flannel shirt coming down to his knees.

"Her name is Brianna Rivera," Wolfie continued. "She's five—"

"Five and a half!" Brianna wailed. Rudy coo-cooed a bit of soothing down without looking at her, and Wolfie continued with a bit of a laugh. "See, Dad, her father left when she was a month in front of two. She refuses to eat anything but fried chicken skin, chopped-up hot dogs, and Fruity Pebbles. She's good at hopscotch and remedial ceramics, but still has difficulty making friends in preschool. She writes poems, likes drawing pictures in the dirt under the tire swing in the back yard, and once had a pet hamster. She also likes chewing things because they make juice, like her hair and the strings on her Flyers sweatshirt."

"What's that to do with me?" Rudy said defensively.

"You're a match," Wolfie said, coming close now. "People are linked psychologically and physiologically. They are cross-wired; biologically drawn to each other, and they spend most of their lives denying it. So sad."

"She's five," Rudy said, teeth gritted down.

Wolfie sat cross-legged next to his father, and Brianna reached to touch his hair.

"So pretty," she said.

"You are," Wolfie teased back, much to her delight. He looked back to his father. "And I'm joking with you just a bit. You and the girl are only linked because it's passed down. Present's in the bedroom. Check it out."

Rudy handed over the girl, her feet pigeon-toed and dragging a bit on the floor, and he barely noticed that Wolfie already possessed the strength to bear her weight straight-armed before hugging her in. He popped a knee on the way pushing up and his walk had a bit of a disoriented sway, but he pretty much knew what was waiting for him in the bedroom.

He turned the corner and she was sitting at the edge of his bed, face flushed and long black curly hair tangled almost as badly as was her daughter's.

"I . . . I . . . want to . . ." she said. She touched her face, smoothed her skirt. She looked up at Rudy with guilt and wanting, face shiny with nervous anticipation. She had charcoal eyes, dark skin, a studded sliver cross resting on the left breast, and a red sash pulled tight around her waist. She was a Puerto Rican beauty named Ann-Marie, and her breath was high. She'd been a good girl all her life, hating the clichés about women of Spanish descent having big asses, fake fingernails, and the desire to pop babies out as if they were peanuts in a vending machine, but she loved flashy colors and she was going to flaunt them. Little Brianna was her sweet mistake, but the two of them were facing the world together. Ann-Marie worked as a hostess at the Howard Johnson's on West Chester Pike by the motor parts store, and she was going to community college for business management. She was poor, but generally happy.

"Cease," Rudy muttered into his collar, and Wolfie's sticky little bio of Ann-Marie stopped rubbing and droning on in his head. Ann-Marie folded her hands, sat up straight, and tried to explain.

"We were taking a walk. My Brianna likes the way the sun sparkles off the reservoir, and he, your son, called to us. We came in. He promised . . . you."

She looked up at Rudy, eyes half-lidded.

The Witch of the Wood

"I don't know why, but I've dreamed of you, or a man like you."

"And I you," Rudy said softly. And it was true. He'd always had a thing for the Spanish flair, but more importantly, he'd always possessed somewhat of a specific picture, partly in the back of his mind, somewhat in the forefront, of an "Ann-Marie," personal and unique, sometimes with a little nick on one knee from when she must have fallen off a bike or a skateboard, or possibly some soft dark hair on her forearms that embarrassed her as a child yet she managed as an adult . . . some flaw that had made her human, and not some two-dimensional Macy's advertisement. And even though it was probable that this Ann-Marie didn't have a nick on her knee, it was clear as day she'd look sexy standing in a doorway, or lying back on his bed with all that hair fanned out behind her. It was as if he knew her and he didn't, and it was rather exciting to fathom that for whatever reason, he fit her sexual profile as well.

Rudy paused. Ordinarily, he would never talk to the hostess at Ho-Jo's. Stare at her, yes. Fantasize about running his hands along the small of her back, the swell of her bosom, sure. But asking her out? Meeting her parents? Dealing with her crazy brother? Babysitting her kid while she went off to class? Driving out to the Interstate where her used clunker had broken down again? The thought would just never advance like that, not for most of us anyway, as we sat there "making appropriate plans" in the Ho-Jo's booths we were anxious to vacate.

So sad.

We let our ideal partners wander off into the shadows of their cultures. Then we both disappeared. It was a class thing, and it was stupid.

Rudy moved closer and knelt on the floor. He delicately pushed the hem of her dress up and almost gasped when he saw a small nick in the skin, left knee, a tiny indentation, long healed.

"I'm a professor," he whispered, looking up into her eyes. She moaned, and when he bent and kissed the imperfection she came right there on his bed. At the same moment, Wolfie made a playful whooping sound on the other side of the door to mask the sounds of it.

For the sake of the daughter.

And it was the second best sex Rudy Barnes had ever had in his life.

Ann-Marie came out of the bedroom adjusting her dress, Rudy right behind her, running his hands through his thinning hair. She gathered up Brianna and turned back to Rudy, looking at him and the floor at the same time.

"I don't usually . . ."

"I know," Rudy said.

Wolfie was sitting Indian style and he caught Ann-Marie's eye.

"Sweet maiden," he said. She smiled back, and Wolfie waved his hand across their shared plane of vision like a windshield wiper. Her expression went blank for a second, and then she switched Brianna to the crook of the other arm, smartly tossing her hair back over her shoulder in Rudy's direction.

"Thank you for the tutoring session, Professor. I'll work on that pronoun antecedent issue. And I'll pay you next time, I promise."

"That won't be necessary," Rudy said. "Good luck with your business writing course at community."

She flashed a last smile and walked out, oblivious, shutting the door carefully.

"It's better this way," Wolfie said. "No expectations, no social obligations."

"Right," Rudy said, feeling sad about it, but only philosophically really. He moved past toward the door. "There are a lot of items I need to return—"

"I read your books."

"Really?" he said, turning.

"Every one. I liked Hemingway's *For Whom the Bell Tolls* best. Great scene by the gorge. I also liked *Macbeth*, but the wrong side won and Shakespeare's portrayal of witches is insulting. But you know that already, now don't you?"

Before Rudy could laugh along, Wolfie did the "blink" and reappeared in front of him, blocking the exit. Rudy almost pulled a muscle in his neck snapping his head around.

"Father . . ." Wolfie sing-songed. He came forward slowly, backing Rudy away from the door a step or two. "My patriarch. *Daddy* . . ." He stopped, and then, to Rudy's wonder, he started to levitate. When he came eye to eye with his father, he leaned in close nose to nose, breath smelling like honeysuckle.

"Your books are interesting," he said, "but they are rather one-dimensional. Like your mind." He leaned in and kissed his father's forehead, slowly, deeply. Despite himself, Rudy bent in to the warmth of it and had his eyes closed even after the release. Wolfie patted his crown. "I need for you to bring me to the library, Dad, where I will spend a day and a night. Not the public library on Sproul Road, but rather the one at the University of Pennsylvania. While I realize that history texts are your most dangerous examples of fiction, I must see with my own eyes the patterns through which you prefer to be lied to. I need to study your philosophy, your most intricate rationalizations, and your science . . ."

He trailed off and lowered himself to the floor, absently taking hold of Rudy's hand on the way down.

"Your science . . ."

Rudy squatted down to his level.

"What about it?"

Wolfie smiled, and it was the first time Rudy had ever seen him appear wistful. The boy removed his hand gently.

"Ancient puzzles."

"To aid with the destruction?"

Wolfie laughed outright, gazing up and off to the complicated future he was planning to unveil.

"No, of course not, Dad. We really only need psychology for Armageddon. Science is for the aftermath." He looked at his father directly then, with a mixture of affection and pity. "You will better understand when there is a context, Rudy Barnes. For now, you need to return all the items you bought this morning and take me on this university field trip Monday. You'll need to either cancel your classes or bring the students along. Computers from here even with a passcode are only useful for searching out scholarly journals, and I need access to the shelf texts as well."

"Won't the pages affect you . . . the wood, the pulp?"

Wolfie's eyes blazed.

"Of course they will. Every book is haunted by the soul of a dead witch, just like the ones on your shelves in the bedroom. But I can't cry over paper and shadows, now can I?"

"No, I suppose not."

"Return the baby products," Wolfie said, walking past Rudy toward the light of the window. "And find a way to get me into that library quietly."

"Couldn't you just insert mental pictures into a couple of security guards?"

Wolfie turned, then lowered his eyes in what actually looked like shame.

"What I did was infantile and crude. Forgive me."

"It was just one man," Rudy said softly.

"You misunderstand. My actions left trails."

"Oh."

"There are better ways."

"Of course."

Wolfie padded across to the kitchen and put his palm on the face of the refrigerator.

"And your food disgusts me. Bring me iodine. A gallon or two if you can. That will keep me nourished. And I will use your laptop and call you on your cell phone to indicate the clothing I will require."

"I think I can handle—"

"No, you can't. Soon I will be a teenager of eighteen. I will stagnate at that growth level for one month, and it is imperative that I blend culturally."

"Why?"

"I need to study the psychological infrastructure of your institutions first hand. High school is the most convenient replica of the mother-port and will provide ideal, low-risk simulation."

"Mother-port?" Rudy said to his son's back. "What on earth is that?"

Wolfie twisted his head around slowly.

"Prison, of course. Where I can amass an army."

It rang out dully and sat there between them for a moment before Rudy politely excused himself and left the apartment.

An army. Of course. Wolfie couldn't singlehandedly murder every man in the world; it was physically impossible. He was a trigger, and they would all annihilate themselves.

Rudy got into his car for the umpteenth time that day and drove out to St. Mary's Cemetery, the place where he'd gone all his life when he wanted to think.

But can I entertain mental activity without Wolfie's eavesdropping?

A good question, and Rudy made the turn through the black gate off Sproul Road, heading in toward the cathedral, a scatter of tiny American flags whipping before the headstones in the entrance grove.

You there, Wolfie? he thought hard, feeling instantly ridiculous.

No answer; no sticky silk. He drove past the gravedigger's shed and two filler-mounds covered with tarps. Could it be that Wolfie's "radar" had a range? A limitation? The Super Fresh was literally three streets from the house, and even though it was similar to St. Mary's in terms of the "time to get there," it wasn't really the same distance. The grocery store took about five minutes with the lights. Once off Maple Grove, you got to St. Mary's by the highway. It was farther, certainly.

Rudy eased the car into his favorite curve, down by some border oaks and mausoleums at the east edge of the property. He put it in park, and a sudden sweat broke out on his forehead. He was sitting here, working out this juvenile math while his son could read his entire collection of literature in one sitting. Who was he fooling? What would stop Wolfie from playing possum right here and now and sitting in Rudy's mind as a quiet spectator to see what he was *really* thinking? Rudy smiled hard and played with the rearview for no reason. What if he said to himself, "Fuck you, Wolfie. I'm going to wait until you're asleep tonight and stick a knife in your chest," but then beneath it, thought, *Just kidding. Don't be so sensitive, kid.* Could Wolfie read the levels? And if he *was* playing possum right now, would he be able to go this one *more* rung deeper (the one that Rudy had just constructed, of course) and know that Rudy wasn't at all sure as to whether he was simply inventing the scenario of joking to Wolfie just now for shits and giggles . . . sort of doing the math for the sport of it, or really testing the idea of murdering his son?

He laughed, shook his head. This is why he hated the movie *Inception*. Once the dream went down two tiers, even the screenwriters had no clue what was going on. Maybe reading minds, even for a superior being like Wolfie, wasn't so easy . . . because of the gradations, the rationalizations, the way we not only lied to ourselves but, at the core, often didn't really know what the hell we were doing until we went out and did it. Maybe it was a rabbit hole Wolfie only lowered himself into just past the rim, retiring carefully to that little room just beneath the lip that unlocked visions of the past, the biographies written in the language he so rapidly learned. And maybe just below this room, churning and bubbling, was the endless pit of "present thought," a chasm of madness only good for an occasional sticky intrusion (at close range no less) that was no more than simple communication: *Come home, I'm bored. Don't forget the iodine.*

The smile faded from Rudy's lips. He did love the boy, and in many ways he despised the world this child was planning to destroy and reanimate, most probably for the better, at least when you thought about it intellectually. But could he really sit back and watch all the men on earth rise up against each other?

There has to be a way for you to stop this. If you were truly some helpless pawn, he wouldn't be offering gifts.

Right. Wolfie was to be faithful to the ones who created him, and therefore Rudy was part of the equation, a check or balance, kept happy (or distracted) by the parade of newly available women, possibly not knowing his role himself until some critical moment. But again, the boy had already figured all this out . . . the pendulum . . . the roller coaster. The question was, Rudy supposed, whether or not this cynical professor, beaten down by the world a bit, quietly bitter, could bring himself to "do the right thing" when he was at one of those temporary moral highs. Clearly, Wolfie was banking on the endgame, where the coaster settled. Fatherly love and a borrower's obligation before allegiance to some lofty ideal.

Rudy got out his cell phone and punched in the number for information despite himself. As hard as it was to admit, there was a definite roundabout going on here—a profound part of him that wanted to see this dark magic unfold just for the wonder of it all. And Wolfie's insisting that Rudy couldn't understand the big picture without context . . . that his mind had been simplistic terrain to navigate . . . that his books were one-dimensional, all had set a sort of fire inside him, jet black and scorching. He wanted more close inspection of the individual pieces of this massive puzzle, almost to prove to himself that he was capable of predicting the more global ramifications without a condescending tutor more than forty years his junior. There was pride involved now, and he supposed Wolfie had already accounted for this, working it into the overall equation after one of his initial picture walks through Rudy's "Biography Room."

"I know that you know, that I know that you know," Rudy muttered, almost like a taunting. Yeah, Wolfie boy, come down into the chasm and play.

When Directory Assistance asked for city and state, Rudy gave it, and when the recording said, "Listing," Rudy asked for the University of Pennsylvania library. It was easy to get past the bored graduate student, and even easier to convince the first snotty, then ultimately warm and articulate head librarian that his Widener kids needed a "real library experience," no tour necessary. He'd bring Wolfie along with the pack wearing a hat and sunglasses, loose clothes, anything that would hide that striking beauty, a paper leaf bag if necessary. Once the kid was in, they could leave him there discreetly. Kids slept over in libraries all the time, and security rarely bothered them once they'd made it past the entrance where they slid their I.D. cards.

As soon as he closed his phone, it rang in his hand, and Wolfie provided Rudy with a list of clothes he wanted from a store called American Eagle. There was nothing in his son's voice that indicated suspicion, and Rudy figured right then and there that they were out of range of each other or the mind-reading was, after all, only skin-deep. And either result confirmed the check and balance. Wolfie had a limitation after all.

Rudy pulled into the road and headed through lot B toward the exit. If there was one limitation, there would be others, and Rudy wasn't finally sure whether he wanted to track and exploit them or protect Wolfie from others who would do so. And of course, all the while he was sitting here measuring his ethics, he was also helping Wolfie infiltrate the library. He was on his way to buy clothes for him, and he was getting ready to register him in high school, almost as if these actions were merely chores, errands, humdrum and commonplace, harmless in themselves when compared to the horror they would eventually add up to. Oh, the devastation was utterly disconnected, beyond the horizon, a dream, a distant, dusty history book that would filter and erase the bloodshed the moment it ceased, whitewashing it with sayings that assured the survivors that their freedom had been threatened, that the sacrifices had been made in the good name of their traditions, and that we only "sanitized" this great land to avoid tyranny, suppression, and subversion. Maybe this was the way that the Hitlers of the world went about their business.

One banal responsibility at a time.

Rudy did the shopping and was numb about it, and the fact that he'd identified the heinous role of desensitization in the overall malignancy did not lessen the all too human lure of falling into it. By the time he got home, entering the foyer armed with bundles and packages, he was exhausted. And Wolfie had indeed become a teenager, dressed now in Rudy's "Wednesday": dark slacks, olive dress shirt, silk tie, black sweater. The boy was simply stunning, blond and angelic, thin almost to a fault yet sculpted under those dress clothes as indicated by his posture.

He was sitting across from a guest.

She turned, and mascara was running down her face like some old-school Broadway cliché. It was Patricia, Rudy's ex-wife, and the professor suddenly had a lot of explaining to do.

Rudy braced himself for the onslaught of questions and accusations that would turn his living room into a Jerry Springer episode. *Who was she? . . . Is she still in the picture? . . .* and the worst of the bunch, voice all choked up and tender . . . *Did you love her and do you still?* as if Pat had come even close to filling that void for the past twenty-two years or so. Suddenly, Rudy missed April Orr desperately and was simultaneously infuriated by the idea that he was obligated to defend himself for thinking he was worth her passion. It was also a pain in the ass to sort out the history he was going to have to invent here on the spot, making it seem that this "ancient relationship" was something he just fell into and couldn't get out of. Wolfie was around eighteen now, so Rudy had had this "affair" in what . . . 1994? What was going on back then, culturally, historically? He'd have to have met Wolfie's mother under *specific circumstances* that Pat needed to let fester, grind her teeth over, and finally accept grudgingly. Then she could block the idea that she was a boring lover, and worse, a shallow and uninteresting conversationalist who preferred to condescend from a platform of ignorance.

So how did he meet this "other woman"? Was there a snowstorm, a missed flight, some day after school that he went and had a drink somewhere? To make it real, he had to add a detail or two, like what was playing on the radio, or what movie was making everyone's head spin, something for context. Grunge, right? *Forest Gump* and *Pulp Fiction*, no? Or was that '95? Had Andrew Dice Clay done his blast and fizzle yet? Was Daddy Bush still President? Had Rich Kotite singlehandedly tried to destroy the Philadelphia Eagles franchise by then?

But Pat didn't demand an explanation. She stood shakily, took a tissue from her pocket (*God!* how it annoyed Rudy when he used to find the pieces of one of those things shredded through a wash), and wiped her face, smearing everything.

"I'm a mess," she managed. She put her hand on her hip and leaned on the corner of the chair dramatically. "And he's gorgeous."

"Oh, Mom," Wolfie said.

"Don't call her that!" Rudy snapped a bit too hard.

"I want to be involved," she said.

"No."

"Why?"

"Because you're not involved with me. Not anymore."

"I was when you went and had him."

Rudy's face went scarlet.

"Old history, sweetheart. My history. A history you really had nothing to do with except at the fringe."

"And whose fault was that?"

"Yours."

"Guys," Wolfie tried.

"Quiet!" They'd both said it simultaneously, though her command was filled with motherly caution and his was laced with a misdirected venom he immediately felt bad about. She folded her arms and held her head high.

"It was not my fault, Rudy. You shut me out."

"You never listened."

"You repeated the same things over and over again."

"Yes, to dead ears."

They were both smiling brightly now, and her fists were at her sides.

"O.K., Rudy. You've got me. I admit that I don't care one hoot about semiotics, syntax, and the wonder of the formulation of rhetoric."

"Clearly."

"So sue me."

"I did better. I divorced you."

She stepped back.

"Why do you hate me so much?"

Rudy looked off into nowhere.

"I don't hate you. We just got old, that's all."

"People get old, Rudy."

He looked at her directly.

"I meant the relationship. The attraction." He touched the seam on the back of the chair she'd been sitting on and ran his finger across it. "I just got tired of lying."

She gazed down listlessly. She was wearing tan pants and a sweater she'd knitted herself. It was lime green with black buttons. She had designer cat's-eye glasses, a short haircut with streaks in it, and earrings with golden spangles, but it was all poor window dressing. She'd developed dour age lines around her mouth and had to wear a custom-designed sweater to hide the double fanny in front and the wide ass in the rear. She looked like a fat boy who had raided his "hip" grandmother's wardrobe for a lark, and while there must have been pity somewhere inside him, Rudy felt nothing now but a deep-seated resentment for that "untended neighboring residence" he'd had to look at across the bed for so many years while he'd done a fair job maintaining his own metaphorical keep.

She stumbled over to Wolfie's footrest, and when she sat, the cushion wheezed. It almost made Rudy laugh outright, God help him. Wolfie slid down to join her and put his arm around her shoulder, causing her to lean into him, her hands sliding between her knees. She peeked back up at Rudy through her short bangs.

"You never understood me," she said.

"I tried."

"You didn't, not really."

Wolfie rubbed her shoulder.

"There, there, mum. Everyone here knows you always did your best."

Rudy was about to explode over the "mum" reference, but there was something in Wolfie's eyes that made him swallow it. Wolfie turned and kissed her forehead, bringing the other arm around for a big, warm hug. Then their foreheads were together. "Breathe," he said softly, and she took a deep one. He did it with her, then turned to Rudy, taking a second to shake the corn silk hair off his forehead.

"Try to understand," he said.

Rudy nodded. "I understand that we were young once."

Pat broke softly from the embrace, and her face brightened.

"We were, weren't we?" A cloud then came across her brow. "But you're right, Rudy. We grew apart. You had your hobbies and I had mine: you with your . . . writing and me, my knitting. You, your lectures, and me, my watercolors." She folded her hands and pursed her lips as if she were conceding something. "We're both just talented in different ways. Two ships in the sea."

Rudy almost went through the roof. Both? Talented? As if there were an equivalency to be drawn between his scholarly articles . . . his hours upon hours of meticulous research and drafting . . . his ability to publish regularly in seven major academic journals without a Ph.D. . . . and knitting? His lectures on navigating the more difficult rhetorical structures, differentiated for up to four separate ability levels simultaneously, and specifically designed to reach perfect climax every class period like fucking symphonies . . . equal to watercolors? The most intricate design she'd ever completed was a rather cluttered-looking paint by the numbers!

"You're kidding," he said quietly.

She looked at Wolfie as if his father were a bad little boy.

"Knitting," she said, "painting, cooking, stained glass, ceramics. He never cared." She stared over at Rudy ruefully. "They were important to me! They defined me!"

Wolfie nodded.

"She's right, Dad. 'Hobby' is such a silly little word. Our activities are what make each of us special." He took Patricia's hands in his and looked into her eyes meaningfully.

"Now mum, Daddy and I have to talk about things. I have a lifetime to catch up on, and I promise that you will be included.

'Stepmother' is as bad a word as 'hobby' for different reasons, and we are going to change its connotation this very minute. You matter, and this will—not—change."

She stood and waddled past Rudy to the door, wounded but a survivor. Wolfie was quick in tow to open the door for her.

"Bye, mum," he said. "I'll see you soon. And look on the bright side. We just analyzed the words 'hobby' and 'stepmother' in true phonetic, semiotic fashion, or whatever Daddy would call it. And we both made it through to live another day!"

They had a big laugh at that one, and even Rudy had to forfeit a genuine grin. Oh, Wolfie was good, there was no question about it. Pat paused in the doorway and said to Wolfie sort of through the side of her face,

"I have other hobbies. Projects. Things I want to share with you. Can you stop by for a visit?"

"Promise."

"Once a week? Fridays?"

"We'll see," Rudy said.

She leaned in to her stepson and reached to touch his face.

"So gorgeous."

She walked off to the dark hallway, Wolfie closing the door behind her.

"Over my dead body," Rudy said, arms folded. Wolfie put his hand in his pocket and came forward, skipping little spaces of time with a rapid version of "the blink," which gave a flickering effect. He stopped and let himself be seen "continuously" when he stood chest to chest with his father.

"She's a woman," the boy said, "part of a tragic race that has traditionally given all and received little. You condemn her for 'letting herself go,' but her allure was cursed with a shelf-life. She instinctively knew what you needed, but was denied the ability to evolve, for years trapped in a state of slow decay. It was absolute torture for her, and you can blame your male ancestors."

"It is what it is, Wolfie. Beauty withers, and I'm still a male animal for all intents and purposes. Maybe she's cursed, but you can't blame me for the biology I was left with."

"No, but I can stop you from hurting her. She's not some defective toy."

"She complicates things."

"Not really, Dad. She's as pure and simple as the rain. And she'll always be beautiful, like all her poor sisters. The withering part is your issue."

He reached past Rudy and pulled the half-gallon jug of iodine out of one of the shopping bags on the floor.

"A generic," he said, unscrewing the top. "Next time get a name brand, please."

He chugged half of it, Adam's apple bobbing up and down like a buoy in a storm. No burp at the end either, a true gentleman, just a pair of curving stains yellowed at the corners of his lips giving him a slight case of circus mouth.

"I'm going to sleep," he said, "straight through until tomorrow morning. If it makes you uncomfortable, I can position myself in your bed with my head down at the foot end, though the difference of that particular custom really escapes me."

Rudy put up his hand.

"No matter. I have a lot to do today, and by the time I join you neither of us will notice the other."

But Rudy was wrong.

After a day of rearranging the apartment for two, downloading (and filling out) state registration forms, and heading back out twice (once for Wolfie's preferred body gel called "Axe" and the second time for a book of stamps), he lay down next to his son. The boy was breathing softly, the moonlight and shadow cutting across his face like scripture.

Two hours later the boy woke up screaming.

Rudy had been dreaming about shadows. They were pitched from the angles and corners of the bedroom as static lines that slowly began to waver, then swirl to a dark, ghostlike version of April Orr, standing there at the foot of the bed, reaching behind to unzip the back of her dress, slipping a shoulder through, letting the fabric flutter down. She protectively covered her breasts with her forearms and then shivered.

"I miss you, Rudy," she said.

Her skin then flaked and peeled off, exposing the bright white epidermis beneath, and those sparkling eyes bubbled to black. Her lips turned violent red and her face went skeletal.

"Don't look at me this way," she said. "Please. Please?"

The word echoed, turned to sound waves that pounded and screeched across the room, and she became a white burst, so sheer, so high-pitched that it burned Rudy's eyes, and he sat up with a jerk into the semi-darkness, and next to him Wolfie was crying out at the top of his lungs, high and sheer, eyes huge, sweat shining along both cheeks. He was sitting upright against the headboard with his knees drawn in to his chest, and he looked at his father as if he didn't know him.

Rudy slapped him hard on the jaw. The boy's head snapped to the side, then came back, his frantic eyes clouding over, then moving to slow realization. Next was weeping and recovery, hands to the face, and his body shook with it. The positioning was awkward, but Rudy pushed over and engulfed the boy in his arms.

"It's all right," he said. He kissed Wolfie's slick forehead. The boy turned in to his father's chest and tried to slow his quick, shallow breathing.

"Daddy," he said with a hitch.

"I've got you," Rudy soothed. "I'm here."

"I saw him."

"Who?"

"The Dark Guardian." He pushed away, hair hanging in his face. "I've had 'The Coming of Dreams,' Dad. It's part of this."

"What does that mean?"

Wolfie wiped his cheek with his palm, and spoke out front as if the words were ingrained in his very core.

"'The Coming of Dreams' is my birth rite. I knew of it even from the first moment you pulled me from the stump, but only intellectually. I couldn't predict its intensity." He looked around the room as if inspecting it for a sudden intruder. Rudy rubbed his shoulder, and Wolfie went on.

"Since your forefathers imprisoned their witches, they engineered a failsafe into the genetic code, each generation birthing a knight of sorts, a Dark Guardian who waits."

"For what?"

Wolfie laughed softly.

"Not what, Dad. For 'whom.' Your ancestors made sure to balance the scales and protect the world from me." He drew his knees in. "He is prophesized to be unyielding and heartless. He is mortal as I am, but immune to my ability to disappear. He is the epitome of masculinity in its raw, savage form, and will be emotionally impenetrable. And before all this is done, I will kill him or he will kill me. There is no possible middle ground. The problem is that he is also resistant to my ability to read his biography and will therefore know of me before I know of him. This also cannot be changed, though the difference could wind up being no more than a moment."

"And you dreamed of him?"

"Yes, but his face was masked." Wolfie curled up into himself even more, chin almost between his knees. "He looked a bit like the lead character in a horror movie whose poster I saw in your history. It was called *My Bloody Valentine.*"

Rudy nodded. He'd never seen the movie, but he remembered by the advertisement that the villain was a miner, face hidden by a gas mask with goggles and a forehead lantern. Wolfie shivered.

"The Dark Guardian wears some sort of headgear, and the lantern light is no lantern at all, but something odd, something circular with ridges. I saw it in silhouette, however, and could not discern its context and identity. And he wears a massive cloak of darkness that somehow shimmers with stabbing light when he moves.

"The second you see him you have to kill him, you know. There can be no hesitation at all."

"Ya think?"

They both entertained a soft chuckle. Rudy pulled on his earlobe and massaged it for no reason.

"You said this was a 'Coming of Dreams,' plural. Was there another vision?"

Wolfie went cross-legged and pulled the sheets over his legs.

"It wasn't a vision, but more a saying, a riddle. I was born to destroy the men of the earth, but that victory would not shatter the spell your forefathers cast upon the wood. My mother race is still trapped in the dirt, and I was put here to try and release them as well. Whether I am successful in either endeavor is not guaranteed, but it is in my nature to try."

"What's the 'Riddle of the Wood'? What did you see?"

Wolfie smiled, and this time it was his reassuring hand on the shoulder of the other.

"It's science, Dad. Not your discipline."

"Tell me anyway. I'll try to keep up."

"'The Riddle of the Wood,' as you call it, has to do with a nova."

"Like the sun blowing up?"

"Yes, and that is why I most need the library visit. I have to make a study of the stars, the moon, astrophysics, astronomy. I dreamed these words in direct reference to freeing the witches from the bondage of the root: *'The sun must burst forth a hundred golden rivers.'* The phrase was visible, in Gothic print, and there was a number in the background."

"What was it?"

"The digit was partially hidden, but I am certain it was the number three."

"That's it?" Rudy said. "That's all you have to go on?"

"Yes. That along with the fact that the saying is a paradox, which in itself sort of causes one, but you already knew that, didn't you?"

"Hmm."

"To sleep now, Dad. I will not leave this room until Monday morning, and you can spend your Sunday preparing. Registration papers are one thing, but you will need high school bus schedules, activity sheets, the works. I hope you have ink in your printer."

"No problem."

"Good." He slid back under the sheets and pushed up with his knees until the bedding came loose from the bottom. He flipped the affair under his heels.

"Piggy-blanket," he said. "Nicer this way."

Rudy slid down and did the same on his side. He turned on his elbow and put his arm protectively across his son's shoulder. Wolfie slid back and let his father embrace him. Dark Guardians? Novas? Mass murder? It was all too big to imagine.

One day at a time.

Of course.

Banal responsibilities on Sunday; an uneventful trip to the library Monday. Steps. A process.

But the library trip was anything but uneventful. And Patricia's phone calls were a constant annoyance.

Rudy was never really good at planning these "field trips," and he supposed that was why he'd always avoided teaching the elementary grades. Those kinds of instructors needed mothering skills. It wasn't really about word walls, picture cues, and the best ways to asses fluency, but more helping Johnny find his inhaler and stopping little Denny from melting crayons on the radiator. It was not in Rudy's "wheelhouse," so to speak, to construct paper hats, play the "King of Ing," and get everyone's bookbags packed on time for the assembly, and it showed Monday morning. In his mind, the day started once they got to the Rare Books and Manuscripts Library, not before, not really. He was mostly concerned with stuff like everyone remembering their Widener I.D.s as he'd indicated in the e-mail. Would they keep their cell phones off as he'd specified? Would they stay in a group and have the decency to respect some of the ancient and classic texts they'd have access to? Rudy remembered this particular facility from his days at St. Joseph's a decade and a half ago when he got his masters in literature, and on *their* field trip, he'd sat at a table paging carefully through an original folio version of *Hamlet*. It was an astounding, humbling honor, and he didn't need some careless freshman spilling his energy drink on Gertrude's counterfeit presentment of two brothers, thank you very much.

There was also Wolfie to think about, not only in terms of Rudy's fear that he'd be an instant attraction to the kids no matter how discreet his disguise, but the fact that the boy's excursion needed to go further than the first target location. When Rudy initially made the arrangements he had spoken to the head librarian at the Annenberg School for Communications Library, who had given permission for Rudy to take his kids to Rare Books and Manuscripts. It had been so long since he'd been there that Rudy mistakenly remembered the two as being in the same building, different floor. But with his casual Internet search the next day, Rudy found that Penn wasn't like the smaller universities with a main library and another for law. There were more than eighteen library centers, all with materials of various disciplines, some up to two city blocks away from each other, and Wolfie was insistent that once they made camp at Rare Books, he be given the freedom to go on his own to Math, Physics, and Astronomy. The kid was highly perturbed, to say the least, since his reading of Rudy's "biography" was only as good as what the man could recall, and now they had to romance some sort of generic gate-pass from the Annenberg librarian instead of merely retaining initial access through one entrance door. Moreover, Rudy could barely convince his students to go to a library within his own subject area, let alone some science think-tank where most of them couldn't even begin to comprehend the abstracts.

And of course, during their bickering Sunday night over whether or not a librarian would actually answer a phone call or e-mail on the weekend versus a song and dance live and in person, Rudy had been on the Net trying to find a place for everyone to initially meet up for coffee. He picked the most obvious winner, a Starbucks, even though it was a few blocks off campus at 40th Street.

Bad mothering. He must have looked in the wrong column for the address, because what should have been a Starbucks turned out to be a still-closed Allegro Pizza, and Monday morning they were waiting for him there, half his class, mostly guys trying to up their grades, and two lacrosse players who happened to room together, Katie Dulaney and Bethany Durst. Many had their arms folded and were stamping the cold off their feet. Rudy came up and gave an awkward greeting, then fumbled through an introduction of his young cousin from Vermont, Drake Barnes. Wolfie gave a slight nod, and no one really paid attention to him. He had on a sweatshirt with the hood up and convenience store sunglasses, looking more the dock worker than some ravishing Prince of Darkness. He was in a sullen mood, carried over from yesterday, that pretty much echoed everyone else's sentiments when they found they had to walk all the way to 36th and Walnut, through the back end of a shabby neighborhood that had nothing better to look at than run-down fraternity houses and some zoned-off construction areas.

By the time they got to 38th Street, a couple of the guys were bumping shoulders playfully, then stepping on one another's feet. One of the girls had to pee.

"We're almost there," Rudy said, keeping it level. This wasn't high school, where he had to mark his territory and use "teacher voice"; those days were gone. But being out of the college classroom took away a bit of his power and mystique. It was disorienting, and he came close a couple of times to grabbing one of these asshole kids by the back of the neck, walking him away from his friends, and reading him the riot act, finger in the face.

Then he lost Wolfie.

They had just passed the parking garage connected to the Wharton Steinberg Center just north of Spruce Street when he noticed his son was missing. Rudy had been lagging in the back of the group watching Ben Alspach text and walk, absently relating it to chewing gum, and he literally felt the vacancy behind him.

He stopped, then snapped his head all around, looking at everything and nothing all at the same time: A Steak Queen Food truck across the street, a Flex Box, a rather dirty and dented POD storage unit half blocking a maintenance entrance, a Penske Rental truck parked too close to a hydrant.

No Wolfie.

Some of the kids had turned and slowed, and Rudy waved them on.

"Thirty-sixth and Walnut! Go ahead, I'll catch up in a minute!"

He walked a few steps in reverse, turned, and started to jog back toward the walking overpass where he thought he'd last registered Wolfie there at his elbow. He got to an alley on the left and gave a glance. It was an alcove where there was an outdoor café, currently closed, its yellow table umbrellas folded in.

Wolfie was there on the brick walkway, and he was dancing.

With a bird.

Rudy stepped forward, mouth slightly ajar. Wolfie had drawn the hood of his sweatshirt tight around his head and almost looked alien-like. Above and around him, a small black bird was gliding and diving, making figure-eights while Wolfie, in perfect rhythm, waltzed along the brick cobblestone. They were beautiful moving shapes, as if held together by some invisible set of cosmic wires, and then Wolfie started doing "the Blink." The bird followed, darting to where the image had just been erased, then anticipating and sweeping back around within centimeters of where the boy reappeared. There was something classic about it, cutting and clean, almost as if boy and bird were meant to share these lovely, erratic patterns that sketched themselves upon the February breeze.

Wolfie stopped suddenly, snapped out his hand, and grabbed the bird from mid-air. The thing screeched and one of its feathers popped loose, cutting half-moon arcs to the ground.

"Fucking tree rat," Wolfie snarled. Then he clapped his hands together. There was a wet popping sound, and Rudy saw one black eye burst loose, caught on a dark tendril that wrapped under at the base of Wolfie's thumb. Out of the other end a runner of shit, white with black streaks, had burst from the bird's anus and squirted down Wolfie's wrist.

"What—" Rudy managed. Wolfie tossed the carcass aside and went to one of the tables where some moisture had pooled in a dent. He pressed down his hands and then rubbed vigorously.

"What?" he said.

"That was disgusting."

"Was it?" He flicked the wetness away and wiped his hands on his pants. "Are you sad for the little worm-eater? The bark-bum?

The one who pollutes the sky with the exhaust of his swooping brethren? A bird's brain is smaller than a fingertip, and the thing camouflages itself behind the fluttering leaves of the prison stalk in absolute cowardice. It feeds on the screams of the inmate of the grain and mimics the sound with its idiot chirping. How do you think the name 'Mock-ingbird' came about?"

"You can't kill them all," Rudy said evenly.

"Why not try? Will it fuck the ecosystem out of seed dispersal and pollination, making it so we can't pretty up the landscape with the flowers and plants that make the trees look more as if they blend? Will car washes go out of business? Will the men who service horizontal phone cables suddenly starve?"

He strode over to a decorator tree, still a sapling really, growing through its black protector foot-grate that was of rather intricate Greek design. He toed it with distaste.

"This here, Daddy-o, is a thornless honeylocust. Isn't it lovely? Eventually it is going to grow to about fifty feet, but even in its infancy it has a little secret there under its roots that twine beneath the firebrick. Due to her eighteenth shadow-transfer from her original prison thousands of years ago, here lies a beautiful shapeshifter. She has pure white skin, lips of ruby, and her heart is still beating down there. Her name is Belinda. Would it be funnier if it was Sabrina? Or Samantha?"

"Wolfie."

"What, Dad? I'm a teenager and I'm angry. I have certain powers, a ton of advantages, but I'm part human too."

Rudy smiled thinly.

"Well, I don't buy the 'I'm just a kid' excuse. I didn't when I taught high school, and I won't now. You need to manage your emotionality, or you're going to draw attention to yourself."

The boy stared for a moment and then the air seemed to go out him. His shoulders drooped.

"I'm sorry, Dad." He removed his sunglasses and revealed that he's shed a couple of tears. "It's just that like the birds . . . I can hear her screaming."

Moved, Rudy wanted to reach out for his son, but he didn't want to be the one to cause more of a scene either. Strange. The kid was sophisticated in certain ways beyond imagination, yet had chinks in the armor, socio-emotive deficits common to his surface age. In terms of mood, he'd retained more mastery as an infant.

Rudy's phone rang, and he struggled it out of his pocket.

"Yes?"

"Roo?"

"Yes?"

"It's Pat."

"I know."

"Oh."

He put his palm over the face of the phone.

"I'm hesitant to leave you on your own, Wolfie."

A muffled voice buzzed in Rudy's palm,

"Is that my angel? Rudy? Rudy! I want to talk to him!"

He jerked the phone to his ear.

"I'll call you back!"

He closed the unit and raised his eyebrows. Wolfie shrugged.

"I'm going to high school tomorrow, Dad. You have to trust me."

"But that's tomorrow," he insisted. "Even stuck as a teen for a month, your growth pattern within it is exponential day to day. And in high school you know what to expect from my biography, at least to an extent. Out here in the city we don't know who or what you'll bump into."

His phone rang again, and he ignored it. They talked through the ringing.

"There's a spy-link for the father," Wolfie said. "If you're going to worry so."

"A what?"

"A spy-link . . . a way to see what's going on the way I see it, as I see it."

The cell went to its silent voicemail, and Rudy briefly pictured the tale full of pain and injury that was being presently recorded in his message center.

"Do tell."

Wolfie kicked at a loose stone and watched it ping off a recycling container that assured in bright white letters that the world was a beautiful place to keep clean.

"You grab your thumb. The left with your right hand."

"Just like that."

The phone rang again, and they both grinned.

"Let me talk to the poor thing," Wolfie said.

"A minute," his father replied. "Explain what happens when I grab my thumb."

Wolfie leaned over and spat, kind of a hanger-on he had to hover over for a second before it released itself. Rudy had to talk to him about that, either to teach him to do it better or not at all. Wolfie wiped off the residue with his sleeve.

"You become a passive passenger in my head," he said. "Not for sharing thoughts or anything, but like watching a movie."

"Passive."

"Right."

"Can I communicate with you?"

"No. You can only watch. Go ahead. Check it out. Grab it."

The phone had stopped ringing and Rudy put it in his pocket. He grabbed his left thumb.

There was an instant exchange of vision. While Rudy could still feel himself holding his own thumb and sense the vibration against his thigh as Pat began ringing his cell phone yet again, he was suddenly looking at himself holding his thumb with the other side of the alley as his background.

I need a haircut, he thought, *and this is a great way to find out if I have food in my teeth.* He saw himself grin and then heard Wolfie's voice come from directly beneath where his new vision was.

"What's so funny?"

Rudy let go of his thumb and was instantly switched back to his own perspective.

"Nothing." He dug the phone out of his pants and opened it. "What, Pat, for God's sake?"

She was weeping.

Wolfie approached and took over, turning away, saying sweet nothings into the mouthpiece. He returned, forfeiting the phone sadly.

"Such a sweet spirit," he said.

"My ass."

"She wants to see me Friday."

"Same answer, Wolfie. She's not a part of our lives. She's clinging and draining and an absolute nuisance." He studied the decorator brick for a moment. "And even though we fell apart, I don't want to be reminded of things. Nice things. The way it started. I'm still letting her go."

Wolfie smiled warmly.

"That's the first piece of sense I've heard from you in hours."

"So?"

"So."

Rudy shrugged, a bit annoyed that he'd picked up on a mannerism he would have rather left for Wolfie to enjoy by himself.

"You have no problem with my 'popping in' through the thumb-link whenever I want?"

"Of course not, Dad. I've got nothing to hide from you."

"Can you pop in on me?"

"No." His eyes narrowed playfully. "Why? You scared I'll catch your technique jerking off? I've already seen it, Dad, in your biography." He started walking away toward the alley entrance. "We're going to be late. If there's something I want you to see, I can send you an indicator by grabbing my own thumb. You'll get an alarm in your left ear. It's quite specific, and you'll know beyond the shadow of a doubt that I'm calling."

Rudy chuckled wryly and stepped along the brick cobblestone to catch up. Grabbing thumbs? Spy-links? Indicators? He almost felt cheated, as if he should have been aware of this foreshadowing earlier. Would have helped knowing the baby was all right in the house! It was also rather silly, at least the way it came off with the "code names."

But then again, Rudy wouldn't have been informed of this aspect earlier, because the baby had been more emotionally stable. This was a failsafe built into the growth pattern. While Wolfie was advancing intellectually, he was regressing and "humanizing" in terms of his feelings, and Rudy as protector was informed of his ability to be the watchdog when it had become relevant. And maybe the code-names weren't so odd after all. They were first to be utilized when Wolfie was a teen, and so the word associations would reflect what one at his socio-cognitive level would naturally come up with based on the image of teens in Rudy's biography. Even in terms of Wolfie's language patterns, far more sophisticated at their base than even Rudy's most decorated superiors, the boy was wired to "fit in" with the age group he'd adopted for this relatively significant period of time.

And really, when you thought it over, was the thumb-grabbing so silly? What would a space traveler think of men shaking hands . . . actually touching each other in such an otherwise homophobic society? What would he think of air-kisses between casual friends, pledging allegiance to a piece of cloth, crossing oneself and kissing it up it the sky before stepping in a "batter's box"?

A bright wail of a sound exploded in Rudy's left ear. It stopped him dead in his tracks and made him bend over, hand to his head.

"Jesus Christ!" he said. The actual "sound" had only lasted half a moment, but the memory of it was extreme, still ringing out sharply in his mind.

"I told you it was 'specific,'" Wolfie called back with a laugh. "Catch up." He jogged off around the corner and kept grabbing his thumb, sounding the indicator in Rudy's left ear. Laughing, Rudy clapped along the pavement after him, palm pressed to his head. Wouldn't a cell phone suffice here? His own started ringing again, and he frowned, slowed, grabbed it out of his pocket and shut it off.

No cell phones.

The last thing Rudy needed was for Patricia to be calling his son every five minutes, expressing her love and devotion, begging for a visit so she could show him her garbage sculptures, her junk jewels, her hat collection, her pottery junkyard.

He and his son had a world to restructure.

And the first night without him was difficult.

Rudy had always been a rather lonely sort of person. It was part of his makeup. When he interacted with people professionally he could always sense that he was considered "the other," the stranger with the past that was like deep pockets not meant to be turned out to the open. He was the one you didn't really joke around with too much, the one who had been through rough waters. Rudy seemed like the kind who'd lost a close loved one in some tragic circumstance years back, or the type who had been subject to harsh childhood poverty, something that made him put up shields, build that flat, hardened persona that made him the dark, emotionless figure who handled that small corner of your life (like your English grade), then went to perform his personal functions off the grid, mechanically, silently, effectively, until he was next needed to do a holistic edit of a nursing paper, or focus corrections for a student with a tense issue. In all actuality, it was more like what Ringo had said, "It's really just me face," but through the years Rudy had grown into what others had made him, now the hardened border-soldier, showing his age lines but putting on a clinic for the way one would sustain a poker face over time.

Until April Orr, who treated him like a man.

Until Wolfie, who in a single day had filled Rudy's dry world with close and personal humanity: his embrace in the car as an infant, his birth fluids, his incredible intelligence, his magic, his humor, his fear.

He is my son, Rudy thought. He was sitting at his coffee table, face in his hands. *My boy.* He couldn't stop obsessing over Wolfie's vulnerability, the terror in his eyes when he'd woken from his dream. And though Wolfie was a supernatural being, spring-loaded to woo mere mortals into overwhelming fits of love and attraction, either heterosexually, homosexually, or paternally (take Pat, for example), Rudy had to believe that his own deep wanting to hold and comfort this man-child was genuine.

He put his hands in the prayer position and rested his nose between his thumbs.

He had played the role of everyone's "other" for so many years that he'd forgotten what it was like to feel this way, so personally connected to someone. It felt like starving, like dying.

His head suddenly burst inside with Wolfie's indicator, and it made him jump.

He grabbed his thumb hungrily. He had forced himself not to impose this voyeuristic tool from the start, invitation only, and it had been the most difficult when Wolfie had first gone off by himself in the Rare Books and Manuscripts Library. One thing was for certain: whatever powers Wolfie did have over others, he had a shut-off switch. No one besides Rudy noticed him leave for the other facility, not even his lacrosse girls.

Wolfie had been invisible for all intents and purposes. Rudy was aware that the kid was walking the aisles with a cart and taking down books by the foot-pound, but none of his students paid him any attention. Nor did the regular library traffic alter its pattern, and by the time Rudy gathered everyone at the exit Wolfie was long gone.

Following that, the real worrying started.

Rudy had driven home aching to pull over and grab his thumb, but resisted with everything he had. That would be cheating, imposing. Still, as he'd said to Wolfie initially, he was almost paralyzed with the fear that his boy would meet up with someone or something not specified in the biography, forcing him to expose himself too early. The kid was mortal, after all. And what of this Dark Guardian? Rudy had a feeling that it was his job as father and protector to watch out for this beast, as it was fate that Rudy aid his son at least in the process of discovery.

He gripped his thumb so hard it must have turned violet.

In front of him, he saw a piece of notebook paper on a desk at a slight angle. Wolfie's handwriting was at the top.

"Hi Dad. Stop worrying as I know you are. I love you, idiot."

Rudy laughed, and felt tears well in his eyes. He could hear the sounds of the science library in the background, a copy machine's side cover being pushed back into place after an obvious paper jam, an elevator bell, Wolfie's breathing. The boy's hands and forearms came into the vision, and he started writing furiously.

"Look at this, Dad! Three is the third prime and sum of all previous primes. The new space is defined by an L. H. Euclidean 4-tuple consisting of a three space plus time. My birth was the fuse that opened the possibility of this seeming Armageddon, and with the coming death of the last man—besides you and me of course—within the three-year span that has been prophesized, that fuse becomes a trigger, the ensuing nova causing floods of lava on the earth's surface (a hundred

metaphorical golden rivers) and our escape at zero orbital velocity in our life pods, falling directly through the sun at a gravity of 1.175×10^{21} ft/s^2. The tornado-like vortex has a R. H. rotation, and is a conducting plasma. The vortex causes a reverse EMF, and it seems the paradox is how we attain the freedom of the witches before the earth that binds them is burnt to bare rock. But they will be released when the sun's magnetic field begins to collapse. There will be a window, Dad. Hope! The paradox actually is that in this new universe we all will have quantum twins, each the other's potential savior or destroyer. We will be long rid of the virus of men, and you and I will repopulate a new world reflecting this awesome reproductive duality."

Rudy let go of his thumb. Sweat had beaded up on his temples. Most of it he hadn't understood even a little bit, but he'd gotten enough of the ground floor to be awestruck. A new existence with father and son as the new "Adams" roaming like gods through a world full of "Eves." And of course, the check and balance, the alternate selves. Rudy had seen enough *Star Trek* episodes to know that usually those were not happy unions. This whole thing was an exercise in revenge, power, sex, and duality, a saga meant to sustain itself over generations. Whoever it was that said science wasn't directly linked to the literary arts was a madman.

And then there was the prequel to all this, the man-to-man holocaust, the bloodbath to come, the cleansing of the earth from its "virus" in the three-year window. This was going to be no dusty, unopened history book, no remote stanza of poetry, no disconnected mathematical formula. It was to be played out, live, right before Rudy's eyes, at the hands of his son. Any new existence would always be plagued by these horrific stains on Rudy's conscience, and he didn't think he could do it. In cold and factual terms, he'd only known Wolfie for a day. He had to destroy him before this went to the next level.

The alarm sounded in his head again. He jerked to an erect posture and re-affixed his grip.

The paper before him read:

"Though we can't talk to each other directly, I know when you disengage, Dad. I miss you, and I'll be home by early morning, maybe 2:00 or 3:00. Wait up for me and don't worry. I'll walk and use what you call 'The Blink.' It will take me five minutes and the muggers won't even know I'm passing them by."

Wolfie's hands came into view, and he had a pocket mirror, slightly smudged in the right corner, bordered by pink plastic. Clearly, the boy had made a lady friend and borrowed (or stolen) the thing from her purse. His face came into view in the reflective rectangle, and he whispered to his father,

"Love you dearly but not queerly."

"Shh!" someone hissed.

Wolfie put his hand over his mouth, eyes laughing.

Rudy signed off and sighed. Though he had trouble picturing himself as anyone's "Adam," he was no Dark Guardian either. If anyone was going to stop this beautiful, complicated boy from carrying out his mother's revenge, it wasn't going to be Rudy Barnes.

He tried to read, and couldn't.

He tried to eat, and wasn't hungry.

Wolfie hit the indicator a few more times through the night, sometimes with new equations and theorems, and others, while he was staring at some slender coed, like the tall one with the low-cut jeans and the dragon tattoo at the edge of her hip, squatting to get to the bottom row of a bookshelf, or the honey blonde at the reading table, casually taking her long hair and flipping it back over her shoulder while she studied (one of Rudy's favorite maneuvers, even if the breast beneath was fully covered by a high neckline). Rudy got his fair share of high thong straps and tight jeans, cleavage, and eye shadow, believe it, and each time Wolfie provided him these treats, Rudy somehow knew the boy was laughing, at least to himself.

Kids.

When he and his son were sharing these moments, Rudy's more

universal concerns blew off to the far corners of his mind, and he felt almost happy.

Wolfie came in at 2:30, and when they bedded down, Rudy felt at peace with his boy in his arms. When the sun rose, Wolfgang Barnes was going to go off to high school, Franklin Heights, the institution that graduated Rudy back in 1985.

The boy had three years to study the system, to infiltrate and learn the infrastructure, to wind up in prison, to call men to arms against one another, to wipe out the virus, and here in the semi-darkness of the apartment it felt nebulous, like a distant dream.

But Wolfie's first day of classes was anything but vague and impersonal.

And Rudy was amazed at how quickly this shit really started to go down.

Wolfie's schedule was morning-friendly, as Rudy had been lucky enough yesterday when he got home from Penn to connect with a sweet and sympathetic counselor named Emily Chung, who was cognizant of paving a nice path for such a promising new senior. He had a "free" first block (no class, just go to the library and make a friend or two), homeroom and AP Physics second block, B-lunch, which split third block photography into two forty-five-minute sessions, and AP English for the last hour and a half. He was also supposed to drop off paperwork to the office and the nurse, stop by counseling to say hello, and meet with his mentor teacher (a formality for all new students) a Mr. Bond / Room 129 for the first ten minutes or so of photography, from which he'd need to secure a hall pass and a return note.

He looked good: dark tan jeans, black designer T-shirt with soft reddish untucked flannel over the top. Casual, but neat. Handsome as hell. He'd slung his new backpack over his shoulder and was muttering something about sneaking in his iodine in an emptied bottle of Snapple, getting his little mentor interview over with during his "free" if the guy had a spare minute, and the fact that he needed an iPad, a pair of iPhones (Dad, your Samsung is simply archaic), and a laptop, pronto.

"Facebook, Dad. Tweets. Trending. That's the way the kiddies do it. If I'm going to infiltrate the system, I have to be an integral part of the communication network."

Rudy pushed away from the table and put his plate of half-eaten scrambled eggs and catsup in the sink.

"All true. I just don't relish your stepmother having a conduit, that's all."

"She'll be the first one I text."

"Funny."

"Not kidding. Bye."

He kissed his father on the cheek and made for the door.

"Take it slow on your first day," Rudy said. "Measure the field."

Wolfie did neither.

Rudy was in the middle of explaining Hemingway's subtle illustrations of formalized masculine rites of passage to his Widener Comp 102 students when he got the indicator. His left palm shot to his ear and Greg Hynman looked up from his notes with half a grin. A couple of girls in the front stopped chewing their gum and stared. Rudy winced, recovered quickly, and told everyone to write a response paragraph illustrating all the theatrical elements exposed in italicized pre-chapter six of *In Our Time*. He was going out to his car to get an aspirin while they did the assignment, and he was collecting.

Rudy rushed off to the bathroom down at the end of the hall, hoping it was vacant. It was a safe bet. By 8:10 A.M. all the early morning classes were in high gear, and students didn't often excuse themselves that early in the session. It wasn't polite. He ripped open the door and headed for the corner stall, the indicator wailing in his head for a second time. His eyes bulged. In the back of his mind he registered that he'd left his roll book back on the podium. Not professional; there were grades in it, and it was too late now. He grabbed his left thumb.

He saw what Wolfie was looking at and gasped. It was a polished block wall in what felt like the far corner of a dark basement hallway, and there was graffiti here, old sayings merged with the new, a layered kaleidoscope of word pollution. Standing out at eye level was, "Until the year we graduate, Franklin Heights is three years of hell," but the "Until the year we graduate, Franklin Heights is" and "years of hell" portions were faded and dull. Pronounced was the "three," more so because the artist had scrawled it as the Roman numeral "III."

"What does it mean?" Rudy said out loud. It echoed there in the stall, and he hoped no one had come in to take a piss in the last fifteen seconds or so. Of course, Wolfie couldn't hear him, but Rudy knew he was thinking along the same lines. The number three was supposed to be his timeline to architect the future massacre, not some prophetic piece of wall-art here in the present.

Wolfie turned to the left, and there was a thick steel door, deep maroon with a small dark window at the top, that had diamond wire crossed inside of it. Above the jamb was the room number 129. His mentor teacher, Mr. Bond.

Wolfie's hand closed on the knob and pulled.

It was the wood and metal shop: two stationary bandsaws in the center of the space, a lathe, a portaband station with the oblong tool mounted bottoms-up on a stand, a pegboard to the left with power tools, their cords wrapped neatly with wire-ties, and a wall of steel saw blades hung by size and tooth number, as the taped and retaped label-tabs indicated. Wolfie moved forward across a cracked and oil-stained concrete floor with a drain grate in the middle, slightly sunken where the rinse-hose had worn the cement down to its aggregate over time. In the far corner there were a couple of industrial basins, paint-splattered and shadowed with old grease and soot, and a worktable along the back wall with a huge bench vise. Over at the other end of the worktable facing away, there was a man bending slightly and welding something, sparks jumping on either side of him.

Wolfie approached, and the man must have sensed him, turning slowly, blowtorch hissing in his hands.

He had on a welding helmet with a dome light affixed above the tinted eye plate. Behind him in the catty-corner, the wall had old rubber soundproofing material glued to it, black with sparkles in the design. A "cloak of darkness" that shimmered.

"Move!" Rudy cried out to no one.

Of course, Wolfie didn't hear him, but he'd recognized the tools and trappings of the Dark Guardian most probably sooner than had his father. The edge of the vision Rudy was connected to actually bristled red, and Wolfie closed in fast. Rudy was gripping his thumb so hard he thought he might have been cutting off his circulation. The vision was slanted a bit and for a horrible moment Rudy associated what he was experiencing with the original audience for Carpenter's *Halloween*, not watching Michael Myers, but taking the steps *as* Michael Myers after he put on the mask.

Mr. Bond had been playing possum, and he swiped the welding torch right in Wolfie's face at the moment before contact. Rudy didn't feel the heat of course, but he knew Wolfie had at least gotten a first-degree burn across the nose from it.

Bastard! Even if he couldn't kill him, he'd planned to maim him, weaken him by nullifying his weapon of beauty!

Wolfie's right hand came into view at the bottom corner of Rudy's vision, and it was tensed and hooked into a claw-shape. Then it slashed up across Mr. Bond's chin and neck area, ripping the helmet clean off the head.

The rest was a flurry of slash and gouge, Wolfie's hands windmilling across the vision he shared with his father in a blur of slants and angles that raked deep furrows and curled the skin along the sides of each, rending so quickly and in such fury and cross-hatch that it was difficult to picture what Bond had looked like the moment before. He was suddenly ribbons on bone. There were exposed tendons that had held like stubborn circus wires on the left side of his neck and beneath the right cheek, and both lips were sheared clean, the teeth beneath grinning with the bloody residue they repelled, like dewed-up moisture on a car recently waxed.

Wolfie's bloodstained fists grabbed Bond's welding cloak at the chest and bunched. Then was the lift, and Bond's head lolled around like a zoo-balloon on a stick. Wolfie hoisted him onto the table with a thud, jumped up after him, straddled and hunched and then leaned in close . . . so close the vision lost focus.

At first, Rudy thought his son was kissing his victim.

When the vision pulled back, Rudy saw that Bond had been further violated. His chin was missing, the vacancy defined by an arc that looked like a frown beneath the skeleton's grin above it. Rudy almost threw up. The vision he shared was moving slightly, jogging a bit up and down, and there was a muted crunching sound.

Rudy disengaged, stumbled out of the stall, and pushed through the door to the hall. Somehow, he made it back to the classroom without zigzagging like a drunk or catching his toe on the edge-trim in the doorway and taking a header. His shirt was pasted to him beneath the cover of his black sweater, but he couldn't hide the sheen on the sides of his neck, his brow, the top of his head. He looked ill and he played it.

"I'm not feeling well," he said. "Read through 'Cross Country Snow,' the last of the Nick Adams stories before we get to 'The Big Two-Hearted River.' Write a response for Thursday that links Nick's father the doctor, Ad Francis, Krebs, Mr. Elliot, and the husband of the lady with the cat caught out in the rain with our lead character in terms of feministic shadowing outside the metaphorical arena. You're dismissed."

That would hold them.

When he got home, Wolfie was already there. He was in the bathroom, retching.

Rudy got to the doorway and held himself there, chest heaving.

"Hi, Dad," Wolfie said. He had his legs curled under and folded to one side. He reached up and gave a mercy flush, and in any other circumstance Rudy would have made a dry joke about holding the kid's hair back, or the fact that he looked as if he'd partied till he puked, something relating to those war wounds of youth that we all looked back on with pain and fondness.

"Let me see you," Rudy said.

Wolfie turned and shook his hair out of his face.

"What?"

"You're not burned."

"I jerked back. You saw the entire path of the flame, Dad. Perspective. If it had scorched me it would have actually disappeared from your vision."

He turned suddenly, shoulders up in points, palms pressed down to the porcelain rim. Then he vomited so hard there was upsplash that made it out to the floor. Rudy came in, slipped a bit, and got him a towel. The boy came up wet, wiping his face and grinning weakly. He flushed again.

"There he goes," he said, "down into the bowels of the earth, his underworld, through the dirty pipes he would have been proud to forge and seal. Now each time you flush, you'll be able to distinguish his moan inside of that hollow refilling drone." He cocked his ear down. "Do you hear it? *Home* . . . he's saying." Wolfie looked down to the toilet and screamed into it.

"At home in your own filthy mechanism! The ghost in the sewers! Eating my sewage the way I ate your face!"

"Is that all you ate, Wolfie?"

He looked up soberly.

"Of course not."

"But you can't have gotten everything."

"Can't I have?"

He was smiling now, but his face blanched and he turned and bent to retch once again. After what sounded like a particularly violent (and meaty) eruption, he flushed and held his hand on the knob-spoon for a second in recovery. He kept his face away.

"I ate all the evidence, Dad. His privates were no particular joy and his liver stunk like poison. I'm not stupid. For all intents and purposes he disappeared, nothing more. I'm not ready for the police yet. My arrest has to be ceremonious, almost religious. Mr. Bond would have been anticlimactic, at least to those around us."

Rudy let breath come through his nose.

"But it isn't only the body . . ."

"I didn't just study collapsing stars in the library, Dad. I am familiar with the rudimentary devices law enforcement would use in their initial investigations, that is, when they'd gotten that far. My tongue . . . are you sure you want to hear this shit?"

Rudy swallowed. Wolfie's linguistic spikes and socio-emotive retrogressions would have been entertaining if not for their content. And the stench in here. "Sure," he said. Wolfie turned and gave his profile now.

"My tongue is a sponge, Dad. Wood, concrete, and cloth are only so absorbent, and what would stain and retain form under normal circumstances becomes solvent almost upon initial contact, not even accounting for the pressure I can apply."

"So you're saying you literally licked the crime scene clean."

"Coveralls, floor, table, everything. Why do you think I keep puking? I am half human after all, and I didn't really enjoy eating dirt and WD-40, let alone . . . everything else."

Rudy looked around.

"How about this room?"

"They won't connect those dots, but if it makes you feel any better I would suggest a contractor's specialty store and some sort of industrial acid cleanser you disperse with a pressure tank and a hose with a nozzle." He grinned. "I wouldn't want to take a piss in a room where there was evidence of a man being flushed down the can either." The grin vanished. "But you'll never get away from the sound, Dad. The ghostly moaning in the pipes after you flush, and the laughter on its heels from the witches buried nearby, celebrating his journey to the waste water treatment plant as he rushes past them down there in the dirt."

Rudy folded his arms.

"What if someone saw you go into the shop?"

"They didn't."

"How do you know?"

Wolfie turned and sat cross-legged there on the floor.

"Just like I was able to see all the blood evidence as you would best imagine in a violet light scenario, I remind you that I can read and study things at a lightning pace. In terms of my initial approach to the school, I was instinctively wary. I could see from across the street and through the glass doors, the main console that had the grid of live video shots mounted up above the records receptionist. I had a 'free' and entered the building through an open gate back by the trailers, therefore avoiding the surveillance cameras sporadically positioned in the main entrance, the cafeteria, and various hallway points most populated by underclassmen. I blinked into the library, slid behind a book rack with a cloaked route to an exit door by a tech closet and warehousing space for English and history books, and then moved downstairs to the shop area. I assure you that my alibi is sound, and in fact will never be questioned, unless I don't return immediately. I have to shower, change, and make homeroom by 9:27."

"All according to plan."

"Faster than you think, Dad." He stood and started removing his clothes. "I need to rehearse the manipulation of the social network, but the practice has a purpose that will cause my departure earlier than I'd originally figured on, especially since I've disposed of the only fucker that could have stopped or slowed my progress. You'll need to get ready for us to split up, Dad." He looked down. "It never goes as you plan."

"How soon, Wolfie?"

He slipped out of his pants and straightened.

"It will take me two days to divide them. By Friday, the student body will be ready to explode."

"And you are the detonator," Rudy said.

"Oh, yes."

"And you are going to kill someone."

"Most certainly."

"Publicly."

"It will be the number one hit on YouTube for months."

He removed his underwear and stood naked before his father. Such a specimen. Suddenly Rudy felt he was going to burst into tears, but he held it.

"Theme?" he said.

Wolfie let his eyelids come down slowly, then reopen in that marionette's crystalline stare.

"Undetermined. For now, I have to go back to school and study the grid." He pointed casually to the pile of clothing there on the floor. "You can burn those if you like after I've sucked them clean. Or stick them in a trash bag and dump them in some gas station garbage container back by the detailing vacuums. Whatever makes you feel better; I just don't want to look at them again. Easier for both of us to move past the footnote."

Rudy nodded, backed out numbly, and gave Wolfie his space. Once he bagged the clothes and dumped them he was an accessory to that footnote, and he wondered if his son's new world standards would make it so that fact would no longer matter.

On paper maybe . . .

Rudy spent the day brooding, making scattered attempts at lesson planning, halfheartedly trying to fulfill a promise to read a colleague's paper on postmodernistic foreshadowing in medieval margin art, puttering around the apartment, measuring his life.

He was becoming a crooked equation.

For dinner, Wolfie brought people.

The apartment was packed with kids, and Rudy had already been out twice, the first on a run for guacamole and chips, and then for diet soda and Red Bull. Wolfie had made a whole lot of friends it seemed, and Rudy was the "cool dad," weaving his path between groups of teenagers, some quieter than others, yet none really animated except for two girls by the front door who kept poking each other and shrieking because they couldn't seem to get over the fact that they'd both worn the same sweater. There were a number of young men salt and peppered about, mostly shy-looking types that flipped hair off their faces with an air of practiced noncommittal, and then those who had too many blemishes, or noses too big, or waist sizes too broad, all with an open sensitivity they wore on their sleeves. Rudy couldn't be sure of course, but he would have bet dollars to donuts that the chess team was well represented here, along with band, the tech crew for theater, the anime appreciation society, and the debate club. On the other hand, the girls were a smorgasbord—the quiet and insecure side by side with the Barbies.

And from the running conversation, Rudy had quickly gathered that Wolfie had organized an anti-bullying meeting, the subject of everyone's discourse, a junior named Brian Duffey. The case against him was blunt and familiar, almost cliché, but no less intensive.

He was a football player (starting defensive end) who lived in one of those saltboxes up on the hill overlooking the Blue Route, his father the type with a ponytail that you didn't fuck with, a roofer by trade, and his mother a "crazy bitch" with a missing front tooth and hair too long for a woman her age, commonly seen at her son's football games sitting in the back bed of their pickup with the tailgate turned down, drinking Coors Lite and shouting obscenities at the refs.

Duffey was six foot three and two hundred and fifteen pounds. He had had bad acne when he was in middle school and now wore an older man's pockmarks on the sides of his thick neck. He had cold little eyes (one of the girls described them as watermelon seeds that gleamed), and a fighter's bowlegged ramble of a walk.

His grin was almost friendly, kind of dopey and silly, but it was a lie. Duffey's favorite move was what he called the "cell cramp," where he'd rip the phone right out of your palm while you were texting and crush it under the heel of his sneaker. He roamed the hallways with his wolfpack, fellow football players Gerry Rush, Bryce Wallace, and Frankie Hanrahan, along with part-timer Ricky Fitz, a stoner they kept around because they liked his ability to come up with awesome nicknames for all the "fags" and "brains" like "Cunt Bubble" or "Ass Monkey."

Duffey didn't like Jews, even though yarmulkes had grown in popularity with the cable show *Weeds*, and a lot of people greeted one another nowadays with the word "Shalom." He didn't like skinny intellectuals who won the science fair, he didn't like sand-niggers, he didn't like sensitive long-hairs who played the acoustic guitar, and he didn't like dirty little cheap-ass dot-heads who thought they were comedians. Black guys were O.K. because they shared the line with him out on the field, but he never invited them over the house for burgers and Ore-Ida onion rings. And sure, he liked hip-hop . . . he'd even drink a cold Miller with a "Blackie" or two down the back end of the quarry by the stacks of concrete pipe and abandoned front end-loaders, especially if they brought weed. But that usually ended up going sour and tense, as the drunker Duffey got the more familiar he tried to become, thinking that doing a mock "nigger" accent with mock "nigger" mannerisms would make him more real to the "brutha's."

He'd invented "The Duffey Fountain"—a dousing from a bottle of Deer Park he'd give you from behind in the cafeteria. That meant that he'd be watching for you in the halls, the bathrooms, or out past the tennis courts.

He knew the combinations of the gym lockers as a result of his access to Coach Sullivan's file cabinet, and had defecated in Brandon Fowler's bookbag last year. When the kid got to Spanish class, he reached in for his text and with instant revulsion withdrew his soiled hands, holding them up in mute horror, earning the name "Shit-Finger Fowler" for all eternity.

Duffey snuck up behind guys in the hallway, punched them hard in the back of the thigh, and then screamed "Run!" as he and his friends laughed like hyenas. He'd pushed a few faces into toilets and had gained schoolwide fame for walking up beside the given dude, whacking him in the nuts backhand, all knuckles, and shouting "Take a bow!"

And this was just what Rudy had picked up on the fringe, walking the room, offering bowls of Ranch Doritos and trying to remember more than three or four soft-drink requests at a time.

Evidently, like two prize bulls sniffing something different and threatening in the arena, Brian Duffey and Wolfie Barnes had become aware of each other from the minute the "new kid" stepped foot in the front lobby.

Duffey had been coming out of the nurse's office, a couple of Tylenols in his palm for the pain he always had in his ankle midweek when he practiced his signature swim-move/cut-left the afternoon before, and Wolfie had just checked in with the secretaries in the main office area. Evidently, Wolfie approached Duffey, who was bent over at the water fountain.

"Nice," Wolfie had said. Duffey snapped his head up and turned.

"What did you say?"

"Nice," Wolfie repeated. He nodded to indicate that he was looking at the mural behind Duffey's shoulder. It was a wide collage of photographs: students and teachers with their arms around one another, all smiles, in some pictures marching together, in others working at outdoor stands at last year's "Spring Fling" and at tables by the auditorium backgrounded by the signs advertising Oscar Wilde's *The Importance of Being Earnest*.

Wolfie smiled warmly.

"It's a nice presentation. In my old school, I was the chairman of the Gay-Straight Alliance and it looks like you have an awesome group here. Are you a member?"

In what Wolfie had described as "a beautiful moment," Duffey moved his mouth without saying anything, fists bunched, the tips of his ears turning red. He took a step forward, but the assistant dean came up suddenly from the stairwell, pushing open the door with a bang, and asking both of them rather sharply where they were supposed to be.

Before going their separate ways, Duffey had quietly hissed, "You're dead."

Wolfie had replied in a voice slippery and honey smooth, "Sounds like you're really looking for a date."

Later at lunch, Wolfie was sitting with a group of girls when Duffey came up from behind with a Deer Park. But Wolfie moved at the last second, seemingly inadvertently, and Duffey wound up dousing Linda Birch, one of the most popular girls in the school.

Tonight, she'd brought all her friends, hence the imbalance of male nerds and girls who had crossed the boundaries of their cliques to unite for the cause. Sure, Duffey had gained credibility by taking his team to states last year. He had his followers and fans, but when you got right down to it he was not going to win anyone over by embarrassing someone like Linda Birch, who had the gmail name "Pretty, Pink, and Perfect," who had been voted "Best Ass in the School" two years running by everyone's Tweet tally (*God*, Rudy couldn't believe what these kids talked about so openly), who was in the running for prom queen this year, who was known to party a bit, could rip-cord a beer with the best of the boys, but didn't have any problem staying after school to sell cookies so they could donate the money to the homeless.

The crazy thing about it was that Duffey liked her and everyone knew it. He also liked her best friend Brittany Sinclair, and before lunch today it had been up in the air as to which he was going to try for.

And with one wrist-flick of an opened water bottle he'd lost both. Worse, he'd had to save face, and when she'd called him a stupid jerk, he'd come right back with, "Stuck-up bitch."

The cafeteria had gone silent. He'd made Linda Birch cry. He immediately dropped a rung on the social ladder, but neither Linda nor any of his prior male victims really felt vindicated.

They wanted blood.

"Guys!" Wolfie called. "Guys, c'mon, quiet down!"

Everyone gradually came to a hush and turned to Wolfie, standing on the footrest with a Sunny Delight in his hand (secretly spiked with iodine of course). He looked around at everyone.

"So? What's our move here?"

"We come forward," someone called.

There were murmurs of agreement and Wolfie put up both hands.

"What's that going to get us?" he said. "Duffey gets suspended for absolutely trashing Linda in front of everyone? He gets a three-day vacation and a lecture? Then what?"

"Yeah," someone said. "I gotta walk by his locker between third and fourth block or I'll be late for calculus. Last year he pushed me into the fire hydrant and chipped my tooth because I wouldn't give him a dollar. Said he'd kill me if I told. What if he finds out any of us ratted on him?"

"Yeah, we'd be dog meat," someone replied. An especially pretty girl with flaring nostrils and hair tumbling down in jet black ringlets folded her arms.

"If you're all too chicken, leave it to the females."

"I agree," Wolfie said. "This is a woman's job, but telling on Brian Duffey isn't going to hurt him. By the time he gets his own version spread all around, he'll end up looking like a champ. I know his type. He's never going to be any famous doctor or lawyer, but he knows how to win the cafeteria."

"That's so unfair!" Linda Birch exclaimed. Voices backed her, and Wolfie quieted them again.

"Yes, it's unfair," he said. "And to solve this, to stop the abuse, to . . . *hurt* Brian Duffey we've got to be brave, and rash, and maybe a little bit unfair ourselves. The only question is whether we've all got the guts to go all the way, to stand strong, to face those in the school who would not approve of what we know in the end was the right thing to do." He tilted his chin. "Do you have the courage to fight back or not?"

"How?" Rudy said. That really quieted the room, and Wolfie carefully moved hair off the side of his face.

"We need more soda, Dad. Be a pal and run down to the store for us. Last time, I promise."

A sea of eyes turned back toward Rudy, and what he saw in those eyes was pain, frustration, and impotence just aching . . . *dying* just this once to turn into something stronger. They'd found their light in the tunnel standing on a footstool, and they were saying to Rudy, *What you don't know won't hurt you,* or more importantly, *If you do know, it will.*

Rudy stood his ground for a moment, wondering how he could stop this. Everything he knew as an adult and an educator screamed that whatever they were planning wouldn't really solve anything, just prolong it. Additionally—and he hated himself deeply for this one— he was considering the liability here, possible lawsuits, litigation, investigations identifying his own specific role in what was to come.

A footnote, Dad.

Rudy started and looked up at his son, who had done one of those close range silent communications. No, he couldn't quite read minds, but he knew his father. Like a book of old morals. Wolfie's lips didn't move, but he spoke clearly into Rudy's mind:

No one will care about you in all this, Dad. It's too big. I'm not planning a "Columbine," so don't worry your head. Trust me, none of it is going to matter in the end anyway. You're free of it, just . . . let this happen.

Rudy worked his jaw and looked at all the faces telling him to leave, quickly if not awkwardly. They'd had their fill of the Brian Duffeys of the world, and to tell the truth, Rudy knew full well that they had a right to strike back. "Punishments" for bullies were rational, corrective devices tailored for people with compassion, geared toward those built more like the victims. Did that make sense even a little bit? The targets had already been scarred. And to their heartless adversaries, the ensuing detention, suspension, piece of community service, or sensitivity meeting was no more than a bother they had to smile through. Where was the justice?

Rudy turned toward the door. That was Wolfie's gift, pointing out what was truly deserved rather than what might be more universally acceptable after the smoke cleared. Yes, universalities were invented by those sitting in a boardroom somewhere, spinning ideals and wearing masks of virtue while down below their feet in the trenches kids were getting whacked in the nuts, punched in the thigh, and tricked into reaching into bookbags filled with feces. Wall Street was blatantly stealing the money right out of the Main Streeters' pockets. Wars were being waged because we needed an enemy to blame. An old sin kept an entire race of women trapped in the dirt beneath the trees.

By the time Rudy went, got another case of soda, and returned the place had been vacated. It was a mess, but not that bad. Wolfie was sitting on the footstool he'd used as a pedestal, and he looked tired.

"So," Rudy said.

"Tomorrow."

"You're going to fight this boy? Maim him? Kill him?"

Wolfie smiled a bit sadly.

"No, Dad. That comes the day after. Remember, I am practicing the division of a mass, a necessary simulation with a dual purpose, the latter of which will indeed send me to the incarcerated men who will become my initial puppets of destruction. For tomorrow, though, I'm not even going after Brian Duffey; in fact, I'm steering clear of him."

"Who then?"

"Someone he cares about."

"His father?"

Wolfie laughed.

"Hell no. I'm not going to do the bastard any favors. I'm talking about Duffey's coach, Mr. Sullivan, the guy who picked the son of a bitch up off the street corner and made him into something."

"And you're going to kill him?"

"No. Destroy him. Humiliate him in the ugliest arena there is."

The Witch of the Wood

"How?"

Wolfie looked at his father with the slightest hesitation and then his eyes steeled.

"Something I found, Dad. In your biography."

The next day was excruciating. Inevitability hung over Rudy's head like a storm cloud, and he barely made it through his classes, fumbling across instances of Hemingway's use of the Aesthetic Theory of Omission in the base text, making halfhearted sweeps at linking more modern examples and coming up empty. There was a clear disconnect here, static in the broadcast, but the students didn't seem to notice or care, all of them listening blandly, writing robotically.

He did not use the spy-link except for one brief glimpse he took up in his office after class with the door closed.

He grabbed his thumb and saw legs, bare legs, a chorus line of them, and there were pink shorts and white shorts and tan khaki shorts, and black shorts, yellow hot pants and blue jean shorts with white dangling frays . . . all the colors of the spectrum and all the timely styles, most of them crotch-high, and some so brief you could see three-quarters of the exposed hanging pockets, others so tight they looked like silk undergarments.

Rudy disengaged immediately, sweat popping up on his forehead and above his upper lip. These were high school girls, and the vision he'd just been exposed to had a pedophilic feel to it, akin to robes, lotions, sex toys, and old perverts. Of course, he didn't know the context here, but it sickened him to know that whatever Wolfie was doing, it was inspired by something he'd found in Rudy's biography.

The day crawled by.

No cell phone calls, no texts, no indicators. When Rudy got home there were no messages on the machine, and he turned on the 4:00 news.

What he saw shocked him.

It was his ex-wife Patricia standing at some sort of outdoor podium, making a passionate plea, mascara running down her face like Tammy Lee Baker. She'd had her hair recently cropped into a boy's crewcut and she was wearing a black hat with a pin in it. Within half a second, Rudy recognized the background as the curved stone wall at the entrance of the high school, and at the bottom of the screen the story-tag said, "High School Teacher Suspended for Inappropriate Conduct."

"He should be arrested!" Pat was in the middle of claiming. "We trust our educators to protect our children, not leer at them."

"He was looking at the cell phones!" someone shouted from off camera.

"Why was he looking down there in the first place?" Pat snapped back. "The young women of our community should feel safe and secure in their classrooms, not threatened that some monster is going to be studying them in a sexual manner."

"He was doing his job!" someone else called out, voice cracking a bit at the end, causing an uncomfortable laughter to ripple through the crowd. Pat's eyes went wide.

"His job? To ogle underage girls as if he's in a strip club?"

"Why were they dressed that way in the first place?"

"Yeah!" another voice agreed. "Your (bleeped) kid set him up!"

Pat grabbed the edges of the podium, eyes shut. Tears squeezed from the corners, running down the streaked paths of those previously made, and she managed:

"My son . . . my *love*, had heard from his new friends that this invasion . . . this *abuse* was a sick and longstanding tradition between the female students of this community and this particular *instructor*. Do not blame my son! He offered the girls a way to fight back, and he should be applauded!"

Rudy was shaking his head in disbelief and disgust. He had rushed through the forms at Wolfie's request and listed both himself and his ex-wife as guardians, just in case he was unavailable. He'd done it as an afterthought, thinking in the back of his mind that there was no way, unless someone was bleeding to death, that they would contact *her*. But "Pat" came before "Rudy," and she'd been involved first here. And the fact that it was all part of Wolfie's plans didn't make it any easier to swallow.

The camera suddenly cut to another podium, this one positioned outside of the district building three blocks away. A tall, slump-shouldered man in a blue suit with quicksilver hair was addressing another crowd, this one even more raucous than the one that had been positioned offscreen at Pat's confrontation. His voice was soft, but his eyes were steel. Below him, the graphic said, "Joe Winslow: Union Representative for accused teacher Bill Sullivan."

"We are not accepting this," he said smoothly. "And we are ready to take on the district, its supporters, and those who have let the morals and standards we all hold dear slip to the point where none of it makes sense anymore. The young women in this country are to be protected certainly, but we will argue that they consistently dress in an inappropriate manner. According to the student handbook, no skirt is to be shorter than where the tips of the fingers would reach with the given student's hands at her sides. So why on earth would security let these girls through with shorts on? Should not that article of clothing be banned? And what about gym class? How can we effectively enforce a rule, when we contradict that very rule in analogous circumstances?"

"Speak English!" someone jeered, and Winslow didn't miss a beat.

"If we outlaw short skirts, why on earth do we supply field hockey kilts and cheerleader uniforms that break the original code? We absolutely sexualize our children, cheering them at pep rallies where the 'fliers' are taught to hold up one of their outstretched legs, exposing the private area beneath the skirt in moves like 'The

Scorpion' and 'The Heel Stretch,' and then cast blame when a male instructor notices that all his female students wear short shorts on a February morning. First, you must prove he wasn't inspecting his class, in spite of the contradiction I just mentioned, in reference to a dress code he is advised by administration to enforce. Secondly, cell phones are not allowed in class, and it is Mr. Sullivan's job to confiscate them. Third, there is no law that I know of that claims 'looking' is illegal, or even inappropriate."

The camera cut back to the newsroom anchor, who clicked a thin stack of papers before him, and set up the dramatic "cap-off" to the report.

"The case is under review at this time with the superintendant's office. For those just tuning in, a student who will not be named admitted to school administration at Franklin Heights High School today that he engineered a demonstration to prove the lecherous nature of Health and Phys. Ed. teacher William Sullivan, by convincing female students to wear revealing clothing in their 3rd block health class and put cell phones in their laps, recording Mr. Sullivan's alleged ogling. Whether Sullivan's behavior reflected the responsibility of enforcing a dress code and confiscating cell phones or some gross invasion of student privacy is to be determined soon by school officials."

Then came the thunder, and Rudy's mouth dropped open. They showed the recording(s). Clearly, Wolfie somehow got the cell phones to the newsroom, whose editors did a fine job of splicing together the images.

The establishing shot was a rough pan of the classroom. It was one of those "amphitheater" set-ups, where one white desktop curved across an entire given row, therefore leaving exposed the legs and waist areas of the students. There was someone in the background throwing a balled-up piece of paper at a trash can and someone behind him looking out the window. The next image

The Witch of the Wood

came from a different phone held low and aimed at the first two rows of students, many of them female, most of them crossing their bare legs. In the background a man's voice said, "Come to order, ya knuckleheads, let's go."

There was then a cut to a sightline from low and far to the side. At the periphery of the shot you could see the edge of a thigh and a knee, and in the center of the screen was Bill Sullivan, standing at the board. He had short hair, thick twelve-o'clock shadow, a black-collared shirt, and black sweat pants. He was thin-waisted and top-heavy; clearly a man who lifted weights, and as a girl wearing a tight white top, pink shorts, and sandals entered late, he looked over, eyes falling north to south and then sliding back on up again, strike one. Next was a camera change, now on the side of the room by the door, this particular cell phone so tilted it almost gave a view as if you were lying sideways. Sullivan was talking about a pre-class paragraph on the subject of STDs, and right after assigning it he told them they were "on the clock . . . write until you feel like your hands are falling off." Then he scanned the room, slowly, carefully.

"Strike two," Rudy said softly. Sullivan clearly occupied them with the writing assignment, all their heads down, and he was checking them out, girl by girl, row by row, you could see it.

Then was the last camera cut, a last cell phone more in the center of the room, first row, slightly stage left, positioned in the operator's lap so perfectly the image was straight up and down. Sullivan was sweating, it was sheened up on his forehead like glass, and he was darting his glance side to side.

"Hey," he was saying. "Put those cell phones away. Hey!"

Back to the newscaster.

It was strike three, slam dunk, end of game, end of story. As usual, the media had formed a dramatic line, and whether or not the individual shots were telling, the combination was absolutely damning. Of course, the context trashed the teacher—it best sold the story. And he was probably guilty. Of looking and enjoying it. So were the cops who beat Rodney King, guilty of beating Rodney King. But the first minute and a half was never shown to the general public. Was there footage that could have saved Sullivan here?

They'd never know.

And Sullivan was going down. No doubt about it.

The newscaster ended with:

"More news from Franklin Heights High School, shop teacher Frank Bond has been missing for a day now. He signed in for work yesterday and never showed up for his classes. Authorities are investigating, but do not expect any foul play."

Rudy clicked off the set.

It was staggering, what Wolfie had managed to churn up in a single twenty-four hour period. Absolute division, confusion, cultural antinomy. Rudy wouldn't have been surprised to see this on the national news at 6:30.

Sullivan was guilty, but stained with a crime he shared with many of those who would condemn him. And everyone was forced now to undergo some real soul-searching, possibly making Sullivan a victim of the larger societal contradiction, therefore erasing cheerleading and gymnastics and track and field hockey, not to mention lacrosse, ballet, ice skating, and all the water sports. And if you took the other side, claiming it was O.K. to watch those things in certain contexts, how did you rationalize harsh judgment on a man who very well could have been looking because he was paid to look, to enforce dress code, to confiscate electronic devices? Was he looking at the cell phones, or were they looking at him?

Then back to square one, everyone saw it in vivid Technicolor. The bastard was looking at the girls, not playing cop. What was expected in the pep rally was a crime in the classroom, at least in the court of public opinion. And if you did slam-dunk Sullivan on the platform of context, you had to live with the contradiction that these latter events (and outfits and uniforms) were designed for male audiences, manufactured for the specific practice of "studying girls."

It was the perfect vicious circle. If you backed him, even in the policing scenario, you admitted you supported "looking." If you condemned him, you were a hypocrite the minute you went to a football game. If you played middle ground and claimed context, your motives would be under the microscope now, and even in this new light, coming in hard from the side so to speak, there would be a strong majority, of women mostly, cheerleader moms just as fanatical as the Little League dads, who would wonder what was fair about telling their daughters to just cover up and dilute the leg stretching, especially considering all the camps, practices, pulled muscles, and turned ankles they'd endured since the age of nine in the name of the sport(s) that they loved.

Division? This was nuclear. And perfect in the chaos it caused, pristine in that there was never a good answer and it made everyone's blood boil, like those essay questions we leaned on so heavily, making the students argue for something impossible to solve like the death penalty or abortion.

Oh, he'd divide them all right. And Pat had been the perfect pawn to set up camp on one side of the fissure.

Rudy snatched the phone out of its holder and dialed Pat's cell. She let it ring almost the full five times.

"Yes?" she finally said.

"Where is he?"

"Oh. Hello, Rudy."

His teeth were grinding together and he spoke through them.

"Where is my son?"

There was a pause, then a blurting that had tears and righteous defiance in it.

"He's here in the car, and we're going to the house for some chicken soup. My precious sweetheart has been through hell today, and he needs a mother's comfort."

"You turn that car around and bring him home. Now."

"Rudy . . ."

"You are not his mother."

"I'm the only mother he's got!"

Rudy stood.

"Patricia! It's a legal issue. He may be eighteen, but he's still in high school. I don't care what it says on some random set of registration papers, I am his guardian and I want him home. Don't make me call the authorities!"

"You go ahead and try!"

"Mum," Wolfie said in the background. "It's all right, please."

"No, it's *not* all right," she said.

"Mum, you'll have to take me home right away. Turn the car around, yes. I'm so sorr—"

The connection broke and there was silence. Rudy tried the number three times, but got voicemail. He was seething; *God,* she infuriated him! Patricia was the epitome of melodramatic emotionality, weak excuses, painting the picture rosy, and winning because the opposition felt sorry for her. She was all the things in life that made Rudy cringe, and though there was no concrete harm in Wolfie being coddled, it filled Rudy with a nearly uncontrollable rage. How *dare* she!

He stalked around the apartment, opening the fridge, not really looking, turning on Comcast, not really watching. Minutes ticked away, hours, years, centuries. Finally, the door opened and Wolfie came through, unaccompanied by the coward, of course. Rudy was in his boy's face immediately.

"I told you, no contact with that woman."

Wolfie backed away and waved his hand in front of his face.

"Whoa, breathe, Dad, yo."

"Not funny."

"Not laughing." He walked around the sofa and plopped himself down. Rudy followed and stood over him.

"Stay away from her."

"Why?"

"She's an influence."

Wolfie looked up.

"On me? A bad influence? Really? Did you just say that out loud?"

Rudy ran his palm across his mouth, trying to calm himself. He moved across the room and sat on the footrest. He sighed and turned toward the window.

"My biography?" he finally said softly. "You got this from me?"

"Yes, Dad."

"I'm not like him."

"Yes, but you look at them too."

"Well, there's looking and then there's looking, Wolfie."

"Potato, potaaato."

"No!" Rudy said. "It's not the same thing!"

"Really?" Wolfie stood up. He looked as if he were about to say something harsh, but he shut his mouth, reconsidering. He put his hands in his pockets, looked down, and said softly,

"Dad. I know two girls from Franklin Heights who would each be a perfect sexual match for you."

"No!"

"But they are."

"That's not the point."

"Isn't it? One is eighteen."

"Wolfie . . ."

"And the other turns eighteen next week. Would it be O.K. for you then? I could arrange a threesome, I'm sure of it."

"Stop it."

"Why? Does the week really make a difference? Really? They are both beautiful, one a redhead with a sour apple pout and freckled cleavage the way that you like it, and the other is a blonde with long, athletic legs. Both have a daddy complex and neither is a virgin."

Rudy's fists had tightened and his neck strained with it.

"No!" he shouted. "I won't! Not with a minor, and not with a student, even if she's twenty-two! I don't care what the law would let me get away with the moment a girl sees her eighteenth summer, and I'm not interested in the way you can twist things! I notice a young woman's sexuality because I'm a man, but I choose my lovers as a human being with a conscience. There are certain things that are off-limits, even in your new world order!"

The room rang with it, and the silence afterwards felt thick and unhealthy. Wolfie shook his head and walked off to the bedroom.

"So sad, what you deny yourself, Dad."

Rudy followed, speaking at his son's back.

"But it's my sadness. I'm happier living with it, Wolfie, and it's not going to change. Ever."

"So sad," Wolfie repeated.

He sat on the bed and opened the laptop.

"What are you doing?" Rudy said. Wolfie looked up.

"You want to come in and see?"

"No. I'm happy here in the doorway, Wolfie."

The boy shrugged and looked back at the screen.

"It starts with the Facebook war, Dad. Duffey will be looking for me on here, gathering friends and supporters, and I've got to address him. Sullivan was the most popular teacher in the school, always voicing 'cool' things on the inside track, like 'I don't understand this book either,' or calling money 'serious coin,' or joking about farts and telling stories during class time. He was a bit transparent, but an easy A and a hearty laugh. And then there was

Duffey, the poor little rough kid that got signed up at age ten for football by his parents because he'd lit a fire in a field behind the paper branch after a long summer of rock throwing, shoplifting, and shooting out windows with a .22. He needed a focus. Since the first Pop Warner game that this frustrated, warped child played years ago out on the grass-worn field at the Dermond complex, Coach Sullivan has been a close friend of that family. He took a disadvantaged kid who could rush the quarterback and built dreams inside of him, of a D1 school, a full ride, and the NFL from there. I've destroyed Duffey's savior. He'll want to kill me."

"And you're going to fight him."

Wolfie closed the laptop gently.

"It won't be much of a fight, Dad. I am going to try to reason with him at first, apologize. He will shove me around pretty good, and there on the asphalt, possibly down on my knees by that point, showered by his taunts, I'm going to stand up for the downtrodden, the abused, the violated, and the weak. I am going to . . ."

He stopped thoughtfully.

"It's best not said aloud." He looked at his father. "But the violence will be so profound and extreme, it will erect a sort of religion."

"So you can be worshipped in prison."

"By some. Division. Remember?"

Rudy ducked out and closed the door gently. He tried to eat and didn't have the stomach for it. He tried to sleep on the sofa and couldn't.

Only someone pathetically weak or utterly insane could possibly let this continue, as father, as citizen. It was no longer some abstract, intellectual concept, a nosy neighbor here, a shop teacher there. It was going to go global fast, and once Wolfie was lost inside the prison system, there was no stopping this grisly, loathsome machine.

Witches underground?

It was a sin, certainly.

Did he believe it?

Every word.

And now the kicker. Would he try to put a stop to this horrific and unacceptable vision of revenge while there was still time?

Rudy Barnes tossed and turned out on the sofa all night, trying to fend off the heaviness that lay on his heart whenever he thought of any kind of harm coming to this beautiful and dangerous boy. Then he questioned the heaviness itself and fought to stay rational about it.

Yes, Wolfie was his son, his blood, but where did this "love" really come from? Was not this emotion something you developed over time, learned to trust, nurtured, built layer by layer?

He'd known the boy for barely more than a weekend. If this was fiction he wouldn't believe it was worthy of the page, so why trust it here in real life?

He stared at the ceiling in the semi-darkness. Wolfie was a warlock. He cast spells of love, so this feeling was not real. It was imposed. It was rape. And the idea that this state of mind lay on his emotions like some terminal cancer gave a perspective, at least intellectually.

He knew that in the end he needed to be true to himself. Rudy hadn't asked to be king of the universe, but he'd gone and signed on when it was offered to him, yes he had, and the blood of two men stained his hands.

Time to undo this mistake.

The question was how. The question was whether Wolfie could actually be defeated.

And also, Rudy wondered whether there would be anything left of his own heart when the spell was ripped clean? Cancer had this clinging ability that made it a tough trick to split it from the tissue.

Rudy had until 7:00 A.M. to figure all this out.

But at 7:10 the next morning Rudy hadn't figured it out. What he had done was wake his boy with a snuggle and a muffling of his hair. He'd made him his iodine shake and sat at the table across from him.

This was going code red, and he couldn't do one thing to stop it. It was easy to picture heroics on the sofa in the dark, but in the pale light of the kitchen those things seemed like dreams and mist.

Wolfie put his glass down hard and gave a little burp.

"Amen!" he said, and something clicked in Rudy's mind. Something tangible, something insightful, it was that sudden, like waking up with a cold shock of water straight in the face.

Amen.

Religiosity.

Perspective.

It was all about riddles, about looking at things from different angles, and Rudy sat at that kitchen table fighting to retain his outer "calm" while on the inside he worked desperately now, point by point, facet by facet, blowing smoke and dust away from the forms and lines that made up an alternate interpretation of Wolfie's "Coming of Dreams."

Rudy had never quite bought into the nova theory. It was not that he hadn't understood the terminology (and he hadn't), but there was something about it that seemed off-kilter. Scientists had formed a way to put the witches under the dirt, but release-codes, propaganda, and prophecies were typically architected by politicians, those who wouldn't know the first thing about life pods, or R. H. rotations, or new reproductive dualities.

Politicians were more like Rudy. They were wordsmiths.

What was the first thing people tended to flock toward during social crisis or change?

The clergy, or something similar depending on the culture.

Rudy's heart pounded in his chest as it all came together. Beautiful and horrific. Holy and violent. The paradox was that the freedom of the witches was not synonymous with the death of all men, and the protective clause was win-win, lose-lose on both sides.

Wolfie's dreams were actually connected.

The number three was a traditional religious reference.

The "Riddle of the Wood" with its flowing golden rivers was a play on words, and the black widow was the most venomous in the shadow of her lair.

"Wolfie," Rudy said smoothly. "I think that before your . . . *event* with Duffey, you should pay a last visit to Patricia. You never quite made it over to the house, and it will be a long time before the two of you will have a chance for reunion."

He'd tried to make it sound like it had been a tough decision he'd really fought over within himself. Overcome with emotion, Wolfie stood and almost stumbled on his way around the table. He took his father's hands in his.

"Finally, Dad," he managed. "You see her beauty. There's hope for the new race of man after all."

He bent to kiss his father, and Rudy stopped him by gently placing his palms on both sides of the boy's head.

"I'm the one who needs to kiss you, Wolfie. Take it with you where you go. Remember it."

He pressed his lips to his son's warm cheek, amazed at his amazement at how much it hurt inside to do so.

In the car, they did not speak. Wolfie was evidently preoccupied with what he was going to do with Duffey, and Rudy's face was a mask. Beneath the surface he was terrified. Sitting beside him was a demon, loyal only by birth-tie, trusting him solely because of the brief history of subservience Rudy had worn about himself like a soaked poncho.

Wolfie could read biographies. That was exactly *like* reading minds, except if he made the mistake of thinking the last one he analyzed had remained stagnant, hadn't been updated so to speak.

THE WITCH OF THE WOOD

Wolfie had "read" his father on first meeting and had no idea things had changed. Rudy hoped beyond hope it would stay that way, at least for the next five minutes or so.

They rounded the corner of Hamstead and Elm, and Rudy was flooded with memories, some bitter, some pleasant. He and Pat had "grown up together" here and then grown apart, married at twenty-seven, divorced in their forties. They had put all their dreams in this place, a Queen Anne Victorian with its wrap-around porch and asymmetrical roofs, the external basement entrance out back adorned by a slanted wooden "Dorothy" door and a yard leading down to Patricia's "craft" area at the rear of the property where a black iron gate separated her work shed from a stand of thick and rather tangled woods. As Rudy had settled himself indoors through the years, making his dens into offices and eventually overtaking the upstairs where he'd demanded silence while he worked, Pat had gone eccentric with all her "projects" outside, erecting her many sculptures soon to be abandoned, her gardens that wound up bug-eaten and wilted, her paintings that eventually got moved and re-moved to the far corner of the basement, dirt-spotted with their edges curling down.

Ironically (considering all the new information Rudy had about the world and its underground inhabitants), they'd initially bought the place for the foliage. The collection of regal elms that stood sentry along the west side of the place and two humongous weeping willows at the other edge of the sloping back yard had given them a perfect sort of privacy.

Rudy guessed she was back there now doting over her little "inventions." Or maybe she was inside making that foofoo specialty coffee he'd always secretly despised along with one of those "healthy" fruit salads she fooled herself with, soon followed by eggs, and toast, and the Special K she refilled the bowl with at least three or four times. When he'd married her, Patricia was barely one hundred and seventeen pounds, hourglass waist, round breasts, and those cute two front teeth turn-buckled together. But then she'd let herself go through the years, fattening up to a whopping two hundred and twenty-five pounds impossible to cloak. She'd gone red in the face and fat in the ankles.

Physically at least, she was the most masculine female he knew.

Wolfie got out of the car and walked up to the door. It was ungodly warm, but there was a breeze, making the porch swing sway just a bit. There were tubular wind chimes hanging from the eaves, softly bonging together; that was new. Wolfie rang the bell. He pushed his hair across his forehead, waited, turned, shrugged. Rudy lowered the window.

"Get her on the cell," he called innocently. "She's here somewhere."

Wolfie smiled, evidently tickled that his father would think of using technology even a little bit. He dialed and put the phone to his ear, one arm folded across his stomach. Then he was turned slightly away, talking, schmoozing. He held the phone away from his head and said, "She's out back. She wants to show me something. I'll be back in a second!"

Rudy waved casually, dismissively. Wolfie stayed on the line with Patricia so he could talk to her on his approach, soaking up every possible moment they could connect before the planned departure he thought she was unaware of.

The second Wolfie rounded the corner of the house, Rudy got out of the car and followed, trying not to run and make noise, struggling out his own cell phone, half looking at it to find the recording button on the side.

At the border of the back yard, Wolfie pushed through two butterfly bushes that had grown across the pathway, shedding a litter of yellow petals to the ground in his wake, and Rudy prayed his own feet would take him the rest of the way on their own without obstruction. He'd been back here thousands of times, the landscape memorized like an old song. He palmed the cell phone in his left hand, leaving the thumb out as if he were hitchhiking. With his right hand he grabbed the digit.

Now he was twenty feet ahead of where he'd just been, inside Wolfie's head, Pat's voice in his ear.

"Keep coming, Wolfie," she was saying. "I have a new project that I simply *must* show you . . . something I've been working on for months, something special, something so . . . *me!*"

"And Mum, you are beautiful!" Wolfie said back. "I cannot wait to share this with you!"

There was a garden of what looked like particularly thorny roses poking through a tangle of chicken wire, and Wolfie turned the corner. Down a short hill, maybe sixty feet away, was an old gray tool shed, a wheelbarrow filled with old mulch, a rain barrel, and a scatter of wood scraps. Kneeling with her back turned was Patricia. Next to her was a sawhorse set up with a piece of plywood on top, slightly bowed in the middle. And behind her was a scattered array of dollhouses on stands, some with flat roofs, some with pitched roofs, some with fake windows, others with shutters. There must have been thirty of them, all so pretty, some darkened with woodstain, others painted up in basic block colors, some no more than a foot long and a foot high and others as large as bathtubs or bureaus.

Rudy was at the crest of the rise and almost took a header as the ground sloped. He stopped where he was and figured he had enough of a view for what was necessary. From beneath the vision he shared with his boy, Wolfie's voice said, "Mum! These are awesome! You made these yourself?"

She started to turn, and Rudy almost betrayed himself, calling out a last warning to the only son he'd ever known.

For the number three was a universal trinity, in this case adding up to the Father, the Son, and the Stepmother. And "The Riddle of the Wood" was no more than a sentence with a homophone, and it was fortunate that Wolfie hadn't picked up the possibility of this in Rudy's biography. For the same rudimentary word-twist had been used in one of Rudy's favorite old *Star Trek* episodes, titled "Bread and Circuses."

The current riddle stated,

The sun must burst forth a hundred golden rivers.

Rudy had simply replaced "sun" with "son," and considering the fact that Wolfie's main source of nutrition was iodine, he was betting the farm on the possibility that Wolfie was not going to bleed red.

The Dark Guardian turned and Wolfie gasped, realizing that yesterday he'd done nothing more than kill an innocent shop teacher. For Patricia was wearing headgear and protective goggles with a plastic nose and mouth guard. And she had on her favorite hat, a black baseball cap with a huge plastic sunflower on the forehead, one that in silhouette would look like a strange headlamp with ridges as it had in the "Coming of Dreams."

"These are my birdhouses," Patricia said. "Aren't they just lovely?" Then she pulled a cord, fishing line connected in a spider web effect to all the doors.

They all snapped open and from the wooden compartments erupted a black swarm, all flapping madly and chirping and chittering in a collective, continuous screeching. Patricia stood, spread her arms, and smiled beneath the plastic face guard now misting a bit with her quickening breaths, the storm of birds rising behind her like a massive black cloak, the February sun stabbing through the spaces. Rudy disengaged and thumbed for the record button on his cell.

Wolfie ran and the birds followed in waves. He tried the "blink," but there were too many adversaries guessing right, and within a matter of seconds he was covered, a dark scarecrow utterly overcome and infested, the multiple wings snapping and beating madly like old rags in the wind.

He hopped around as if he were on fire, swatted, swiped, rubbed, tried to stop-drop-and-roll.

Wherever he went, they were on him, like a moving second skin, even on the ground where he tried to cross his hands before his face. They shrieked, they wriggled and burrowed, squirming forward, tail feathers up, working the creases and filling the spaces so the boy just couldn't lay still.

By the time he'd regained his feet an eye was gone. He gave a last brisk hard-palming to the face and they came off in a wavelet, exposing the multiple punctures and the bursting golden runners, forked and streaming down to his neckline.

Like bees to a hive they were on him again, and his head was a black, fluttering skull; and when a particularly fat black and gray barn swallow pecked in, Wolfie's second eye popped in a stringy burst. He cried out, but it was muffled by wing and rump and feather and mantle.

He had stumbled to the base of the rise and stood there below his father. Rudy was murmuring "Oh my God," over and again to himself, but still managed to hold the phone steady, getting it all in the shot. There was a mad screeching now about the swarm, and Wolfie in his shame and disgrace put forward his hands palm up as if asking, *"Daddy, what should I do?"*

"Say it," Rudy croaked. "Say it and I'll make you immortal."

Wolfie swiped at his mouth area for clearance and choked out, "Father!"

The birds stormed his face and he mashed them away.

"Father, why have you forsaken me?"

He stretched his arms out slowly to the sides then, making his body into the shape of a cross. A pair of black junco sparrows wriggled into his mouth, then another bird, and yet another. Wolfie kept his stance as his throat bulged and they forged through him, raked across him, consumed him utterly, his thin body an opened thoroughfare.

When they finally came off him, he fell face down on the hill, his clothes mere tatters drenched in dark gold, the back of his head a wet swirl of matted blond hair pulled up in tufts.

The birds were above him now, suspended in layers of rolling waves. They rose, formed a massive V shape at roof level, and burst off into the February skyline.

Pat was nowhere to be found.

Rudy let the hand holding the cell phone rest at his side. He felt like weeping, but he was dry. From beneath his feet, he felt a vibration. Then another, and a third, like some gargantuan underground beast coming slowly awake with a guttural rumble.

He looked around him, and the earth seemed suddenly unsteady, rocking, pitching, buckling.

It was all the trees. At their bases.

They were starting to move.

Chapter 3

Wolf

First was the great rumbling, vibrations that sent numbing shooters through Rudy's feet, pebbles and dirt seemingly from nowhere rolling and threading down the hill toward the shed, Patricia's plywood work board trembling and shivering on its supports, then falling off at an odd angle. Next was the rocking, the skyline come alive, trees all around pitching to and fro as if engulfed in some strange hurricane that painted arcs on the horizon.

From beneath, there were great pulling sounds, stretching, yawning, a muffled army of high-tension bows being drawn as the massive network of intertwined root systems strained to the absolute breaking point.

Then the earth erupted, a million buried circus whips cracking all at once as the embedded roots ripped up from underfoot in a damp throaty roar, soil coming up in bursts and cascades, peppering the house, showering all around Rudy Barnes who covered his face with his forearm.

He thought he heard screams: a neighbor walking a dog maybe, a jogger, who knew? It got drowned out quickly by the fantastic collapse, the purging of the skyline as every tree came crashing down to the earth.

Rudy was lucky he was not killed. The border elms like the slats of some massive gate-barrier thundered down in a diagonal pattern, first smashing through the roof atop the detached garage, then the kitchen and laundry room, the rose garden, and all along the hill Rudy was sidestepping down, the ground feeling like shuffling floorboards in a funhouse. Rudy turned and tried to run. A gargantuan trunk pounded the ground, missing him by inches, and he dove off to the right. The weeping willow on the far side of the back yard smashed down into the shed, turning it to splinters, and three trees plunged across Rudy's path a few feet ahead of where he had fallen to his stomach. He covered his head with his hands for a moment, the scratches and abrasions up his forearms wet and stinging.

The thunderous booming of it was overwhelming, rolling shockwaves pounding the ground, a riotous tumult that felt like the end of the world. It reached a tremendous peak, then slowed, thinned out, and scattered to isolated shivers, the final showers of soil and rock pelting down, then drizzling off like an engine ticking down as it cooled.

There were dull echoes. There was aftermath silence, but then came a mad skittering in the grass. Rudy raised his head and there, coming on at ground-level from the felled ruin of the wood beyond the iron fence, was a mad rush of wildlife flooding over and between the crooked nest of trunks and branches: white and gray fieldmice, chipmunks, squirrels, rabbits, gophers, small foxes, deer, all jumping and crawling over each other in a mass exodus from a world that had been turned inside out.

There were more screams now from over the hill, honking horns, cars crashing into things with gritty finality, hoarse shouts.

"Good acoustics all of a sudden," Rudy thought wildly, as he pushed to his feet and made for the tool shed, its opened back corner still standing on its own like some ancient monolith. He moved, climbed, stepped across the jigsaw of foliation, lost his footing and raked his shin, then doggie-paddled over to the "monument." The catty-cornered shelves had held, and Rudy swiped the remains of a collection of gardening trowels to the ground along with a stack of clay flowerpots. He climbed two shelves high and wrapped his arms around the corner post for dear life.

The evacuation swarmed underneath him, yipping and rustling, and what looked like a bear cub loped right past his ankle nipping and snapping at the air. The mass covered the hill, a rippling hoard of clawing, retreating hindquarters that scurried off to the jungle that had become Hampstead and Elm Avenues and beyond.

The dust and dirt that had risen in the air was now settling to a resinous haze. There was almost a dramatic pause then, like the time for a deep breath where one could take inventory, cut his losses, and measure his options.

But along the slope of the near hill there was new movement. A sneaky sort of creeping.

It was a spread of strange coloring, an outpouring, and Rudy's breath caught in his throat. Bone-white hands and arms were creeping out of the holes in the ground, skeletal fingers feeling about the perimeters, palms settling, then pressing, and then was the emergence.

Rudy focused on the closest cavity across the yard, where an elm had toppled down across the forest gate, bending the corner into a twisted black dog-ear. Back at its dark uncorked root-cellar, a form pushed out of the hole, black beetles and other vermin swimming off her in a sort of unveiling, white skin stretched bone-tight and spotted with filth, tangle of black hair peppered with dirt. Her bulbous black eyes shuttered open and closed in reaction to the glare of the sun, and she pushed up to a standing position, bony knees almost buckling.

Her hand was at her forehead then, in a protective salute to shield her sensitive eyes, and Rudy noticed something. He still had a clear view of her face in an odd sort of bare perspective.

"No shadow," he thought.

She let her hands fall to her sides and took a step forward, careful not to touch branch, leaf, or stalk of the prison column that had held her underground for so long. She gave a slight curtsey and then spoke in a voice rough with dirt, "Rudy. Rudy . . . Barnes."

She began to change, and there must have been a seam around the back of her, because the pale epidermis dragged from the rear to the front, coming around the arm, the thigh, the shin, the waist, then down over the face hugging the contours, a sheet slowly drawn from a petrified statue. There was a brief moment when she was a skeleton, heart beating in the cage of bone, veins pulsing, muscles quivering as the receding cover of skin met in folds and creases going into her open mouth. Simultaneously was the regrowth, a burst of supple skin spreading from the vagina out, and before Rudy could make the rather juvenile symbolic connection between the consumption of the real and the birth of the façade, he came to recognize the masterpiece coming to form.

She was April Orr, bob hairdo hanging in limp strings and clots, soil-spots on her forearms, dirt caked on her pretty bare knees. But even covered by the filth of the hole, she was gorgeous. Rudy had never seen the woman naked, only bent at the banister with her dress up over her hips, and here, bared to the world, she was without a doubt the most potent sexual presence he'd ever known. The long fingers, sharp face, and sparkling eyes reflected an elegant humor that was absolutely magnetic. Then as if in sweet contradiction to the air of sophistication she downplayed was that body, lithe and engineered for passion and sweat. Those small, firm breasts had their nipples up. Those long dancer's legs stood firm now beneath slender hips defined by squint-eyed dimples slanted on either side. There were two freckles to the right of her belly button, and a daring rose tattoo to the left, long stem snaking down to frame one side of her neatly shaved pussy-stripe.

Rudy wanted her. Now. He pictured it in his head, making his way through the clutter of branch work and kissing her, cradling and melting to the ground with her.

He climbed down from his mount and closed the distance between them. It was awkward. He almost tripped and took a header but recovered abruptly, and as she reached out her hands to him he had a sudden and awful vision of his son in the same positioning, absolutely covered with birds.

"No," Rudy whispered instinctively.

Her head exploded then with a wet burst. Rudy squeezed shut his eyes and gave a half-turn, raising up both arms as bone shards and hot pith splattered over him. He was soaked and cut on his hands, his forehead, the right cheek, and he heard pieces landing in the grass. He opened his eyes just in time to see the headless body before him careen, walk in a drunken step forward and back, then fall in the hole it had crawled from.

There was a murmuring now, a gritty hum coming from along the hill, the Gregorios' back yard, the space on the other side of the property now exposed where there was a vacant area overgrown with clover and ragweeds, and of course the broken heap of a forest spreading out past the black iron gate.

It was a massive, rising congregation, a sweeping haunt of skeletal forms with red lips and black eyes, thousands of them pushing up to standing positions beside their prison holes, focusing hard on the man at the foot of the hill and droning,

"*Rudy...*"

Then came the gory fireworks echoing across the landscape, wet ruptures of blood, bone, and brain torching upward like exploding party favors at Temple University's Cherry and White Day, then raining down on the headless bodies collapsing upon the wood and grass in an awful sort of haphazard symmetry. Rising behind the carnage were more witches, a blurred mass closing steadily.

"Rudy!" someone said from behind.

It startled him, but the voice was clear, no drone, no grit.

He turned, and it took everything in his willpower to do it gracefully, without putting his arms and elbows in front of his face, cowering.

The Witch of the Wood

It was Caroline Schultz from up the block. She was a thirty-something blonde who worked for the water company, or the gas works, one of the utilities, he couldn't remember. She'd traded recipes with Patricia a couple of times, and they shared the same lawn service company; that's all he knew about her. That, and the fact that she liked wearing hats. Today she had one with army fatigue colors. No coat, white T-shirt, black yoga pants that flared at the bottom, and pink Converse All Stars.

"Come with me," she said. "Unless you want to kill a thousand more witches."

Rudy's mouth opened a bit and hung there for a moment.

"What?"

She came down to his position at the base of the rise.

"It's now or never, Rudy. You've got to trust me and ask questions later. Kill any more and you'll gain the wrong followers."

"Me? Kill more?"

"No one can look in the face of God and live, Rudy."

"I'm not—"

"To them, you are." She took his elbow and looked off to the west. "I've got to get you out of sight, and if you don't cooperate I'm going to have to kill you." The corny, outdated phrase was offered as almost an afterthought, a ghost of what seemed her "pre-disaster" offbeat humor, but when she turned toward him she was only smiling a little.

"O.K.," he said quietly.

There was a new round of wet bursts to the right, and it sent them running off to a hoarse and breathless escape, leapfrogging and hurdling together through the Gregorios' yard, then the Goldbergs' and the Denardos', all cluttered with a cross-hatch of wooden debris and fallen construction, and in the distance was a wide, opened panorama, now exposed all the way down to the Schuylkill Expressway. It was a mass of halted traffic, scattered fires, downed trees, and crawling human forms, the calico and then the pale white following close like a virus.

Bald, he thought. *The world has gone bald,* and the second wave of exploding craniums in the forest was overshadowed by the ones coming on right behind them, marching numbly across the bodies of their fallen sisters, and calling Rudy's name with voices of dirt.

Brian Duffey was trying to do that cool fucking trick Nickie Walters had shown him in bio class, where you snapped your index finger to the middle one making a "whapping" noise, when the kitchen roof caved in. Ma was at the stove cooking scrambled eggs and cheddar on the long griddle pan, and Pop was coming through the archway. Brian had turned to give him his usual grunt of acknowledgment, and the man didn't respond, heel of his hand pressed to his forehead. Duffey turned back to his finger trick. Pop was too hung-over to work again and was saying, "Both of you can just shut the fuck up," when the rumbling started.

The house shook as if it were made of balsa, and the first thing Brian thought was,

Aqua's working on the water main this early? followed quickly by, *Yeah, it would take an earthquake for that Wolfie motherfucker to get out of a fight, just my luck.*

Then came the great crash from above. Duffey had his eyes on his mother, looking around in disbelief, pink terrycloth bathrobe, long wisp of hair hanging in her face. The ceiling split open like the end of the world and the maple from the front yard smashed through, crushing her against the oven, splintered floorboards and insulation showering around her. Duffey pushed up out of his chair and turned to the shattered doorway behind him. The massive trunk was on Pop's back, severed branch running him straight through between the shoulder blades, coming out through his chest like a throwing spear. The point was embedded in the floor, and the man slid down, re-slickening the peeled and splintered shaft, arms and hands quivering and going still the second he hit the linoleum.

There was muffled screaming from next door now, and Ma was screaming in here, good arm waving out like a spastic trying for a cab. She was sizzling, face pressed to the hot plate, tree on top of her like a rapist. Brian leapt across and saw that her head had ruptured, sending brain matter into the eggs, curling like maggots. He moved calmly to the pot rack and went for a frying pan. Then he changed his mind and got the heavy black skillet, turning, bunching his muscles for it. Her one good eye may have focused on him, he couldn't be sure. He smelled burning hair.

Brian Duffey brought down the skillet with all his strength.

Caroline Schultz didn't have a finished basement, to say the least. It was dark, though the new shadowless phenomenon exposed details that were rather startling, like the serial number on the Westinghouse washing machine's label plate over in the far corner by the dehumidifier, and the cluster of flies caught up in an intricate spiderweb fastened between rafters. It was cold down here, concrete floor with a layer of sediment that made that gritty non-echo beneath your shoes, water boiler with rust stains leopard-spotted up the wall side, exposed piping, rickety stairway. There was an old couch sitting in the middle of the space under the glare of a bare light bulb, and Rudy didn't ask why. Didn't matter. In the back of his mind he wondered if it was infested with mites or something, but he didn't complain. Caroline had drawn over an old barstool with one leg slightly shorter than the other and was in the process of dressing his wounds. The sports adhesive tape didn't stick all too well, and he didn't complain about that either. It was kind of nice. And he had questions. A ton, to say the least.

"So how do you know about the witches?" he said finally. She sucked at her bottom lip and put a Band-Aid on a cut across his elbow.

"Right to it, huh?"

"Is there a more appropriate time?"

"Guess not." She stood and stretched her back, then took a place next to him on the sofa. She sat there, hands on her knees, thinking. He was about to say something, and she shushed him, putting up the stop-sign hand and closing her eyes, organizing it. After a moment she gave a short laugh.

"I've had a strange life, Rudy." She glanced over, measuring his reaction. It was stone, and she sighed.

"O.K., here goes, clumsy and all at once, but you asked for it." She'd crossed her eyes, but he wasn't laughing. She started off slowly then, building up steam as she went.

"It started with the read-alouds," she said. "You know, like when I was a baby. There was 'Curious George' and all that, but for as long as I can remember there was another book, a special one that my grandmother passed down to my mother filled with graphic arts stories and riddles about witches and trees. As I grew older, I believed it came through so many generations that the tale originated before print was invented, though I had no real basis for that idea; I just knew, you know what I mean?" Rudy gave a slight nod, and she continued. "Gosh, I loved that book, as a baby, a toddler, all through elementary school. It was my bedtime book, the old teddy bear you never threw away, coloring my world sort of thing." She paused. "But then were the weird activities, the eccentricities shared by my mother and me that I could never tell my friends about, things she and I did together that didn't make sense."

"Like what?"

"Like keeping a lifelong tally of the trees in the world, by name and number in a log with a leather cover. Like being compelled to spend seven years digging the tunnel that goes from the trapdoor under this couch, five hundred yards down to the high bank at the edge of the river." She leaned back, drawing her knees up and hugging them. "I missed middle school and high school for all intents and purposes, but I know how to brace underground walls, track erosion patterns, and dig, Rudy. I know how to spend years building a fake, collapsible second floor that masqueraded as the walls of the living room, den, and kitchen above us for so many years, and I knew when I heard the great rumbling that it was time to pull the tripwire as soon as I secured you down here. I did it while you were making your way down the stairs just now. Pretty smooth, huh?"

Rudy didn't answer. She shrugged.

"Well, no one will find us here. There's no entrance from upstairs anymore." She took off her hat and started braiding her hair into a long warrior's lock. "Now all the puzzles make sense. With 'The Great Fall of Timber' I become *The Provider,*' here to help the new messiah gather his flock. There will be massive power outages, chaos, looting, murder."

"That's one hell of a children's book, Caroline."

"Yeah, right." She shrugged. "But it's typical, isn't it? Messages in nursery rhymes are often dark as all hell, and there are more dirty jokes in the old Bugs Bunny cartoons than we ever care to acknowledge. And what about the story of Lot's wife, or Noah's ark, or Jonah and the whale? One horrific context to the next, intensive storyline presented in childlike verse and animation then brought to some sort of ethical epiphany, it's the Anglo way. And believe it, Rudy, all we have known is gone, like your apartment, like the rooms above us. They will be ravaged like all the convenience stores, the supermarkets, the toolhouses, everything. Cars will be useless for awhile and many of the weak will die of starvation. The governmental structure will temporarily falter, and there will be a brief period where hunters, gatherers, and those who work the saw will be the only ones to truly master the landscape. It will take more than seven years to clear all the downed trees, and until new ones are planted and grown, there will be a global effort to construct a generation's worth of oxygen-filled domes."

She paused and looked at Rudy, who was looking back at her closely.

"What?"

"Nothing," he said softly. It was information overload difficult to fathom, and his mind had drifted, back when she had started analyzing the structure and intent of children's literature. Caroline had been an acquaintance of Patricia's he'd inherited at the periphery and written off as the "artsy" type, more a pain in the ass than anything else . . . someone who would rope you into an argument about feminism when you thought you'd been talking about tax shelters. Her wide-set eyes also made her look kind of ditzy, and her nose was a tad too big. But the impression was a bold-faced lie. She was intelligent, strong vocabulary. Plus, her pants were tight and she had good legs, nice and sturdy, powder-blue eye shadow that went nicely with her blond hair, all totally beside the point, but he was more aware now than ever of the never-ending manner by which men studied women, an act almost shamelessly woven into the fabric of every conversation, every gesture. Wolfie had proven his point.

Wolfie . . .

Rudy's throat caught, suddenly, unexpectedly, and his shoulder's hitched. He glanced down at his shoes.

"What?" Caroline repeated, this time concerned.

"My son. His body. It's out there and I want to bury him."

"You can't." Rudy looked up, eyes reddened.

"Why the hell not?"

Caroline took the braid she'd been working, knotted it off, and tossed it back over her shoulder.

"Because he's surrounded by witches, and you shouldn't kill any more, Rudy, if not for humanitarian reasons, then for those of dangerous publicity. There is a lot unexplained out there, and many of the living will think you're a cold-blooded murderer. Others will view Wolfie's death as a beautiful religious sacrifice, but your casual explanation of it all, leaning on your shovel, with the heads of naked witches bursting all around, isn't going to help your cause in either scenario. You've got to measure and limit your appearances. And I'd wear a mask when you do surface, unless you want to paint the town red with the blood of your followers. Or your own for that matter. Wolfie and the necessary propaganda aside, I'd be willing to bet there are three million dead under tree trunks and timber in the United States alone, civilians, mothers, grandparents . . ."

Rudy put his head in his hands.

"What a mess."

"It's going to get messier, Rudy, and there's no witch alive who would blame you. There is collateral damage on both sides, and they've been ready to die for their freedom for thousands of years. It's time to lead them. Fresh out of the hole, they're trancelike, looking for a man to transform for. Thousands will be throttled and stabbed, beaten and shot for fear that they are some sort of outworlder or plague carrier. The number of the 'first dead' will be staggering actually, but the second and third sweeps will adapt. They are fast learners. All they need is a chance to shower, steal a set of clothes, and transform, and some of them will actually cheat and cross over."

Rudy's breath came hard through his nose.

"Cross over, as in they become men. Women with the greatest gift ever bestowed upon the human race and it's wasted."

Caroline raised her chin.

"I didn't say all. I said some." She stood, did a little dance straightening down her pants from the sides and then folding her arms. "And I love my mother-race, but their daughters still have something to offer."

Rudy smiled, but only a trace.

"You sound like the enemy now."

"I'm just saying, Rudy. All might not be quite equal in the end, but when feelings are involved, it's not like just picking flavors, you know?"

He didn't. He didn't at all. Was there a signal here? Was she contradicting a learned belief for one from the gut? Was this philosophical or personal? He put the points of his elbows on his knees and folded his hands, index fingers pointing straight up. He rested his lips against the affair and closed his eyes, knowing that she'd know he was changing the subject rather bluntly, and also knowing that she'd immediately forgive the poor transitioning for the sake of expediency.

"All right," he said. "Rules and facts. How many trees are there in the world?"

"Four hundred billion, two hundred forty six million, three hundred thousand, two hundred and one. Give or take a few."

"But they all couldn't have come down. Even with what my son referred to as 'shadow-transfers,' new trees were planted since the original imprisonment, right?"

"Check. Around thirty million witches went under. But all the trees came down. Part of the revenge quotient. With the uprooting, no prison stalk nor lookalike would remain sealed and seated."

"So some places just have downed trees? No escaping prisoners?"

"It'll still appear pretty even. Blame the jailers. Thirty percent of the land mass is populated by trees, but they're spaced to 'cover,' as painters would say, to give the illusion of completeness. And the burials inside that thirty percent were spread just as aesthetically. For all intents and purposes, the earth has been ravaged, and the coming-out party will appear to be a complete infestation. Or liberation, depending how you look at it."

"And it's that 'depending' that makes my presence a continuing requirement," Rudy muttered.

"Exactly. Unless you want the haters to win without a fight."

"And they are who exactly?"

She sat down next to him, hands between her knees.

"Hard to say. There will be factions. It won't be black or white all the time."

"It will if a gun is in my face, Caroline."

She smiled.

"Measured and cautious appearances, right?"

"Right." He rubbed his nose. "So how do we start?"

"You start by knowing which enemies drift between vague loyalties and undefined ethics, and those who are a clear and present danger."

"Like who?"

"Like Patricia."

"Oh God," he said, face going pale.

"No, not God. That's you, to some. But she was pre-chosen to defy you as I was destined to lend you support. She's not dead, and she's five times as dangerous as she was before Wolfie's passing."

"How?"

"My book says the Dark Guardian is awarded a gift if things have advanced to this particular level."

"What gift?"

"The ability to shape-shift. At will. No receding epidermis either. Instantaneous transformation."

Rudy looked at her critically, and she gave a short nod.

"That's right. She could be anybody, even Caroline Schultz, and your biggest ongoing struggle will be whether or not you can trust me. So decide, Rudy Barnes. Me and my tunnels, or the teeming labyrinth out there?"

Rudy stared, and she didn't falter.

"Here," he said. "I'll stay here, at least for awhile."

"Good. Then help me move this couch. I've got food in dry

stock I've been hoarding down there at the base of this tunnel for years, and we should take fresh inventory of the expiration dates. Then we need to get out your cell, pray you have service, and look at Wolfie's crucifixion so we can splice it to your first public address on YouTube before all the laptop batteries go dry."

Rudy's eyebrows went up.

"Pardon the old-timer's ignorance, Caroline, but, uh . . . the power must be trashed out there. You're saying I can still use the Internet?"

"Like the world's newest cockroach; you can't kill it. Power isn't out everywhere, just most everywhere. And there's always a way to tether functionality . . . a personal hotspot feature on the settings menu here enabling wifi on an iPad there . . . browsing on the unit using an iPhone as a 3G transceiver, you know."

"Sure."

"Anyway, the news will be back up and running sooner than you think, but that doesn't mean we can't beat it to the punch. You have some explaining to do, and believe me, there are a lot of people who will want to hear it. There are also those who will throw their own hats into the virtual ring, using your logic as tinder for the view that will oppose you, so pre-planning some sort of counter-response wouldn't be such a bad thing either."

They were standing on each side of the couch, preparing to push it across the floor.

"And who might these 'opposers' be exactly?" Rudy said.

"Conservatives to start. Those who might not feel quite right about new religions and shape-shifting witches entering the bloodline." She made a sign to push, and they started to move the sofa across the floor, more of an effort than it had seemed it would be. Rudy suddenly felt older than dirt.

"Conservatives, huh?" he said when they'd uncovered the trapdoor completely. "They sound like a pleasant squad."

The Witch of the Wood

She grinned ruefully.

"They're not your main problem, Rudy. Old bluebloods preaching family values in the Bible Belt won't matter as much as the ones who would prefer living in the wild, feeding on the chaos, and finding they have new purpose in a world that had shunned them."

"Yeah . . . the scary warlord rising from the ashes, huh?"

"Not so cute, Rudy. There are those who never understood the idea of sitting at a desk for twelve years, then withering in a cubicle for forty more. In a profound way, this new world will make a lot of sense, a ravaged war zone where one can lead by raw strength and fear, as long as there's a way to keep the engines running."

She stopped suddenly. Rudy tried to say something, and she put the finger across the throat, like silence, like now.

There were noises, muted but hurried. Footsteps from overhead.

A lot of them.

Brian Duffey was not stunned nor saddened. There was no time for that shit. He pushed open the back door, stepped out, and saw that Mr. Nardo had been out checking his laundry line, as usual, thinking he'd be so quick that none of his neighbors would notice he was just wearing boxers. He was pinned beneath a tree, face-up, squirming, eyes rolling. Duffey ignored him. To the left, the Valentines' place had been hit with three massive trees from the street side, and through all the branches and leaves there was a thick black smoke gaining momentum.

A cold voice inside Brian Duffey's head checked off the Valentines in the same way it had dismissed Mr. Nardo. They were all over retirement age. Expendable. Lying at the foot of the steps in the yellowed grass was the game ball from states last year, signed by all the players and coaches in white-out because they'd been so excited they hadn't taken the time to hunt around for a Sharpie. Dad, the drunken prick, had taken it off the mantel to fuck with again last night and left it out here. Duffey jumped down to grab it, and when he turned back to the kitchen doorway, there was a figure standing in it.

A pale naked figure spotted with filth.

Brian Duffey didn't understand it, but he didn't fear it either. He dropped the football. He met her stare and waited, watching her change. He also remained cold and emotionless when she was transformed into a quite dirty and naked version of Linda Birch, shyly pushing one knee against the other, looking at him sideways, and playfully hooking her index fingernail on one of her bottom teeth.

"Hi, Brian," she said in a voice of grit.

He went to her then, mounting the short steps, arms reaching out, eyes cold flint. He took her head in his hands, and just as she was beginning to mew and rub her cheek against his palm, he gripped hard and snapped her neck with an audible "pop." She went ragdoll and he dropped her, stood over her, heart pumping, fists balled up tight. His breath was heavy now, and he only wished he could kill this stuck-up bitch one more time.

Another pale figure appeared in the doorway.

And it was at that moment that Brian Duffey knew the world had changed just for him.

Set in motion by the noises upstairs, Caroline strode to the far side of the basement and pulled across what looked like a set of thick vinyl shower curtains one might use to mask the more deteriorated area of the space or the corner with the French drain. Revealed was a set of green storage lockers, and she snapped open the doors.

Guns.

Hundreds of them.

"You're kidding, right?" Rudy breathed.

"No need to whisper," she said. "The bottom of the fake floor up there is made of a soundproofing material like one of those po-

THE WITCH OF THE WOOD

lice interrogation mirrors; we hear them, they can't hear us. Ignore them." There was the sound of something heavy falling over up there, the faintest tinkle of shattering glass. Rudy was the one who flinched, shoulders coming up like a frightened little turtle.

"Who is it?" Rudy whispered, not able to help himself.

"Neighbors," she said. "Probably looking for medical supplies, food, water, weapons. Too much racket to be do-gooders checking for those in need, and too feeble for the out-of-towners who will ultimately decide to become looters for a living."

"And we're going to confront them with guns?" Rudy said.

"No, of course not." She turned toward the stockpile. "But the breach up there is a time check of sorts, and I'm due to introduce you to your birth-trove, like your son's 'Coming of Dreams.' It's owed to you for gaining the title of 'Father.'" She let her hand go across, palm up, in ceremonious presentation. "I've spent a lifetime collecting for you. The first section is hand guns, the middle compartment a battery of rifles, and to the left over there are the shotguns. There are divisions of breech- and muzzle-loaded weapons, and more trivial subcategories, especially in the pistol area. Below each storage section you'll note the ammo container, and to the far left are the straps, shoulder holsters, and ankle bands, anything you think you might need." She looked down bashfully. "There's also fireworks in that black footlocker at the end there. Nothing in my storybook about them, I'm just a real Fourth of July kind of girl. I like the colors. They're pretty."

Rudy nodded off this last odd detail and gazed at the arsenal in amazement. The weapons were arranged by size, manufacturer, and style, all the marquis players standing in their slots like silent merchants of doom—Beretta, Colt, Glock, Ruger, Smith & Wesson, and Winchester. But then there was what seemed the specialty talent, the ones that made Rudy know he was not deserving, let alone savvy enough to pick up, load, and fire one of these bad boys: Benelli, Browning, Bushmaster, Ithaca, O. F. Mossberg & Sons, Stoeger, and a slew of them he just couldn't process on the first sweep.

Something fell overhead with a muted crash followed by a skidding sound; china bureau, had to be. Both of them cowered at that one, and Rudy moved away from the cabinets.

"How about the possibility that someone might notice it's strange there's no basement entrance?"

"Smartass," she said.

"Sorry," he said. "It's the deconstructionist in me, always looking for logic errors in the plotline." She came over to join him at the base of the stairway and looked up at the doorway with him.

"It goes by the principle that in this kind of emergency no one will be looking that hard or staying that long," she said. "We're trying for an illusion that would survive a passing glance." She put her hands on her hips. "Besides, if you did want to get through from up there, you'd need pneumatic breaker tools, Rudy, and I doubt anyone would be interested enough to go dragging in those kind of heavy hammers to get into my little old basement. Unless they knew who I was hiding, that is."

"Thanks for making me feel so safe."

"Don't mention it."

Rudy backed off and walked over toward the lockers, shutting a door or two, pausing to slide his index finger along the barrel insignia of a Taurus Tracker revolver.

"Hey," he said. "What about the storybook up there as evidence? Isn't it like a blinking road arrow board pointing to your little compound down here?"

"Burned it. Checked the cinders too."

"You got any family out there?"

She paused. He turned; he'd hit a chord.

"Funny you mention it," She said. She approached and took over closing all the doors that were left standing open, slowly, methodically. Then, to Rudy's amazement, she came and took both his hands in hers. She was close enough that he could feel the warmth of her breath.

"I'm . . . uh . . . not good at making bargains, Rudy." She looked at the ceiling, and it seemed she was going to cry. "I was never good at advocating for myself during job interviews where you tried to enter at the highest pay rate, and asking for raises always terrified me. I'm the one who would inevitably settle for a title instead of a bonus." She met his eyes. "But in this case I want to make a deal. And it's not negotiable."

He wanted to kiss her for some reason, quite badly in fact, but he didn't. Of course not. He was the polite guy at the edge of the picture, the wallflower, the one who would never dream of playing off a girl's clear vulnerability. And it was a cold reality check to be sure. He was back to true form, the puritanical patriarch who didn't have a warlock conveniently providing him "gifts" anymore.

"What kind of a deal?" he said.

"The kind of deal that will save a life."

"Whose?"

"My mother's."

"Is she upstairs?" he said. She laughed, and he gave a stupid grin. It was a good tension-breaker. She let go his hands, and walked off a step.

"No, Rudy, she's not upstairs. If Ma was here she'd be with us."

"Where is she then?"

"At St. Elizabeth's, in the cancer ward. And she's got it bad, metastatic, terminal, spread all through the pancreas, liver, and lungs."

Rudy nodded. This was an easy one.

"No problem. When do you want to go get her? St. Elizabeth's is at the top of a rise at the end of Everett Street, right around the corner." He stopped himself and smiled stupidly once more. Was this one of the trade-offs in the new reality? He was "God," but told his compatriots things they already knew like some doting grandmother? He coughed into his fist, and said, "What I mean is . . . hospitals have generators, right? I'll bet with its position on the vista, the damage from the 'great fall of timber' was minimal."

She shook her head.

"No. She stays where she is for now, but you're right, we need to risk venturing out to her as soon as our business allows."

"So your price is an abduction no one would really care about in these circumstances?"

"No. It's what we bring with us." She went over to the area to the far left of the gun cabinets where there was a small end table with a carton sporting the "St. Elizabeth's" insignia stamped on an angle.

"What's in the box?" Rudy said, almost bursting out in crazy laughter from actually speaking aloud his favorite line from his favorite film, *Seven*.

"It's filled with plastic bags," she said flatly. "Tubes, rubber straps, a big pair of scissors in a sheath, syringes, needles."

"I'm going to give her my blood?"

"Oh, yes."

"And why?"

"Trade-off for my services, Rudy. In this 'new reality' you gain a power called 'The Healing Blood.' It not only puts disease in a holding pattern, but enlivens the senses. The problem is that it's temporary. The good news is that it's potent. She's in stage four, and a full donation buys her three years."

"And when I've rejuvenated enough to give again?"

"Another dose for another three years and so on, for as long as I assist you."

"Right," he said thoughtfully. "It potentially adds up to so many doses that it basically assures she'll die of old age before the disease gets her. It's a noble thing, a good thing, and I'll give you all that I have."

"No, Rudy. I'm afraid that you won't." She was staring at the table with the box on it, running her finger along one of the creases. Her eyes were fluttering. "It's in the book I burned, Rudy . . . part of the story I didn't tell you." She looked at him, bottom lip trembling. "It's prophecy that 'The Provider' isn't supposed to live very long."

Duffey had had to make himself stop. It's not that he'd gotten tired of killing the monster-bitches; in fact, the hunger had grown with each slaughter. It's that he needed his strength for what was to come. After tossing aside the eighth dirty corpse, he'd made his way through the back yard and paused to look down the cliff to the Interstate. It was a total clusterfuck; God had ripped open the world for him. Instinctively, he knew he had to get out of the neighborhood, and he saw store-raids in his near future: lanterns, camp gear, wilderness clothing and generators, not to mention fishing equipment, hunting knives, and firearms.

Back in the house he said a small prayer by the body of his mother and gave the finger to his dead father as he straddled the great trunk, making his way to the street, to the circus. There was wailing, screaming, sirens in the distance, people running past, a flock of wildlife bursting into the road and flooding across the fallen timber in two sets of rolling waves.

Duffey worked his way down the block, busting windows and screen doors to hunt through the rubble, helping men lift fallen ceiling joists off the dead and wounded, rolling tree trunks out of their landing grooves to get to the crushed and the trapped, finding children caught in small spaces with broken legs, broken heads, broken backs, broken arms. He pushed a heavy bedroom cabinet off a ten-year-old girl who had lost an eye and three toes when the back yard pine had smashed through the wall, and he yanked the door clean off a pickup with a crushed cab, tree laid across in diagonal, the driver inside pressing his nose to the horn over and over. He peeled back twists of siding and dug through piles of crushed stone and brick. He saw a man abandon an infant in a car seat left on the hood of a black Acura when one of the monster-bitches started to change for him. Duffey grabbed the dirty thing and snapped her neck, cutting off her inhuman wail as if he were throwing a switch. He turned in disgust, and the man was pointing, jabbering wordlessly. Duffey punched him in the face, breaking his nose. One of the men with Duffey called out that the guy was a "sympathizer." Duffey liked that word. It sounded like "sympathy," or "empathy," or one of those other pathetic terms that usually went along with fat ugly girls with allergies and issues. But there'd be no more of that noise. No more "talking," no lame excuses, no *weakness*. The man with the broken nose sat on the curb for a second, using the tail of his dress shirt to pad up the wound.

A minute later he was carrying his baby in the car seat and walking with the group, all of them taking turns killing monster-bitches along the way, keeping a tally. When Brian Duffey got to Front Street, he had twenty-five followers.

By the time he reached the Interstate, they were two hundred strong.

"Tell me about the prophecy," Rudy said softly. He'd made his way to the sofa, hoping she would follow in tow.

"It's nothing."

"Not true. It's all relevant, and I need to know, Caroline." He smiled gently. "No deal on the blood donation until I have all the facts, miss. No ticky, no laundry."

"So you're tough as nails, huh? Balls of steel, the poker face of the century?"

"That's right. Sit, please." He patted the area next to him. "One old couch-pillow, no waiting."

She came over and took her place next to him, close enough so the other side of her cushion was raised up an inch.

"It's prophesized in my storybook," she said, "that the Provider only serves you briefly. The symbol for 'The Father' is a face with no features. It scared the shit out of me when I was a child, to tell you the truth." She went pigeon-toed, knees together. "My point is that the icon for 'The Provider' shares space with the Father for a page and that's it. The only other mention of her is the very next page where her symbol is surrounded by skulls."

"A page could mean fifty years, Caroline. It's a book of riddles, and the timelines sound blurry."

"Easy for you to say."

Rudy nodded acknowledgment.

"So what's you're symbol," he said, "your icon?"

She smiled ruefully. "It's the letter Y, but drawn in a curvy way that always made me think it was a vagina. Made me feel naughty as hell for thinking so too." She glanced at him sideways with slitted eyes. "Don't get any ideas, mister." Rudy laughed it off like a gentleman.

"If it's not . . . well . . . *that*, then what is it?" he said.

"A fork. A crossroads."

He considered this for a moment.

"Anything else on the page?"

"Yes."

"Do tell."

"It's a sign at the bottom, a squiggled line with an optical illusion, like an Escher picture."

"What's the illusion?"

"There are two dots above the line, but when you turn the book upside down, the two dots are on the top again where the underside was. And if you look at it long enough, the dots disappear altogether."

"What's it mean?"

"I can't be sure, Rudy, but I think it's a symbol for irony."

He smiled. That was clever, he had to admit it. He looked over, ready to say something complimentary, but she was making study of her nails in a way that made him pause.

"You know," she said finally, "my favorite of yours is the one titled 'Word Choice and Politics: A New Semiotics.'"

"You read that?"

"I've read a lot of things. And I liked the . . . *irony*, Rudy. You're really a funny guy; your humor is just so dry a lot of people might think there's no wine left in the wrinkled old vine."

"Thanks for the image."

"Don't mention it."

They smiled at each other. She looked down first, and Rudy had no idea what exactly that meant. But he was suddenly sure that any "skull" coming within fifty yards of this particular fork in the road was going to have to deal with this old professor's protective wrath, even if it took a baseball bat or a tire iron. Again, he had the strong desire to kiss this young woman, but of course he couldn't bring himself to initiate it.

"Caroline," he said softly.

"Yes, I'm right here. No need to shout."

"Ha ha."

"Ha ha back at you," she said. She looked up eyes dancing just a bit, but she was scared too, Rudy could see it.

"The skulls might not symbolize your death at all," he continued. "They could mean that, well . . . that *you* are the one killing the bad guys."

She laughed at that one.

"I've never killed anyone, Rudy! I don't even kill spiders; I throw them outside. The gun collecting was part of the compulsions, but I've never even dry-fired one."

"You're kidding, right?"

"Not even a little bit. I did my job hoarding, and now when the shit hits the fan you can go pick your favorite. I can tell you all the brands and serial numbers by heart, I can break them down, wire-brush them with oil, and load them. But I can't fire one, Rudy. I've just always been afraid of that part, and I wouldn't even know how to aim it. There. I'm a dweeb. My secret's out." She looked up at him from under her lashes. "Some 'Provider,' huh?"

"Wait now," Rudy said. "Maybe you're not 'The Provider' at all. Maybe you're 'The Preparer of the Basement' or 'The Gun Collector' or 'The Digger of Tunnels,' someone subordinate to this character with such a dark future."

She reached for the bottom of her shirt and hauled up a bit so he'd get a good view. And there, on her hip, was what appeared to be a tattoo. It was a squiggly line with two dots over it. Rudy didn't bother testing it by moving up and behind her to see if the dots would still appear on the new upside, but after a few seconds, as advertised, the dots seemed to disappear from view altogether.

"This was raised up on my skin right before the trees started falling, Rudy. I am your Provider. I just have to face the fact that my time may be short, and pray that I'm the right girl for the job when push comes to shove." She got up. "Speaking of which, and I hope you'll excuse this poor segue, we didn't shove this couch over for nothing. Help me pull open this trapdoor. It's made of six inches of concrete and I don't have Mother to help with the up-n-over anymore."

She turned the bolts on three sides of the square cover, and even though their hasps were anchored with what looked like contractor's wedge bolts, Rudy seriously wondered how difficult it would be to break in from the underside. He dismissed this, however, writing it off to the theory that all this was built on the idea of illusion, passing glances failing to register the truth in the architecture both upstairs and out at the bank of the river.

They both took hold of the iron ring and pulled. The door came up, hinges squealing, and they let it fall to the floor with a thump.

There was a noise then.

From down in the hole. They both peered over the edge, and there were eyes down there looking back up at them. Slanted yellow eyes.

Hundreds of them.

The tunnel was packed with dogs, and Caroline was already squatting back at the trapdoor, digging her fingers under to throw it back over. Rudy put out his hand.

"No, wait!"

She paused, and he gave her a half-look, ear cocked.

"Do you hear it?"

"Hear what?"

"Exactly." He peered back down the hole, and the eyes stared back, waiting. He went down to a knee for a better angle and looked over the rim of his glasses. Yep. They were a throng that went all the way back as far as the eye could see. And no nipping or barking, no jumping, no growling. He pushed up and put his hands on his hips.

"I have a feeling about this," he said. "A strong one." He pointed to the floor by his feet and said, "Come! Now!"

The dogs trotted up the ramp single file, quickly, efficiently, a flood of them filling up the basement floor space: collies, Rottweilers, bulldogs, Labradors, greyhounds, pit bulls, Newfoundlands, and Siberian huskies. There were wild dogs and dogs with collars, an English mastiff with one eye and a limp, and a Great Dane standing four and a half feet high. And then came the wolves, gray and black. Foxes too, the lot of them jockeying for position, the biggest canines in the rear, the smaller nose-nudged to the front with a few of the very largest spot-positioned up there like sentries. When the room was filled the parade stopped abruptly, the remaining animals waiting patiently down in the tunnel, one last dog trying to be included up in the light—a tiny Cavalier King Charles Spaniel puppy scampering up the ramp, hind legs low to the ground in anticipation, tail wagging furiously. An Old English sheepdog with an especially sad-looking expression bared its teeth and growled, and the spaniel went flat on his stomach, ears back in terror. Caroline bent to pick him up immediately.

"There, there," she said, trying to cradle him. The puppy kept kicking his soft paws to find purchase on her chest, licking her face, shaking with it.

Rudy turned to the pack.

"Sit," he said, and in militaristic synchronicity they all did. So did the remaining animals in the tunnel.

"What on earth is this?" Caroline said.

"I suppose," Rudy answered, "that it's one of the 'powers' that I was destined to gain after the trees fell."

"But it wasn't in the book."

"Doesn't matter. It's in our collective psyche. And your 'book' could have been a copy of a copy of a copy fifty times over, this one small part lost through the translations. In terms of the last few days, think about the players who have surfaced, all of them classic figures that represent 'the horrific,' those who were actually foreshadowings of a new world order. There's the witch, the warlock, and now the 'werewolf' or the king of dogs. And the prisoners coming out of their ground-holes in a temporary trancelike state are the zombies. These iconic characters were passed down to us first in verbal story-code. Of course, we made them into caricatures over time because it is in our nature to euphemize, but now is the time for perspective. It makes more than perfect sense that my army is canine."

The cavalier spaniel was in Caroline's ear now, licking and nudging with its tiny black nose.

"Shh," she was saying, trying to control him. Finally, she let him down to the floor gently. He had a wild moment where he hunched and gave darting, frightened glances all around, tail wagging madly. The sheepdog gave a quick bark, and the spaniel went over, turned, and backed in between the bigger dog's feet, quieted now in his little safe haven.

"I'm not an expert with pop culture and Gothic," Caroline said, still smiling about the little one, "but aren't we forgetting the Vampire?"

"Your mother," Rudy said. "She needs my blood."

"Hmm," she said. Her smile had vanished, but Rudy didn't think she was offended, not quite. Maybe she was thinking what he was, that it was possible Mother-Dearest had more to do with this than gaining a few disease-free bonus years. Still, it didn't warrant further discussion, not at the moment. There were priorities.

"Get your video camera," Rudy said. "I have a message to send out, and I want the dogs in the background. They make for a powerful visual presentation, and we should capture it on tape, or whatever you'd call it nowadays, before they start having to go outside to piss and poop in shifts."

"You hope," she said, moving through them nervously, the lot making a path for her. "If they make in here, I'm just letting you know, Rudy, I am not cleaning it up." She opened one of the storage units and reached inside. "I'm still a bit pissed that they breached my river entrance. I mean, it's just camouflaged tarp with a slit down the middle, but it's *good* camouflage. I walked past it hundreds of times when it went up, and you literally couldn't distinguish it from the background."

"Old icons and images, Caroline. And triggers. They've had that dressed-up river doorway in their collective consciousness for as long as we have been erecting these cartoonish archetypes with their Halloween storylines."

Caroline came back through the mass with her palmcorder.

"I wish I could have taken one of your classes," she said.

"I never taught Gothic."

She tilted her head slightly.

"I'm not talking about content, Rudy. It's the delivery I'm starting to like."

She was looking at him. It was awkward and electric, and neither of them budged.

A dog growled, another barked to shut the first one up, and a third chimed in to let the second one know he or she was just as guilty as the former for the interruption. Or that's the way it seemed.

"So," Rudy said.

"So." She had a rueful grin, but it was warm, saying for all intents and purposes, *"Another time, maybe . . ."*

Yes. Another time: Rudy's theme song.

"You know how to work that thing?" he said flatly.

"Sure do," she replied, "but you'll still need to hide your face, unless you want every witch who's stolen a laptop to die for it. Hold this." She handed over the camera and moved through to the stairway. Its underside was cloaked by a white gauzy material, and she ripped it down, next reaching under to pull out an old groundcloth that looked as if it had seen its best days in the 70s. She came back through the hoard, and the dogs didn't seem to mind that she dragged the things over their heads. In fact, Rudy could have sworn they felt privileged by the touch of them, smelling up at them, licking their chops after they passed over.

She paused at the couch and nodded toward her hat.

"Put it on backward the way a catcher does," she said.

Rudy did it, and Caroline tossed the gauze back into the crowd of dogs, giving the command, "Eyes, nose, mouth!" as she did it. The dogs dove to it, and when it resurfaced, they had bitten holes in the fabric. Caroline draped it over Rudy's head with the holes coming over his face in the proper places. She then proceeded to put the old dirty canvas over his head in a hood rather than simply across his back like a cloak. The last piece was a hank of rope she took off the top of the dryer and tied around Rudy's neck.

She backed off a step.

"Well?" Rudy said. It smelled like mothballs and old camp gear, and he imagined he looked like some cartoon Western bandito who couldn't afford pantyhose to go over his face. Caroline shivered.

"You're the faceless man in my old book who frightened me as a child," she said. She brought up the camera and shot for a second, next hitting rewind, then play. She touched the pause button and showed him the screen.

The man Rudy saw was a monster. The lack of aesthetics didn't matter; in fact, they made it worse. The get-up was makeshift, childish, his black-rimmed glasses beneath the mask finalizing the low-end bargain-basement feel to this thing, and then in absolute contradiction, the eyes looking through the glasses and ragged holes had a lunatic's certainty. Not the effect Rudy had been trying for, but he was pretty sure people would stop, watch, and listen for a second.

"Film me," he said. "One take. Off the cuff."

She switched places with him so the dogs would be in the shot, adjusted her view screen, and nodded.

Rudy spoke.

"Fellow citizens, there are many changes that have taken place today, grave changes, and you are certainly owed an explanation. I do have answers, but you are not necessarily going to like them. I can identify causes for you, but I admit there is no reason for you to

The Witch of the Wood

believe me. Still, before you write off what I am to tell you as the ravings of some madman, I ask you to honestly assess what you have seen this morning. Logic and scientific rationales don't work anymore, and I would ask you to suspend old disbeliefs for the sake of new ethics. Take a leap of faith and trust me, at least until the end of this recording.

"First, you must know that every tree in the world has been uprooted; there are no exceptions. Moreover, I am sure that after your recovery from 'The Great Fall' you noticed an emergence from the ground cavities. Please note that the beings coming out of the dirt are not, repeat not, monsters or aliens. They are the original inhabitants of this planet, the first of our women, punished for unjust cause and entrapped by a spell, yes a spell that held them beneath the prison-root for centuries. I am asking you, no, I am *begging* you not to harm them. The newly liberated that I speak of are shapeshifters with the ability to transform according to the preferred vision of their given beholders. It is no illusion. And please do not consider this to be any type of sorcery. It is an old reality, what was quite natural for these women back in their original time period, and we should welcome them, celebrating their emancipation.

"And to the newly liberated females flooding our properties, fields, and streets, I have a message for you as well. I am aware that you were incarcerated unlawfully . . . that what you endured was excruciating, that what you are owed in retribution for your pain is more than this modern world has in its coffers. Still, I would plead with you to abstain utterly from thoughts of revenge. Your jailers are long dead, and would be considered irrelevant in terms of any position of defense you might argue following rash actions in this time and place.

"Please know that I am 'The Father,' who was faced with the bitterest of choices. I could have helped engineer your wave of dark justice and destruction, but I decided to employ the alternative: your freedom for the mass acquittal of these descendants of sinners. As a result, it would harm you to look me in the face at this point, and hence I wear this cheap disguise, this mask of gauze, this dirty hood. I am not God, nor would ever claim to be. But I now believe in miracles, and I have faith that from the ashes of today's many disasters we can start afresh from a platform of love. Is that not what all our old religions would have had us do if we broke down all their customs and rituals to their foundations? This recognition, this awareness is our miracle, and the chance to unite is upon us.

"Do not raise your hands in violence! I chose the liberation of prisoners at great expense, and you were not the only ones to lose those held dear to you. This morning, I sacrificed my own son, a half-breed, born of a cavity-dweller and filled with the golden blood burst forth from his skin like a hundred rivers, fulfilling the prophecy of freedom for his sisters entombed. Celebrate his passing by ending the bloodshed of the red. History is now, and we can author this new age together, rewriting the way all this was really meant to play out. Join me."

He had his hands held out to the camera, and Caroline hit the stop button.

"That was beautiful," she said. For a bald moment, Rudy thought she might have been chastising him for the melodrama, but her face told a different story. He looked at the floor.

"We should . . . ah . . . discuss it sometime."

"Promise?"

He pulled up his head and nodded curtly. There was chemistry here, but like the first pass when she'd complimented his vocal delivery, the timing was out of joint, and maybe that was the sum-total of his personal tragedy, his destiny to surround himself with new messages of love and togetherness, yet walk through it all utterly alone. He undid the rope and removed the disguise. Even with the hat protecting his hair, the get-up had felt filthy on him and he was sweating.

"I don't feel too pretty," he said.

"Eye of the beholder."

"You're too kind."

"Not really." She walked up to him and took the material from him. "But you're right, Rudy. There are times and places for everything, and right about now you owe your son a viewing. Let's see it. For your speech to work, the warlock's visual has to be absolutely devastating."

Rudy got out his cell.

They replayed it, looked at it, heads together.

And Rudy wept.

For awhile Rudy didn't speak for all but a few grunts and mutterings as he stood over Caroline's dented red toolbox, looking for stuff. He next busied himself over at the gun cabinets, digging deep into the holster bins, cutting straps and adjusting them, repositioning buckles, crimping clasps, piercing new prong slots. When he was finished, he had a pile of leather six feet high and ten or so wide. Caroline had positioned herself on the sofa to work at splicing the two tapes together and uploading them on YouTube with multiple tags, the spaniel puppy up on her shoulder like a cat, the sheepdog watching it all warily. She had taken a number of breaks to organize the dogs in groups to go outside and do their business, and both she and Rudy had avoided conversation up until now.

"So what are you doing?" she said finally. The spaniel, named "Killian" according to his nametag, was in her lap now, flicking his long tail into his own face and acting surprised by it. Rudy stood straight.

"I'm making new holsters from the old ones," he said.

"No kidding."

"No."

They shared a fresh silence. Rudy had been stunned by the visual representation of his son's sacrifice, so much so that the dread of it still hung around him like fog. Caroline wasn't pressing too hard, but Rudy knew he had to recover. There were things going on outside the sanctuary of this basement that needed attending, and his grief had to be put aside.

"The holsters are for the dogs," he admitted.

"Really."

"Yes." He came over flexing his hands, reddened by the close work of the last hour or so. He felt he'd never be able to look a pair of pliers or a utility blade in the face ever again, and he sat next to Caroline with a tired sigh. Killian waddled over, tail going mad, ears back. He nipped playfully at his master's earlobes, and Rudy couldn't help but forfeit a grin.

"Geez," he said.

"He likes you."

"He likes everybody." Rudy pushed him off gently. "Reality check; there are going to be a lot of people out there who will scoff at that taped speech."

"Yes. The old 'Have you heard the word of God today?' on the bus syndrome. A real aisle clearer."

He ran his palm over his scalp absently.

"And some who do see it will violently oppose."

"No rest for the messenger."

"Right."

She scratched Killian behind the ears, and the dog closed his eyes in pleasure. She had her lips pursed and was making "goo-goo" sounds. Then she said in the "baby voice," "So the holsters are for the dogs, hmm? Is the King of Canines so clever he can train them to shoot?"

Rudy laughed for the first time in what felt a long while.

"No, my dear. I'm just being practical. When I take them out for a stroll, I don't really know what kind of a world I'm going to find out there. I have a feeling the non-believers are going to outnumber the faithful at first, and you don't walk into a gunfight with a penknife, as they say. I figure I can only load up my body with so much reloading ammo, so it made sense to pack all the dogs with heat. With a hundred of them at two firearms apiece, I go into the outdoor arena with more than twelve hundred rounds available to me. Not too shabby, huh?"

"Indeed." She let Killian down, and he went to the sheepdog, who curled him in and nipped motheringly at his flank. Caroline put both palms into the small of her back and stretched.

"Well, before you go for your stroll," she said, "I need for you to give me the healing blood for my mother's first dose."

"Of course."

"And we'll go see her soon?"

"Yes, under the cover of darkness. I'm no Navy Seal, but common sense claims that if I am going to enter a building in stealth I don't want my approach or escape to be a neighborhood show."

She set up the needles and tubes and syringes, and when she was finished the drawing Rudy felt weak. She took the two bags of his blood and stored them in an old cooler she got from the same storage space under the stairs that the groundcloth had come from. He rested for an hour. Caroline again ran the dogs out in shifts, both to "go outside" and this time to hunt for food.

When Rudy woke from his nap, he holstered up one hundred of the biggest canines, arming them with two loaded weapons apiece. He put on his disguise. Right before going down to the tunnel ramp, Caroline told him that their video had gotten fifteen hundred hits already.

Rudy went down the ramp, to the tunnel's opening, to the new world he'd partially created.

And didn't quite get what he'd expected.

The going on the outside was rough at first. Rudy didn't worry all too much about getting flagged at the entrance by some passerby, since the riverbank sat in the middle of what had been uninhabited woods five hundred yards removed from the street. There was even a nice cross-hatch of fallen wood right there at the cutout, acting like a bridge over the cold waters rushing below. But the dogs moved too quickly, packed together like a large diamond with Rudy trying to jog in the middle. Of course, the forest was a tangled mess, and he hadn't gone ten feet into it before turning his ankle, barking his shin, skinning his knee, slipping, and getting stuck in a couple of voids. They made it to a glen of sorts, still bordered up by masses of overgrowth patchworked into a rough circle about a hundred feet in diameter, and Rudy called, "Stop!" They waited patiently, and he tried to catch his breath, hands on the knees, sweat streaming down his cheeks. The mask was off-center, and he readjusted the thing, thinking that the dirty moisture building up there under the gauze was making it cling in places. Yeah, he was a "ten" when it came to "creepy," and a flat zero in terms of practical mobility. He thought of King Richard III and said, "My kingdom for a fucking horse."

Something came from behind him then, pushing under his butt, sliding between his legs. He lost his footing. Dogs to both sides moved in for balance maintenance, and before he could fall backward the body beneath him completed its positioning. His feet were off the ground entirely, and he was perched on one of the wolves, huge and dark gray with black streaks going in two parallel lines up the back of its head. It had gone cold, and the wolf's breath was misting. The side support moved off a bit, a few renegade snowflakes fell, and Rudy suddenly felt comfortable and sure. The animal bore his weight easily, and the seating was so flush and specific that Rudy was suddenly positive he wouldn't need reins. He was sitting on a crisscross of leather, and hanging along the wolf's flanks just behind Rudy's heels were two of the long pocket holsters he had so meticulously jury-rigged. He reached behind for the weapon on his right. It slid out and gleamed in the cold sun, Mossberg 500 Special, and the withdrawal hadn't skewed his balance in the least. He felt the animal adjusting beneath him moment for moment, but it was a natural thing like breathing. He sheathed the shotgun and reached back to his left, withdrawing the Bushmaster M4 Patrolman. Somehow, he was certain that he could shoot and hit a target in full stride. In fact, it didn't seem it would be too difficult to fire both weapons simultaneously, he was sure of it. He raised the gun over his head, and called, "Ride!"

The animal beneath him burst into a dead-run, and the pack galloped along, all close, backbones working around him in bobs and thrusts, haunches pistoning across the ruined forest floor.

They made it out of the woods in about five minutes flat.

And the world was an open wound.

The first thing Rudy noticed was the lack of channels, dividers, "corridors." The trees had acted as natural organizers, making one feel secure in the grid; and now with their leveling, the buildings looked, for lack of a better word, *sporadic*. The south edge of the woods abruptly ceased before a rather complicated highway junction at the border between Broomall and Havertown, and the Barnaby's, the car wash, the closed-down Pathmark, and the houses curving up along the rises due south and northwest all looked like teeth in the cliché hillbilly's maw. Isolated and crooked.

Felled trees were everywhere and traffic had come to absolute gridlock. By now, most of the cars were abandoned, many of them crushed by the mass of decorator foliage that had broken through the graded sound barriers leading to the 476 entrances, other vehicles crimped up trunk to hood from chain reaction rear-endings that wound for miles up West Chester Pike.

There was smoke threading through the air, and it made the light snow look like ash. Victims still pinned and trapped were honking horns, there were a couple blowing whistles, and someone all the way up by the Manoa shopping center was shooting green flares off into the gray sky. There were scatters of do-gooders moving in groups looking for victims, but surprisingly few in Rudy's immediate area. And no police. Yet how could there be, really? They depended on roads for access. Moreover, there were only so many officers, and it was never made clearer than by this stark illustration that they were but tokens, placed strategically to handle the few making trouble or in the process of getting in it, based on the probability that the balance of society basically managed itself.

Rudy then thought of the military, the National Guard, and got the same answer. There were only so many soldiers. No agency or system could help literally *everyone* all at once.

The world was on its own. At least until they got the chainsaws running.

Directly in front of Rudy at the corner, there was a thick twist of street-wreckage including an old station wagon with wooden side panels, a black Lexus, two pickups, three minivans, and a jack-knifed eighteen-wheeler, its cab turned sideways and run half up the light pole. The driver had gotten the passenger side door open like a broken wing, and he was hanging upside down out of it, leg stuck back up in the cab, hands splayed, long salt-'n'-pepper hair dangling. Rudy wondered why no one had tried to help him and surmised that the guy had passed out on impact, then lay hidden by the angle across the floorboards until waking up with a start, reaching down for the door handle, snapping it open, and falling down after it.

"Hey, friend!" Rudy called. The truck driver snapped his head around, took one look from upside down, and started flailing like a fish out of water. Stuff fell from him then like bad slapstick: keys, sunglasses, a pencil stub that had been set behind his ear. Rudy got down off his wolf and ran over, straddling two vehicles and climbing up the backside to get to the driver's door, hard as all hell to open straight upwards, thank you very much. Inside, the guy's boot was stuck between the smashed instrument panel and the front seat, his wooden bead seat cushion wedged into the affair like a seed caught between a pair of molars. Rudy gave it a yank, and the guy's foot came loose, sending him to the street. By the time Rudy got down, however, the trucker was gone. He wanted nothing to do with a masked man accompanied by dogs and wolves, especially those wearing gun holsters and waiting for their master like a battery of storm troopers sitting in the "at ease" position. More personal irony. Not only was the one preaching love and togetherness destined to walk alone, but his paradigm of charity was misunderstood.

"Who are you, mister?" someone said.

Rudy turned, and there were at least twenty-five people looking back at him, clothing disheveled, sleeves ripped, blood and oil stains on the trousers, grease and dirt on the skirts and pants suits. Right. Acoustics worked both ways, and they'd heard him coming, seen the dog pack, then gone to hide behind the cars to watch silently as he climbed up to save the trucker. Up front, there was an African American woman in nurse's scrubs ripped at both knees. She was fingering her I.D. badge, looking at him critically. Three women in business attire and sneakers had their heads together and were whispering; one had her arm in a makeshift sling and another wore a glistening scrape on one side of her forehead. A buck-toothed boy with a back-turned baseball cap held the hand of a skinny guy wearing khakis and glasses with one of the stems broken off, and there were five filthy women huddling together under a huge Phillies blanket, all of them blondes, all of them twins, all shock-blue eyes, high cheekbones, heart-shaped lips, and legs, legs, legs; someone in the group had a Scandinavian fantasy and was secretly thinking he'd crashed into heaven.

Rudy wanted to say something prophetic. He wanted to show his appreciation for what seemed their philanthropic effort up the avenue, and their clear acceptance of the ground-dwellers as people that needed a blanket for the sake of modesty and comfort. They were a signpost for hope and didn't even realize it.

His voice rang out then, but it wasn't him. It was the recorded Rudy Barnes on somebody's iPad, and the group gathered around a guy with wild curly hair, a gray hoodie, and cargo pants. The recording was relatively poor, and Rudy's voice sounded tinny. When he'd made the speech in the basement it had seemed a solid piece of sophisticated prose, but here, out on the street, it came off insincere, almost silly. He had once sent an e-mail to his chair at Widener, casually bragging about making an APA go-to sheet that morphed that awful blue text with bits and pieces from Owl Purdue, and she'd called a private meeting, reading his words back to him, making him squirm a bit for his inappropriate bravado. This felt similar, and when there was the cut to the crucifixion, mouths fell ajar. A little girl buried her face in her mother's thigh, and the boy with the baseball cap started crying. When it had concluded, the nurse looked up at Rudy and whispered, "You did that to your *son?*"

The group just stared, eyes cold judgments cutting across the double yellow line.

"It's obscene," someone said.

"Blasphemy," another chipped in.

"Disgusting."

"Disgraceful."

"Insanity."

"Murder."

They had formed a semicircle and closed the distance a bit. The dogs behind Rudy let out a collective and rather bone-shivering growl, and the group halted. To the left, the witches were on their knees, foreheads flat to the asphalt, hands splayed out palms-down.

The Witch of the Wood

A woman with tight red jeans, a jet black ponytail, and exceptionally high eyebrows came forward a step and pointed back toward the youth with the iPad.

"Do you really want people to see that? These children are in shock!" She dared another step forward and hissed, "There are so many bodies we can't hide their eyes from them all! Then you come and show us a horror movie? A snuff film? How dare you!"

Rudy had no response. How many people wore Jesus on a chain, hung him from the rearview, placed him on the wall above the mantel? Crown of thorns, javelin through the ribs, nails in the hands and the feet, all wonderful in metaphor removed from the current timeline, but horrific, gratuitous, brutal, even pornographic in the here and now.

"It was the way," he managed.

"Well, we don't want you here," she replied. "We don't need your guns and your masks and your dogs and your murder."

Rudy turned without another word. He walked to the pack that made room for him to reach the middle, mounted his wolf, and made a harsh call into the wind. They bounded off in a blur, jumping the guardrail and going back fast to the fallen woodland from which they had come.

"It's all for shit!" Rudy called.

"What?" Caroline said. She was standing on the lip of the cutout, and the rushing water was rather loud beneath her. Rudy and his pack were on the far riverbank. He ripped off the hood and the mask.

"I said it's all for shit," he repeated. "This world, this life, my role in it. They don't scoff at me out there, they *despise*. And they don't come forth with a child's ignorant violence, but rather a hardened, deserving disdain." He tossed the costume into the creek and four dogs splashed in after the articles, loping downstream across the slippery stones to an area before a bend thirty feet south where the canvas and gauze next caught on branches and brush. Rudy started taking off his clothes: shirt, belt, pants. "The world has ruptured!" he shouted, "and I am its prime offender! I murdered my own son . . ." He broke off for a moment to get back control. "I sacrificed my own flesh and blood—"

"A demon bent on revenge," Caroline finished for him.

"I caused this natural disaster."

"That obliterated the many dungeons of the innocent."

"The 'Great Fall' killed hundreds of thousands!"

"And freed millions!"

"But who am I, Caroline? There's no place for my masks and my guns and my dogs. People want to heal. They don't want some new belief system based on metaphor; they want security and order, tradition and the familiar. They want better health plans and stronger retirement programs, hope and opportunity. And what am I to them but a monster? What's my purpose—was that in your book? Is it my job now to shoot teenagers breaking into the Giant or the Super Fresh, looking to steal energy drinks, Nyquil, and a few DVDs? I don't fit into the master plan anymore, and you know what? I'm making a pledge. No more bloodshed, not by my hand. There will be no more broken spells, twisted prophecies, or speeches. I'll rot in your basement, and we're going to set these dogs free one by one."

He stepped into the current, and it was a shock. He halted for a moment, and there in the rushing creek he stood, shivering, fighting off the image of baptism, the barrage of religious symbolism that had become so frequent and common in this new reality it was almost absurd. He was dirty, that was all. He had cuts all over his arms and legs, and he'd been wearing a soiled groundcloth, a squalid veil. This was practical, not allegorical.

He washed vigorously. He kneeled on the hard stones and dunked his head, face freezing, temples pounding, and it gave him no sense of reconciliatory martyrdom. He was just soaked and cold.

Once finished, Rudy climbed up and gained a foothold on the slapdash bridge of felled timber, taking his time going across it, the balls of his feet damp and slippery like polished jumbo marbles trying to gain purchase on concave oil-slicked glass. He reached the tunnel archway, and Caroline had stood her ground there, waiting and watching.

They stared at each other for a moment, face to face, breathing heavily. He put his hands on her shoulders, he pulled her in, he pressed his lips hard to hers. Her arms were tight around his neck, and her mouth was open. He pushed through the split in the tarp and pulled her along by the hand into the tunnel.

The dogs waited outside.

After it happened, Rudy and Caroline lay on the sofa together cuddling, trading breaths and whispers. When they'd entered the space, the remaining dogs had bounded down the ramp and away as if on command, all except Killian, who'd stubbornly remained throughout the moments of foreplay, going up on his paws, nuzzling his little black nose into their ears as Rudy kissed Caroline's breasts and felt her calves there on the sofa, making it awkward, making them laugh.

Still, when Rudy had her stand there before him, slipping the band of her white cotton panties over the swell of her buttocks, the curve of her thigh, the dog yelped and ran down the tunnel. The rest was slow, affectionate, almost careful, and even after he entered her, they just couldn't stop kissing each other. The lack of atmosphere, the bare bulb and squeaking sofa, could have made things seem trivial, but didn't somehow as they worked their hips against each other, lips parted, eyes burning with this evolving storyline. At one point she burst into tears, shuddering, palms braced against his shoulders, and at another juncture he was gasping, working into her desperately, her ankles and heels making friction against his collarbones and ears. After the second round they'd joked about their given exclamations leading up to and during orgasm: hers a high mewing that almost sounded like pleadings for sympathy, and his, a series of hoarse and breathless "Oh's!" and "Oh fuck me's!" and various other classy expletives.

The dogs came back in, the smaller ones taking positions at the far edges of the space, those holstered making a ring around their masters, all facing away. Rudy and Caroline cradled each other, and just before he dozed off Caroline rose to hang up the clothing the dogs had retrieved from the river, clean and wrinkled, shirt, pants, mask of gauze, and groundcloth. One sock was missing, but no one was criticizing.

Rudy slept and dreamed about being an embryo, falling in slow motion down an old rickety set of basement stairs. When he came awake, Caroline was dressed and sitting on the sofa up by his chest, knee propped there by his head. She had her iPad.

"You need to see this, Rudy," she said, "before you go hanging up your holsters."

He sat up, rubbed his eyes, and ran his fingers down the corners of his lips. And somehow, he knew that his assessment of things had been as premature as that of his critics out there on West Chester Pike. By now darkness had fallen, and they had gotten back to their homes finding that many had been destroyed, ripped open to the night.

"It isn't teenagers stealing Nyquil and Marlboros, is it?"

Caroline shook her head slowly.

It was a YouTube video, cued up and paused, the screen a bright blur as the cameraman had been roughly panning across something that washed everything out to stark whites and streaks. The title was "Message to the Dogman," and Rudy said quietly, "Play it."

The Witch of the Wood

Caroline hit the button and enlarged the screen. It was a field somewhere, and there was a massive bonfire thirty feet wide at the least. At the fire's right edge, there were skinned animals, whole-bodied yet headless, roasting on spits, angled up at the moon. The camera panned left and Rudy just nodded to no one.

It was a mob five hundred deep, most of them covered with sweat, dirt, and blood. There were men and women, most of them physical specimens, a few kids, but not many. And there were police officers in the ranks, a few others wearing military fatigues, all with sidearms, some with rifles.

"I wouldn't have thought it at first," Rudy murmured. "The boys in uniform break rank, go against the code. But I don't think these men are a true representation of the law and the military . . . more a vocal minority of rash concrete thinkers moving right to the next hierarchy, the more rigid and practical the better. Law of the jungle, law of the literal, law of . . ."

"Shh," Caroline said. "Watch."

Two men stepped into the shot to face the crowd, and the shorter, stockier one put his fist in the air, shouting,

"Food! Light! No weakness!"

The crowd answered with a resounding roar, and the two leaders turned to the camera. The fist-pumper had a thick neck with pockmarks, and small stony eyes that caught reflections of the fire in ugly pinpointed gleams. He was young but had a stance that boasted a seasoned man's cynicism, a certain cold meanness, blunt cunning. The taller man standing beside him had a wide jaw, thick five-o'clock shadow, and a black Nike sweatband going across his face in diagonal, covering the socket where he must have lost an eye in the uprooting. Rudy recognized him. It was the teacher Wolfie had framed for looking at the high school girls crossing their legs.

So here was the infamous Coach Sullivan, most probably thanking God for this disaster, this distraction, allowing him to reinvent himself as "Lord of the Bonfire" with his criminal stooge Brian Duffey right there at his elbow.

"I'm not going to talk you to death," Sullivan said, his voice a rasp as if he'd been shouting all day and into the night. "But things have changed, and now it's cold and dark, at least out there beyond the fire." He took a step closer. "How many of you came home to the dead? What's left of your neighborhood? Did you raid the fridge and take what you could? Did you bust into the 7-Eleven? Then what?"

He stalked to the side of the bonfire where one man, shirtless and covered with sweat and grime, turned the spits, and three others behind him tossed timber into the massive blaze, throwing twirls of sparks up into the darkness.

"We've got venison here," he said. "Warmth. Water from the river. Three hundred cases of beer!"

That one raised another roar from the formation of supporters, and Sullivan came so close to the camera he filled it with his face.

"I know . . ." he said paternally. "Soon the power will come back on. We'll wood-chip all the trees, clear the roads, put out the fires, we always do. But there's a cancer among us, one that will eat us alive right here and right now while we're scrambling for candles. The 'Dogman' gives you his fancy preaching, but these are not women he speaks of. They are monsters, trying to assimilate, trying to *breed*. Funny thing, though . . ."

He moved aside and let Brian Duffey come into the shot, hauling over a terrified girl who looked very much like Linda Birch, the one who was over at the apartment last night. She tried to push backward, and Duffey gripped her tight, hand over her mouth, arm clamped around her waist. Sullivan came back into the shot with an iPad.

"See," he said. "Professor Rudy Barnes is your masked coward, your boy-killer, your freak-lover, and he has his picture on the Internet." He gave a sour laugh, and Rudy ground his teeth. He hadn't known there was a picture of him online; must have been the headshot Frank Willis took of him last year when he'd volunteered to edit the *Pioneer Review*, Widener's literary journal. Sullivan walked over toward the squirming girl and said, "It seems the monsters can't look their Dog-Master in the face, even after they transform."

He put the screen up in front of her and Duffey held her head in place, both hands plastered hard to her cheeks and temples, thumbs pressing her eyes open. Like a shopper in self-checkout trying for the right angle for the barcode scanner, Sullivan put the iPad in multiple positionings in front of her. Finally he caught a sightline, and her head burst. Duffey retained his tight grip, and the force cracked her face in three places, both eyes rupturing in hearty pops, meaty runners from the top of her crown bleeding down over Duffey's thick knuckles.

The crowd cheered as the witch's body crumpled, and after he dropped her Duffey shook his hands off dramatically, mouth open like a rock star bending a note, up on one foot bunny-hopping with it. Sullivan got camera-close once again.

"No impostors here, Dogman. Every woman to the side of this bonfire is pure."

He ran the back of his hand across his mouth and got sincere with it. Went down to a whisper.

"Dogman, come here. I want to show you something."

The camera followed him away from the fire, past the crowd, and into the darkness of the field. He was but a blackened form on black background for a moment, afterimage leaving ghosted outlines, and then his voice said, "Let there be light."

Offscreen it sounded as if Duffey were pulling ripcords, a number of chokes and grinds, and suddenly the area behind the fire lit up to a brightness so potent it washed everything to near blacks and whites. Rudy gasped. They had obviously utilized Sullivan's access back at the school to raid for football field lights and gas generators, moving them through the fallen woods behind the grandstand, down the slope a few hundred yards off property where suburb abruptly became highway. There was an antenna tower in the background, partially toppled, hanging on by its stubborn wires, confirming that it was the Runnemede cornfield at the edge of the Blue Route, all the crop curled down and blackened from last summer's drought; they'd done a piece about it on the news comparing it in microcosm to the disasters in the Midwest. But now there were crude wooden crosses rising up from the dark mass of dead corn husks, most of them ten to twelve feet high, probably built of the fallen timber two meadows over where the edge of Scutters Woods bordered the landscape for fifteen miles both north and southwest.

The crosses were in rows patterned in rough alternate, and there must have been three thousand of them, all leaning a bit one way or the other, each bearing a witch hanging there like Jesus. They were all blank slates, all of them naked, and Rudy could only assume that they'd chosen to retain their raw form for pride, for protest, so as not to be found out through an iPad weeding procedure that would inevitably make their talent of transformation seem an act of deceit.

One of them was set off from the others, and the camera walked its way over to a full body closeup. Her dark hair was a toss of damp strands clinging to her forehead, curling on her cheeks, spiked to wet points along her shoulders and collarbones. Her black eyes were wide open in terror and her frail white body was emaciated, bony, almost translucent, knees together, one crossed over the other, wrists and ankles chafed raw where she was tied to the wood. The camera backed off to accommodate its narrator, who was joined by Duffey, carrying a torch.

"Here's the thing, Dogman," Sullivan said. "We don't want your Stepford Wives, and we're going to have a pyro party, one per every five minutes until dawn. Then . . . we burn them all and hunt for new ones."

He nodded to Duffey, and the kid ambled over, bending with it, wary of the flames licking backward up the branch leaving black marks along the shank. The blank slate squirmed and strained against the cords as he drew near, the flickering light of the torch reflecting off of her. Then at the moment before contact, she stopped struggling and looked straight into the camera.

"My name is Rebecca," she said. "Rebecca."

Duffey brought the torch to her toes and she went up like kindling, flames spreading up the sides of her, and for a moment she appeared to be wearing a translucent blue aureole. It was the pause before the screaming. Then the fire took her, ate through her. The hair burned the brightest, leaving spots of afterimage on the camera lens. There was a long moment of peeling and curling, eyes liquefied to parallel runners of molten tar, then strange movements within her down low, things dropping untethered. Next was utter consumption, flames snaking the voids, licking clean the openings. It was but moments. It was forever. Finally the angry blaze started to vanish one flickering brother at a time, the hangers-on lapping and flicking at the remains.

Her blackened skeleton grinned, smoke coming off her in wisps.

The scene ended.

Caroline put the iPad aside.

"There's no ultimatum here," she said. "No deal, no ransom."

"Her name was Rebecca," Rudy murmured.

"You can't let this go on."

"I know."

"He'll fill the crosses again; he's not bluffing."

"Quite."

She cricked her neck one way, then the other.

"Elephant in the room, Rudy. He doesn't need you as his hostage, taking you on a leash cleansing the streets as you go because he's got your picture. This is bait."

"Exactly."

"He wants to erase you before you gain a following more practical than a pack of dogs."

"I realize this, Caroline."

"So what are you going to do?"

"Take the bait," he said quietly.

There was a thick silence, and Caroline tried to touch him on the shoulder. She got absolute deadwood and withdrew, next folding her hands in her lap and speaking to them.

"Even with your wolfpack, Rudy, you won't be able to get to your guns fast enough. That bastard has law enforcement and military, let alone the potential arsenal he didn't show on camera, plus the fact that—"

"I can't let another witch die on my watch," Rudy interrupted, "not if I can save her. They're not just blank slates, they're people." He looked at her with what felt like bloodshot eyes. "Her name was Rebecca."

"I know, but your word is currently stronger than your might."

"I'm going in."

"You'll die."

"I know," he lied. It quieted her, and that was a good thing. He didn't need to argue with her and dance around the truth, now that it had come unveiled to him like some hideous primeval sculpture. For he'd had what alcoholics, gamblers, and petty thieves called a "moment of clarity" just now. He wasn't meant to preach, but rather to betray and deceive. For the good of the many, he was destined to delude and destroy the ones closest to him, as he'd done with Wolfie. It was inevitable.

But there were lies and there were lies, and rather than the out-and-out bold-faced variety, he opted for partial truth and avoidance.

"Sullivan," he said, "is a health teacher, Caroline. He's also seems quite a man's man who'd rather entertain barroom philosophy than a more global assessment that accounts for the past."

"Riddles, Rudy. Riddles."

He stood.

"What I mean is, I don't think he really thinks I'll attack with nothing for backup but a bunch of dogs, not tonight anyway. That video clip was more a way for him to gain more disciples, pardon the clumsy religious allusion. The thing was addressed to me but postmarked for the world, a demonstration that proves I won't make a showing, that I'll live up to his accusation of cowardice."

She rose to her feet as well and stepped near.

"So you're banking on the fact that he won't be ready."

"I'm banking on beer," he said. "Three hundred cases of it. That and the lesson of the Hessians."

She smiled.

"And he's a health teacher."

"Right. He's no history scholar, at least I hope he isn't."

"And the lessons of the past . . ."

"Repeat themselves." He put his hands on her shoulders and gave the most meaningful look of sincerity he could muster, hating himself for it. "Will you trust me on this?"

"I'll try," she said. "But before you attempt . . . whatever you plan to do out there . . . you, uh . . . promised to stop in on my mother." She sucked in her top lip for a second. "I apologize for sounding inappropriate, but a deal's a deal."

"Of course," Rudy said, pretending he'd forgotten about it. "Just give me the cooler with the bags of blood and do me a favor."

"Of course."

"It's a dangerous mission."

"No more than yours, I'm sure."

He pointed to the black footlocker at the edge of the arsenal.

"What exactly do you have in there, anyway?"

She grinned girlishly.

"Oh, the usual: aerial tubes, bottle rockets, pinwheels, Roman candles, black snakes, you know. Why? You looking for a big entrance?"

"More like a diversion. And you won't have tree cover. You'll have to crawl around to get these fireworks set up. Can you handle it?"

"I think so. But Rudy, please. It's suicide. It's not worth—"

"Saving three thousand human beings? It most certainly is."

"And you're sure I can't convince you otherwise."

"Dead sure."

"Bad choice of words, Rudy."

"I've made a lot of bad choices in my life, Caroline, and this isn't one of them."

"Whatever you say."

"Right."

She shrugged sadly, like *I give up*, and got the cooler.

"Well, we thank you for this, both my mother and I."

He took it and stuck it under his arm.

"Just have those fireworks positioned, Caroline. That's all I ask. Wait there for me and make sure you're ready to light the fuse."

"And my cue?"

"The dogs," Rudy said, "the moment they make their appearance. And be punctual, please." He smiled a little. "I realize we're going colonial here, but it'll be too late if you can see the whites of my eyes."

The hospital up on the hill had a mass of people waiting at the emergency room entrance for sign-in, spilling across the concrete rotary and into the parking area. There was a construction zone outside the orthopedics wing, and its plastic fencing had been forced to the dirt, the road cones kicked aside, people sitting on the skid steer loader buckets and piles of crushed stone, caution tape fluttering at the perimeter like loose strands of hair. The trailer had been raided and stood open to the night; three groups huddled around rusted fifty-gallon drums with fires in them.

For the sake of stealth Rudy brought his dogs around back along the angle of the rise just below the lip of the access lane, the concourse itself covered with fallen trees and brushwork too dense for those without paws and claws to advance through. At the rear of the facility there was a set of dumpsters, bay doors, and loading zones for maintenance and food service; to the far side, the ambulances. Considering the fact that vehicles had been deemed useless, the area was vacated; were it summertime you would have heard the crickets chirping. Rudy left his wolfpack to sit at attention in a culvert just off the apron and made his way toward the building.

The service entrance was locked, of course, but there was a basement door at the bottom of a ramp that was open.

Lucky.

Would it last? Rudy suddenly had a bad feeling, as if the minute he'd walk through that door he'd be nailed by security, or an orderly, or some RN looking for blankets, or worse, someone from the crowd who had made it inside, looking for comfort, for medicine, for food, for answers.

Rudy turned the knob slowly. This was the lower level, and if the hospital administration and staff were worth their salt, they would have blocked access to the elevators up front somehow and condensed the emergency space to protect from burglary down here. And wouldn't they keep the proletariat away from ICU and the in-patient areas where the beds were already full, especially with the sensitive cases, like those recovering from radiation and chemotherapy? He pushed open the door.

The basement area was vacant, thank God: empty corridor, lecture hall with two columns of spare chairs stacked to the side of the podium, darkened classrooms, bathrooms, broom closets. There was a pallet jack sitting by a linen storage space, and the distinct hum of industrial cooling fans at the end of the hall in the generator room. Rudy took the elevator up to the twelfth floor, where Caroline had said her mother was residing. When the doors slid open with that little *ding,* Rudy was relieved to find the entrance suite dark and unoccupied. There was a floor guide in a glass case, and he saw "Oncology / In-Patient Services" listed as down the hall and to the right, the nurse's station in the middle of the floor.

He was fairly sure that most of the staff had been reassigned to the downstairs emergency space and the floors right above it, but he was taking no chances, detouring through the radiation lab and a waiting area, all dimly lit as the generators were obviously set to power only what was absolutely necessary. He risked a brief stop in a supply closet for a flashlight, and then another in one of the examination rooms, where he proceeded to open cabinets and route through the drawers as noiselessly as was humanly possible. He realized that he was holding his breath and let it out in a shaky hiss. The animated parts breakdowns of the pancreas and colon were staring down from the walls like grinning omens: *"You coming up on fifty, friend? We're just dying to get your attention,"* and he laughed back at them, a bit too heartily. Finally, he found the implement he'd been looking for and stuck it in his breast pocket. He backed off and opened the door a sliver, looking out cautiously. No one.

The hall bent around twice, and at the end of it was a set of swinging double doors, the directional PVC signage on the wall by his head announcing "Cancer Ward" in charcoal block lettering.

Rudy followed the arrow, walked the long hall, pushed through the doors.

There hadn't been anyone up here in awhile, he could tell by the smell. And it was blatantly clear why they didn't use this space to house those with broken arms and twisted ankles. It was the epitome of hopelessness and decay, darkened, two to three beds per room-space, each divided by a set of curtains, most of them opened. The patients were skeletons twisting on their cots, blue lips, dark sunken eyes, skin mottled and sagging and spotted with age. Most of them were bald, arms riddled with bruisings left by multitudes of injections. There was a woman to the right hooked to her infusion pump, and she had no nose, just a stringy blue void with a bone dividing it down the middle. There was a man twitching and squirming, lips curled back, purple gums worn so thin his teeth were exposed to their bottom roots like some hideous version of the 70s "Alien." There were face nodules and head craters, black bumps and brown patches, lesions, blotching, and sores reddened at the edges, pregnant with pus.

There in the back corner, three beds from the end on the left, was Caroline's mother.

She was bone-thin, black knit cap on her head, wide-set eyes like those of her daughter. She was lying on her stomach, head where her feet should have been, and her gown was open in the back revealing a body shriveled and shrunken off a knotted spine. She saw him and clawed at the air, clearly in pain, saliva coming off her bottom lip in a long thread. Rudy almost wept. It was easy to tell that she'd been beautiful once, sharp nose, long proud jaw. She was the type who'd probably been really regal when she was angry, pretty as all hell, now ancient and desperate.

Rudy approached, many around him moaning in disappointment as he passed them. He got to the bed and stood there.

"The . . . Great . . . Father," she said, looking up with lidless eyes. "And he's come to pay what is owed The Provider."

"I have," Rudy said.

She surrendered to a wave of nausea with a short bout of dry retching, then a rattling cough and a couple of swallows.

"And you've brought the Healing Blood?" she said finally.

Rudy patted the cooler under his arm.

"Right here, ready to go."

She looked up with a grin and actually licked her lips.

"Then give it to me."

Rudy put up a finger.

"Are you aware that this is only temporary? That it is no cure, just a massive stimulant?"

"Are you aware," she spat back hoarsely, "that they haven't emptied the commodes in here for a day? That the diarrhea is so bad I'm afraid to eat a piece of toast, that the shooters rip through me like barbed wire? I don't care if it's temporary."

"Caroline says it causes unexpected surges of adrenaline, spikes in bodily strength difficult to channel."

"I'll work it off in the gym."

"Heightened emotionality."

"I'll see a psychiatrist."

He sat on the bed next to her, careful not to weigh down the edge enough to have her roll into him. He took a deep breath and looked off to the side.

"I've got good news and bad news," he said.

"You're kidding."

"I'm not." He gazed down at her. "The good news, Marilyn Shultz, is that you're going to get a dose of the healing blood, tonight, right now."

"And the bad?" she rasped.

Rudy reached into his breast pocket and got out the implement he'd just stolen from the examination room with the organ breakdowns on the wall.

It was an eye-dropper.

She actually bared her teeth when she understood.

"That's not fair."

"Things rarely are."

"That can only dispense enough for an hour."

"But that hour will be your finest." He opened the cooler and pushed stuff aside, careful not to disturb the bag of dark blood, and drew out Caroline's iPad. "I want to show you something," he said. "A recording you might find of interest."

He cued up the witch-burning scene at the cornfield. Marilyn Schultz watched it in a numbed silence, and others in the room were craning their necks for a view.

Brian Duffey tossed another Heineken empty into the pit and let out a long belch. This sucked. Lighting them up had become a chore, and there weren't even people cheering anymore. It was dark back here away from the fire, and since Coach Sullivan had insisted that Duffey was the man to clean up the stuff under them with a shovel, he'd been wheelbarrowing that stinky, bloody shit over to the hole all night. He had a bandana over his face, and he felt like a trash man. Wasn't he co-leader? Why couldn't they get Junior Shipley to do this for awhile, or Rex Cunningham, or one of the police officers over by the tent island, or the home-boys from the Air Force base, sitting behind the sandbags up front showing off their rifles? He'd been killing these monster-bitches all day, and he was tired. He wanted to grab something to eat, make a move on one of the single moms, cop a feel off Heather Doyle or Robyn Stein, right under the ass palm-up as he passed. New rules, right?

There was a rowdy-shout off to the left. Three big dudes with buzzcuts were challenging some long-haired biker types to funnel chug. A fat kid was crushing cans on his head. Some thick guys with tattoos on their necks were throwing knives into an uprooted stump, and there was a ring of shirtless men over by the grub area starting a fight club.

Duffey took the ancient wristwatch Sullivan had given him out of his pocket and held it every which way, trying to pick up a reflection off the fire. The orders were to burn one bitch every five minutes, and it was coming due again. Tempted for the millionth time, he gazed off far left toward the supply area by the reeds and ferns. There under the lean-to were the gas cans. Why couldn't they just do a massive douse and blaze right now, anyway?

"*It's symbolic,*" Sullivan had said, and Duffey hadn't understood him even a little bit.

"*We have to show we're not scared to sacrifice them in broad daylight,*" he'd then said, and Duffey had gotten that loud and clear. But back then (and it seemed like years ago now) his bad ankle hadn't been throbbing, and his back hadn't gone sore right down to the tailbone. He ambled over to the back side of the fire and reached for his torch rammed there in the ground, the layers of sweat socks they'd pulled over the big end almost burned down to the grains underneath. Duffy looked in the rag bucket and saw that no one had bothered tossing in any more clothing; it was getting colder outside by the minute and people were skimping, avoiding him. Duffey ground his jaws together, took off his shirt, and stuck the shank of the torch between his legs, tying it off tight up top, coming around again with the sleeves for a double knotting.

Assholes. *Someone* was going to come to back here for burn-duty if it killed him, and he was going to take a well-deserved turn smoking a blunt and chilling. And he was going to switch up the goddamned tunes. Sullivan had hooked up a system that could work off an iPod, and the old heads had been hogging it, playing Golden Earring and Steppenwolf garbage.

He stuck the torch in the fire, gave it a swivel, and stalked back to the dark swell of corn, working in between the crosses three rows deep where he'd left off. The women closest to him started talking again, begging, pleading, moaning in hot whispers, promising him things, trying to make dirty deals, and for the millionth time he was about to scream for them to shut the fuck up when he got to his fresh one.

It was his mother hanging there in the dark.

The Witch of the Wood

"Brian," she croaked. "Don't do this to me, please."

"Bitch!" he screamed, whapping the torch into her face and throwing a brilliant cascade of blue and white sparks. The witches behind got showered, and they struggled violently, pulling at their restraints, bleeding on the ropes. The witches behind reacted and it was a domino effect, all of them twisting and writhing, shrieking in desperation and pain.

The one Duffey hit had regressed to her form as a blank slate again, but her broken nose had caught fire, spreading across her face, consuming her in a quick campaign south and lighting up the area in blue phosphorescence. All of them were thrashing there in the brightened dark now, whitecaps, wriggling vermin in a massive trash pit, and two rows down, seven girls over, Duffey saw something funny, not funny as in "ha-ha," but funny like "wack."

One of the monster-bitches was doing a gymnastics trick, similar to one of those straddle-sit positions on the uneven bars. It looked so goofy Duffey almost burst out laughing despite himself. She'd gotten her feet loose, spread them wide, and was trying to get to the left wrist with one of her toes, straining with it, making her neck cords bulge.

Not funny at all.

She hooked it and pushed outward, making an extra millimeter of clearance, next pulling her hand through, bunching and ripping the skin.

More movement now, but this was at the periphery of Duffey's vision, outside the mass of cornhusks and crosses. He turned to it, staring as if from down a long corridor, squinting, trying to focus on the disturbance out there across the short field and behind the lean-to where the forest once was. Something was flooding the landscape and advancing.

It was one of those "zoo-rushes," where a pack of animals did that stampede thing. He could see them loping and bobbing over the logs and fallen timber, coming right at him down the dark slope toward the west edge of their campground. Instinctively, he looked back the other way, and out through the corn he saw another pack, this one smaller and wider spread, galloping toward him from the east across the meadow from the Blue Route, catching the light of the moon.

They were dogs, all types, some of them house dogs; he could see the name tags gleaming.

Brian Duffey burst out of the corn and ran around the rim of the broad fire, shouting to no one in particular. He'd had an emergency whistle, but had taken it off when it picked up heat from the fire and scorched him.

Everyone seemed to be partying in slow motion, and Duffey charged into the heart of the campground, a few heads turning in mild uninterest, a couple of guys raising their beer cans to him as if to toast what looked like one of those drunken bum-rushes dudes sometimes did for attention, showing off their happy mo-jo. The guys on watch up front were leaning back against the sandbags, sitting with their knees spread, guns butt-down, muzzles pointed skyward. They were laughing and cheering because a woman with long brown hair and a bad case of horse face was taking off her top, moving her hips. Someone had just switched the music on the iPod system, and Duffy recognized it as "Cold Hard Bitch" by Jet. He burst into the circle and grabbed someone's rifle. There were "Hey's!" and "What the fuck's!" and he turned back toward the western slope, taking a knee.

Now there were hollers of hoarse recognition all around him as the "sentries" and others around them scrambled for positions to defend against the onslaught coming upon them from both sides of the corn.

Duffey fired his weapon. One of the dogs curled down and skidded, and the sky exploded.

The Witch of the Wood

It began with a wide burst of blue and red, a flowering fountain six hundred feet across, flickers, shimmers, a flash, and then a loud boom that sent Duffey flat on his ass. People were shouting, swarming around him like driver ants looking for cover, and he willed himself not to go down to his stomach covering his ears. A couple of the slutty older girls who'd been thinking of joining the horse-faced stripper were pointing upwards with wonder and glee, and a particularly big German shepherd from the zoo-rush smashed into one of them, bringing her to the ground in a hard spray of dirt and sending the other one away screaming. The dogs were on them now, jumping, clawing, going for pant legs, ripping at arms, snapping for throats.

There was a heavy screeching, followed by a harsh whistling like "incoming" in a World War II movie, then a blast of greens and yellows shooting across the sky sideways, a bombardment, five consecutive detonations that sparkled and crackled, then fizzled, only to give way to silver twirlers that made lassoes in the night, hearty bangs one after the other, then the exclamatory "boom" that shook the ground and rattled the camp gear. There were a series of popping sounds, glitter cascades in aqua and pink, and people were scrambling, tripping over things, pushing each other, lying on the ground wrestling dogs off them, running off to the west woods, to the Blue Route.

The enemy was so deeply integrated it was hard to get a clear shot, and one of the biker dudes suddenly ran right past Duffey, jumping the sandbags and booking away across the pasture toward the wide rise ahead that led up to the high school. The guy was pumping his knees at crazy angles, zigzagging as if he knew someone was going to take offense to his desertion, and Duffey moved the muzzle back and forth, cursing softly.

Suddenly, the guy's feet came out from under him as if he'd been clotheslined, and he crumpled down to the earth in a heap.

Duffey had a moment where he actually wondered if he'd pulled the trigger without knowing it, and the sky lit up in grand finale style, total saturation, a criss-cross effect of shooting rainbows and glitter-bombs. The hill leading to the high school went bright underneath, and it was flooded now with wolves and huge dogs coming on hard. Duffey lowered his rifle, mouth falling open.

This was no zoo-rush. It was an army of ghouls riding the canines like horses; they were skeletons with spotted skin and tumors, mummies without the bandages, the living dead, many of them hairless, some toothless, all with their mouths stretched open in hideous war screams, eyes rolling in their sockets, guns blazing.

It was hard to hear anything, but Duffey felt bullets whipping past him, hitting things, dropping people. At the back side of the swarming advance coming down the hill, there rode a figure, tall, hooded, white ghost-mask, cape whipping and flying behind him.

The Dogman.

Duffey fired his rifle dry, making no visible dent in the attack coming on, then dropped it and turned, looking back through the campground, hating himself a bit for not grabbing another weapon and standing his ground, but knowing deep down that he held the ultimate trump card here.

He was going for the gas cans.

The wave came in hard behind him, bullets kicking up dirt, people around him twisting and spinning to the ground, wolves and dogs and foxes pounding through the space, screams, skids, sounds of blunt force. The west side of the fire was an attack zone, flooded and overrun, and Duffey hustled around the long way, bullets whipping past his right ear, blasting some cooking pans hanging on a wire, hitting a guy in the back of the head and sending him sprawling, ripping into the face of a woman he knew who had worked at the Walmart, cutting one of the knife-throwers across the chest on a slant. To the left, there were women and children (and some dads Duffey wanted badly to thrash) abandoning the tent area, and running off into the darkness behind the camp ground like frightened mice.

One of the canvas flaps was thrown open then, and Coach Sullivan came out. He was buttoning his pants, and Mary-Beth Healy, a ninth-grader, came out behind him, slinking off, pulling her shirt back on. Duffey tried to shout something to him, but from the side a skeleton-ghoul-lady riding an enormous white Arctic wolf burst into view. She was wearing a black knit skullcap, eyes wide, teeth bared in a ferocious war-cry. She aimed a semi-automatic weapon at Sullivan and hip-fired it, missing wide right. She kept coming on hard, timing her jump off the animal, and ramming her body into her enemy, snapping the tent stakes, whip-folding the canvas over them like a set of dark wings. Duffy ran past as hard as he could. Back in the corn, the witches were loose, a lot of them, at least twenty. They were untying one another, gnawing at the ropes, yanking their feet and hands through.

Duffey cut across their bow and went for the lean-to, the thirty red gas cans lined there like soldiers. He reached down for the one closest to him and started unscrewing the cap.

Behind him someone hissed, and there was a low growling.

Duffey spun around, major déjà vu, just like when he'd been getting a drink of water and that faggoty-ass Wolfie Barnes had pulled a sneak and whisper on him. This time it was the kid's father, the Dogman himself, down off his wolf, weapons in hand.

They were pointed at the ground, and Brian Duffey knew he only had one chance here. He burst out of his crouch, sprang forward, and "rushed the quarterback," surprised him, slammed in full speed and rolled him hard to the dirt. Barnes hit like a sack of bricks, guns flying out of his hands, spinning and flashing in the air, and Duffey scrambled on top of him. Oh yeah, this was going to be better than a mass burning, for now Duffey had the opportunity to unmask the false prophet, make him a hostage, walk him back through the rows one by one and wipe clean the field. It beat doing it with an iPad anyway. . . .

Duffey held him down and reached for the gauze. He yanked it free and blinked stupidly.

Rudy Barnes wondered if it wasn't hubris, the tragic flaw the classic Greeks had most warned us about, a stubborn sort of pride that had influenced him at the last minute to lower his guns, make the scales a bit more even, a "mano-a-mano" kind of thing. Or was this the blacker side of the binary, the animal in him, raw and primed with the unhealthy desire to surpass the impersonal nature of a bullet in the dark back here and get dirty with it, kill this heartless fucker with his bare hands . . . ?

Duffey yanked off the gauze and blinked stupidly. Checkmate. Both his hands were occupied, one clenched around Rudy's shirt at the collar, the other balled in a fist around the fluttering mask material. And of course, Rudy's right hand was free to grab the scissors he had between his teeth. He snatched them by the finger holes and made to plunge upward.

Like magic, Duffey's throat then blew open just below the Adam's apple, and he was hurled forward and off as if some invisible giant had rope-pulled him toward the dark western slope. Rudy pushed up on his elbows, looking back into the space Duffey had just vacated, and twenty feet away was the blank slate, down on one knee, still looking down the barrel of the Bushmaster Rudy had dropped on the ground. The skin on the back of her prop hand was hanging down in a flap, and the freed witches behind her were pressed to the ground like Hindus, hands out flat, faces in the dirt. The ones on the crosses were looking away, and the shooter rose. She avoided Rudy's eyes, retrieved the face-gauze, and dropped it near him as she passed.

Rudy slipped it over his head and secured it into the rope necklace. By the time he turned, the bloody, naked witch was standing over Brian Duffey, writhing down there in the dark by the lean-to. She leveled her weapon and spat on him across the muzzle.

"You rotten, ignorant bigot," she said. She pumped five shots into him, making his body jump in the wild grass. Discharge smoke blew off in threads, and she lowered the gun, letting it hang by her side.

"We are not used to violence," she said, still looking at the body. "We are a docile people, but men like this have taught us the concept of murder."

"He had it coming," Rudy said.

She looked at him.

"It isn't the way things were meant to pass."

"It never is." He stood. "You're a brave one."

"You are masked."

"Still, your sisters are frail, and they are afraid of more than just gazing at my mask."

"They'll learn." She came closer to him. "It was an honor to defend you. I didn't realize I could do such a thing, but the saying 'The Lord doth not kill directly' has been in my mind since the ancient times, like a law, a commandment."

"I understand."

She made to walk past him and stopped.

"I want to give you a list of the sisters who were burned here. Rebecca is not the only saint who died on the wood."

"And what is your name?" Rudy asked.

"Elizabella," she said, turning. "Will my Lord honor the names of those dead?"

"I'll put them in a book."

Her eyes flickered.

"With new human laws."

"That's the idea."

"You will always have my sincere thanks, my Lord."

"And you mine for your acts of valor."

Elizabella bowed her head; awkward yet sincere, using the moment as an exit strategy to turn politely back to her girls. But she froze right there. The unbound witches were still on their knees face down to the ground, and there was a stranger behind them in the corn. It was a rather round woman standing there shivering, dressed in baggy jeans and an oversized Villanova University sweatshirt. She had a sleeping bag and a couple of blankets in her arms.

"I lost my husband," she said. "My house was destroyed, and my neighborhood turned to a disaster zone. I didn't know where to go, and these men promised food and shelter." She looked down. "By the time I realized what they were doing to these poor women it seemed it was too late. I panicked and hid in my tent." Her voice went down to a whisper. "I am so ashamed."

"Help me get my girls down," Elizabella said. "Can you do that?"

The woman looked up.

"There are others," she said, "more with blankets, back in the tents. I can get them. We can untie the knots together, all of us."

Elizabella nodded, and the two women moved toward a cautious embrace. Rudy looked off, as moments of sentimentality had always made him feel odd and misplaced, and his gaze swept across the campground that had been laid to waste, smoke from the fireworks an acrid cloud floating above it all. There were bodies from both sides lying cold, too many bodies, sprawled in the dirt, lying across things in awkward positions, and Rudy was sickened inside. He'd always been a pacifist. Over at the tent area there was a lot of activity now, men and women gathering in small groups, making their way toward the corn. At the back end of the space a dark spot moved. It slinked and crawled and rose up to make a break for the far side of the pasture where the highway stretched off behind the mass of downed trees.

It was Sullivan running for it, limping, favoring an arm too.

Rudy cursed himself for his dress shoes and briefly considered kicking them off. At the same time he had to admit to himself that on a certain level he was considering just letting the bastard go. But the terrain was rough with debris, and a man didn't run around in his stocking feet out here just to gain a step or two on his given adversary. And men like Sullivan didn't halt their campaigns just because of a bum leg, a missing eye, a bruise on the arm, and one battle lost. These individuals were incorrigible cancers, popping up again and again even if you nuked the living shit out of them with radiation and drowned them in chemo. Best to cut them out with that metaphorical blade if and when you had that first chance.

Rudy cut across the site, pausing only briefly to kick a dude in the face who'd held a stick underneath him, playing possum by the trash pit. Sullivan had a good lead and was fading, despite the intermittent flickerings thrown by the ebbing flames of the bonfire.

Rudy took a deep breath. Then he jumped into the high grass and chased the wounded man in through the meadow.

Professor Rudy Barnes suddenly wished he'd spent more time all these years gaining a higher level of personal fitness. He was a tall man, "big" in a sense, yet blessed with a high metabolism passed down by his mother. It kept him wiry-thin. Moreover, years of practice helped him bottle emotions most of the time, internalizing them, working them down and through the strong and silent way, and maybe there was a little bit of credence to the idea of manufacturing some kind of inner furnace that burned fat off by tension alone. But dissecting student papers with aggressive red slashes, planning lessons with a measure of competitive intensity, and stewing and poring over journal articles that only one percent of the population was interested in reading didn't equal the toning and conditioning one got at the gym. Sullivan was wounded and still outrunning him. And though shadows were no longer existent in this world, there was certainly darkness, the kind Sullivan was steadily becoming a part of.

Rudy called out suddenly, "My kingdom for a fucking horse!" but no dog came running, no wolf conveniently sliding between his legs. He had acted impulsively, running like a madman into the pasturage, and now he was out of earshot, alone.

The meadow-grass was iced over, and the further he got into the depths of it, the more dampness accumulated in the fabric of his pants, weighing him down. Ahead he thought he could hear Sullivan's breathing, but he couldn't be sure if it was just the haunt of his own footfalls, like a residue of dark hope.

Up ahead was the dim spread of the highway curving off right to a fine point that got lost in the rise of the valley. There were abandoned vehicles hulking there in the darkness, and Rudy pounded toward them. By the time he made it to the edge of the blacktop his chest was heaving, and his legs ached as he pulled them over the guardrail. The roadside gravel made loud, guttural sounds beneath his shoes, and after a step or two he paused there, hands on his knees. He wanted to quiet himself so he could continue to monitor the exhalations of his foe, but the more he tried to tone it down, the harder he seemed to pant and wheeze.

Something clanked.

It was distinct, some iron product, two hundred or so feet north. Rudy strode forward through a toss of broken glass in the breakdown lane. There was a shredded tire he had to step over and a bent sign to his right with a picture of a truck tipping on a sharp curve.

Now he heard grunts, cursing, more clanking, and at the top of the mild crest and a bend left he looked down over the guardrail.

There was a graded dirt slope leading to a wide bed of crushed stone. Directly behind was a huge concrete pipe built into the landscape and a massive storm drain at the foot of it; hence the sounds of steel on steel. Sullivan had been struggling to haul off the grate cover. Rudy got a fleeting glimpse of the man's head disappearing down into the hole and then slid down the slope after him, almost tripping over his own feet and taking a header. What he planned to do when he caught up with Sullivan in the catacombs was not entirely clear. He wasn't going down there to talk, that was for sure.

Could Rudy take him?

That wasn't clear either. There were a lot of factors, a lot of unknowns. How injured was the man? Was he really blind in one eye, or was the patch just for show? He was younger, but Rudy was taller. The man was more buff, but Rudy had that wiry leverage going for him. Seemed kind of even.

Right . . .

Sullivan was a football coach, built like a brick shithouse, using the super-gym at his disposal through the school to model the advantages of sheer and brute muscle mass to his players. Even injured, he was the favorite in this little "cage match" to come.

Rudy advanced to the lip of the hole and peered over. There was a rusted stepladder bolted into the wall and the chute was cylindrical. There was the sound of running water and a foul smell akin to swampland, black gutters, and waste.

It was not entirely dark.

There was a light flickering and wavering down in the recesses, and it didn't take long to connect that with the fact that Sullivan had not been in possession of a torch during his retreat from the campsite. He'd been down the storm drain earlier, prepping it. Advantage bad guy.

Rudy bent, took hold of the ladder, and turned ass-backward.

Slowly, he climbed down into the hole.

* * *

The curved block walls were slick with old moisture, dank with mold and networks of stains from nitrates and phosphorus accumulations that webbed their way down the ceiling of the shaft. It gave a distinct skeletal illusion, as if Rudy were trapped inside some ancient, malignant beast. Every one of his steps was trailed by a hollow echo, and there was background dripping. The cylindrical tunnel was fifteen feet high and was riddled with cracks filled with moss and sediment directly across from the entrance point. There were torches jammed into the shattered light boxes every thirty feet or so, burning steadily, leaving black arcs on the damp cement behind them and simultaneously reflecting down their sickly flames in the sludge staining the tunnel's base in a wide, brownish runner. Rudy was no mechanical engineer, but it was clear that this drainage system was a combination of storm run-off and sewage. Somewhere, this nasty stream was siphoned off into the river, probably the Schuylkill, and if circumstances had been different, Rudy would have considered sending a letter to his congressman about it. Thick patches of rotten leaves blocked the dirty flow in places, making it churn up and re-route, and horizontal ghost-lines along the sides indicated that during flooding this place filled near to the one-third mark. Rudy walked first on the right side, then hopped across to the left for haste, letting his momentum bring him forward. The fact that he had no shadow leading him on was a comfort, but his shoes were louder than cannons down here. His glasses steamed up, and he withdrew his mask and hood, almost laughing to himself that he'd sort of forgotten they were there.

At a juncture, he made a right and then halted.

There at the far end of the tunnel was Sullivan, straddling the murky runnel at his feet as was Rudy. The eye band had been removed, and there was a crater there tailed by a recently dried scrape that ran up the side of his head, then curling back down like a ram's horn. He didn't have long hair, but what was there was matted and curled. His five-o'clock shadow had turned to heavy black stubble, and his teeth glistened from within it in a crooked smear.

"Professor..." he sing-songed.

Rudy shivered. There was something about being addressed directly by this individual that was unnerving, like a wife-beater faking some "sincere" plea for women's rights and looking at you with that reddened edge in his eye, ready to thrash you within an inch of your life if you admitted you didn't believe him. And Sullivan was taller than he'd seemed on television. Where was that pair of scissors Rudy had brought with him to the battle? Did he drop them back by the lean-to? What if Sullivan was armed? Rudy would have been if he was Sullivan, that was for sure.

"Why didn't you ambush me?" Rudy said, motioning back with a jerk of his head. "At the juncture there's a concrete edge to hide behind. Seems like something you'd be good at."

Sullivan laughed, and for the big man that he was it was high and sheer and razored, cascading off the curved array of wet polished block like a siren.

"Ambush?" the man said finally. "As in an attack? Like fisticuffs? Like a little barroom brawl down here in the pipes?" He stopped grinning and his eye gleamed out from his dark face. "We aren't down here to fight, Dog-Boy. If you live, you live... all the power to you and bless your sweet soul. For me, I wouldn't dirty my hands with you, but before any of the fun stuff begins we're meant to know each other. Form boundaries, just in case this winds up being one of those... prolonged sort of disputes."

Rudy stepped forward two paces and straddled the sewage water.

"No boundaries for a child molester, Sullivan. I'd die before drawing any lines in the sand with the likes of you."

"Really," he said. "I hope you're willing to stand by those

words. They'd write books about them, different from the old ones."

"What books?"

"Biblical ones, of course. The ones you already have yourself starring in, hmm?"

Sullivan had lowered his voice to that soft, condescending, nearly effeminate tone so often utilized by those careful pricks in Human Resources who were going to nail you to the wall for some minor infraction that was going to go on your record. It bothered Rudy immeasurably.

"What are you talking about?" he said. He was really judging the distance between them, estimating how much momentum he could build in a straight rush. Sullivan took a step closer himself.

"For every action, there's a reaction, Professor. When the zombie-girls came up, someone had to go under." He pointed with the lame hand, its pinkie finger broken and crooked. "You're the king of those dogs, but as subjects . . . as infantry, they're of no use to you here in the sewers, Professor, even if they could climb down the ladders. They're too clumsy, too big-boned and slow, don't you see? In the new world, you've got to think about mastering the smaller, unnoticed parts of the earth, you've got to learn the cracks and crevices, understand the secrets of the dark, at least if you're going to make your way down into the bowels where I'm the one you'll have to answer to."

Sullivan smiled. Allowed himself a giggle, and right on cue something came up from behind his head. Rudy thought his eyes were playing tricks on him, for it looked like a shadow at first, then a curious black cat with its paws clinging for purchase in Sullivan's hair, crawling up and over his crown, then sliding around behind his ear, along the shoulder and up under his jaw, mewing, nuzzling.

Sullivan reached and grabbed the animal by the scruff of the neck and gently pulled it off, pronged paws dangling in little curves, the long gray tail coming to hang down like the back half of a garden snake.

It was a sewer rat ten pounds at the least, and Sullivan positioned his forearm to cradle it lovingly. Its paws played at the air, and he scratched its bald belly, bending to Eskimo kiss its sniveling nostrils, the top of its black muzzle oscillating rapidly up and down to expose two crooked front teeth that Sullivan took a second to flicker the tip of his tongue across.

"That's my girl," he said. He looked up at Rudy with a sheepish shrug that said, *Can't help it, Jack. I just love her,* and then he positioned his bottom lip into a widened clown's grin. He whistled shrilly.

There was a terrific clicking and tacking from the depths of the darkened tunnel behind, and then came the pouring out from around his feet as the army of rats flooded the space, skittering and yipping, jumping and scratching over one another in a bristling plague. In the swarm there were pups the size of fieldmice and others big as terriers, all filling the concrete tunnel in a spreading storm on both sides of the sludge. Rudy turned to run, and Sullivan's voice rang out behind him,

"The Dog King retreats from the land of the Rat God. Put that in a book, why don't ya? Sic 'em, boys! Don't leave anything behind but the bones if you catch him!"

Professor Rudy Barnes sprinted back in the direction he had come, feet clapping along the dank cement, thighs pistoning furiously, arms pumping, neck straining forward. At the juncture he slipped making the half-turn and skidded against the far wall, almost breaking his elbow. Somehow he retained his balance, but he had to restart, feeling as if he were in one of those old Warner Brothers cartoons where the feet spun in place momentarily to the wacky percussion soundtrack. He willed himself forward to full speed again, stamping along the right of the murky runner for five steps or so, then jumping over to the left for the same. From around the corner behind him he heard the pack gaining, thousands of paw-nails clicking as if the entire population of Lilliput had been given tiny tap-dancing shoes and were emptied into some massive orchestra pit to charge through. With the echo it sounded like some sick sort of applause. Rudy heard splashes and sloshing and angry squeals. Nope. It ain't faster in the pond, kids. Better to stick to the gunwales.

Suddenly he was disoriented. The exit ladder should have been straight up ahead about forty feet stage-right, bolted to the block wall about a yard from ground surface. On the high side of the tunnel he saw a porthole in the curve leading to the outside with a faded wash of moonlight funneling through it, but now there was nothing below but shadowy grime-blackened walls leading down the recess where the tunnel dead-ended in a concrete half-moon, acting like a catch-basin for a channel at a higher level.

Rudy hadn't come from that far. There had been no graded concrete apron to jump down from. Of course, he hadn't looked back over his shoulder down to the right upon entering in the first place. He had followed the torches to the left, so no, he couldn't be absolutely positive that this blockade had been at his rear when he'd first made his way down the tunnel. In running from the rats just now, had he ducked back down the wrong exit shaft?

He shotgunned his legs forward, looking at all the context clues. There was the torch jammed into the light fixture box and the spidery cracks underneath with moss growing out of them: check, this was the place.

He ran forward with everything he had, dropping the gauze mask and regripping the groundcloth haphazardly.

The key word here was "shadowy." There were no more shadows. Grime yes, but the walls just weren't that blackened from it. There was something else here, something covering the cement.

Rudy ran for the torch and grabbed it out of its holder, next jumping back across the stream, aiming for the darkest area along the far wall beneath the high opening. Just before impact, he pulled over the groundcloth like a blanket in a house fire and lowered a shoulder.

He banged straight into the right side of the camouflaged ladder, feeling simultaneous and dichotomous sensations: a give and burst as if he'd body-checked a host of leather-lined water balloons, and the hard resistance of the cold steel beneath. It was a bone-shivering jolt that rocked him back a step and detonated a terrible flapping that exploded in front of him and down the shaft; a thick cloud of them all around outside of his makeshift hood, the torch buying him what sounded and felt like a cushion of about a foot and a half.

It wasn't rats, but their winged brothers, beating the air with their membraned forelimbs and shrieking.

Rudy reached out blindly with the hand holding the canvas to catch a rung, and the groundcloth drew up his back, exposing him. He dropped the canvas altogether, turned a shoulder, and waved the torch out behind him.

The cloud pulled back, and the cement at his feet darkened with the torrent of oncoming rats. He turned and climbed, torch still in hand, things jumping at him, three or four rodents clinging to his pants cuffs and wriggling, bats darting in within an inch of his head and retreating. Barely. He moaned, kicked, and shook out his feet, waved and tomahawk-chopped the wand that was quickly losing its magic. He swept it back and forth, making short "whup-whup" sounds against the close air, and then gave it a last-ditch toss back into the fray. He only had four rungs to go, and he vaulted them two at a time, pulling with everything he had.

He scrambled out of the opening, and the black cloud vomited hard out of the drain-chute behind him. He rolled off atop the crushed stone, loving the keen air. There may have been a bat or two stuck to him, but he didn't think so. One or two might have bitten or scratched him, but he didn't feel any pain, only the wide openness of the night and the ground beneath him. Above him, the sky was blotted with the shapes of those Halloween circus tent wings, at first marking the night in a random fluttering squall, and next taking form in a widened arrowhead, the mass making downward swoops across the landscape and dizzying rises up at the moon.

The flock made two passes over the meadow and then returned in a massive plunge, forming a flickering cyclone whose funnel-mouth hissed within inches of Rudy's nose. He was in the process of putting his arms in front of his face, but there was no need. They promptly shot back down the storm drain. It gave the illusion that they were actually being sucked down, like a video recording of an active volcano played on super-fast rewind. Rudy could only guess that they'd expected the outside world to be laden with landing pads, weigh stations, safe havens, trees. No more, and the rear-ranged outdoor furniture had distracted them from their goal of mauling the intruder. He got to his feet and brushed off, raising his arms, looking for tears in the cloth, bite marks, anything.

He seemed to be all right.

But there was something coming, there at the edge of audibility.

It was a whispering, brushing sound gaining body and purpose. Closing. Rudy looked at the opening he'd just come from. Could rats climb ladders? He knew these kinds of rodents could walk along thin rails, squeeze into tiny holes, slip through cracks less than a quarter their size. They didn't have bones, wasn't that right? Or was that a myth? But either way they couldn't scale wet concrete at a ninety-degree angle, now could they?

Maybe not, but they could certainly find alternative exits. They weren't coming from the storm drain. They were advancing through the grass from a ways behind it. Rudy made for the dirt leading up to the guardrail, legs feeling like lead. Halfway there, he awarded himself one last look over the shoulder.

The Witch of the Wood

The high grass going back hundreds of yards past the concrete pipe was moving, like wheat and rye blowing in a soft Oklahoma breeze. Rudy didn't wait until the interlopers started darkening the dirt. He ran for the curve of the guardrail, new sweat breaking out over the layers of the dried and redried, cold wind coming up over the asphalt stealing his breath.

Rudy was going to die here on the highway, overcome by rodents who would disappear into the fissures of the earth like wastewater. He could not think of a passing more insignificant. He was a speck on the horizon, dust on the plain, alone in the universe.

The darkened hulls of abandoned automobiles lined the roadway for miles, yet (just Rudy's luck, it seemed) here at the bend there was a gap and the nearest vehicle was twenty or so feet to the right. Rudy cut across the lane and over the ribbed concrete divider to get to the heavier concentration of traffic that had been going south, toward town. He approached the nearest vehicle, parked at a slight angle. It was some sort of coupe with a red racing stripe going down the center and those quicksilver hubcaps that seemed to spin in opposite directions simultaneously. Locked. He cut across to the cruising lane and got to a hatchback. It had a bumper sticker saying "Be Nice to America or We'll Bring Democracy to Your Country," along with "Obama 2012." Through the back window, Rudy could see duffel bags alongside pillow cases that looked as if they were stuffed with laundry. College kid making his way home to do a wash, ask for money, and most probably lie about his initial spring semester grades. Probably a philosophy major. Probably the type to click his pen up by his ear and interrupt the professor with snide, circular logic delivered in "elevated" vocabulary, slightly out of context. Then he'd get drunk at night with nine friends and go do the "lift and shove" to some freshman girl's Smart car, straight into the handicapped space, leaving it to sit slanted across the blue lines with fucked-up brakes and damaged suspension. Rudy tried the door and cursed into the cold night air. This one was locked too, and from behind he heard that clicking once again. This time, it was the mad Lilliput people turning noisemakers backward fast against the grain and rattling miniature castanets in their flood across the asphalt.

Rudy burst down to the next vehicle and ripped open the driver's side door of a sky-blue sedan, definitely a Ford, maybe a Taurus or a Crown Victoria. He reached for the steering wheel, pulled himself in, and scraped out for the door handle. The rats were in the lane, so close Rudy could see their sloped snouts and whiskers, the configurations of their curved, forked paws scratching forward. He shut the door, and the outside sounds became a muted screeching that dulled in his head, blurred, and grew fainter only because he succeeded in partially blotting it out.

Rudy looked out the passenger window and saw the closest ones scrambling over their mates in a writhing, violent blur, jockeying for position, the ones a stage deeper forming strange swirling patterns as if conjuring some bizarre ritual or communicative effort, the lot a dark throng as big as a forest pond spilling back over the divider, through the other lane, and back over the slope. It looked as if the ones all the way at the rear were heading back the direction they had come, but he couldn't be sure, too dark and nondescript out there to really tell.

He looked down at his hands in his lap and breathed a shaky sigh of relief. Stalemate, and soon they'd lose interest, even the ones right by the car, so he hoped. He shivered. Just the sight of them, even from behind glass, filled him with revulsion. He had a headache and his throat hurt. His shoulder was aching right at its point where he had thrust himself at full force into the steel stepladder, and he'd put a welt on his knee at some point, he could feel it. He rested his forearms on the padded steering wheel. The car smelled new. It was an automatic with enough dashboard controls to warrant the good part of an afternoon figuring out the particular button combinations that worked all the bells and whistles, and there was a dainty little plastic bag hanging off the gear shaft. For trash. Maybe it was the story-doctor in Rudy, but he imagined the owner of this car was a lady, late thirties, pretty but worn just a bit. She was the type that was against texting while driving, yet found it appropriate to put on mascara at a red light, or on the highway if it was straight and she'd gone to cruise control.

Suddenly, the car jerked down under Rudy, as if it were made of building blocks and someone had yanked one out from the back left corner. The rats hadn't been just loitering and making swirling patterns as Rudy had foolishly assumed. Not all of them, anyway. Some industrious bottom-crawlers had been working the tires with their gnashing little teeth. There was a sudden burst rear right now, Rudy actually heard that one, and the car fell back tilting up, giving a wider view of the skyline. He fumbled for the ignition and came up empty, of course. A wry, sardonic laugh snorted down through his nose. Of course, trying to turn the key had been an instinctive response, but was this the best he had? And were the rats flattening the tires in some sort of mass anticipation that he might drive away if there *were* keys left dangling there for him like some all too convenient plot twist in a B-movie? Were they really as smart as he was . . . or as stupid, depending how you looked at it?

Smarter.

Both front tires burst out there, and the car sank down that last six or so inches at its bow, bringing the vehicle distinctly lower than the ones parked in front of it, close enough to the road now to make it more accessible to those little disease-ridden beasts that were just dying to test out their leaping ability. There was a muffled yet distinct thudding as multitudes of rats jumped and swarmed over the Ford from the rear, scampering across the trunk, over the roof, and down the windshield.

And there were sounds of infestation from beneath the floorboards, from under the hood, scratching, burrowing. Rudy wished he had access to a Ford parts and body schematic right about now. How enclosed was the interior of a car, really? There weren't gaps and holes, were there? You wouldn't be able to heat or cool it properly, right? Check. But where were the weak spots? He wasn't encased in solid steel. Could they get in the trunk? Was *that* area steel-encased, or was there possibly a strip made of cheap vinyl or thin plastic fastening one area to the other? And how about the fancy instrument panel right here at his chest? Could they get up through the undercarriage and infiltrate from under the hood? All these buttons and dials were set in recesses, voids, possible entranceways. Rudy could hear the rats presently, right above his knees, gnawing and pawing and scurrying. Any second now, he expected them to get inside the steering column, set off the airbag, stove in the radio unit, pop through the air vents.

Something on the windshield exploded, and Rudy jerked back against the headrest. The moving mass of swarming rats scattered and one of them slid down the glass, leaving a red streak. By the time he came to rest on top of the right-hand windshield wiper, his whiskers had stopped flickering. He'd been impaled, and the bird that had done it in a suicide dive had its head buried almost entirely inside the body of its victim: Rudy could see the point of its beak poking out through the rat's bloated underside.

Now there were pops and bangs all over the car and around it, pounding along the roof, the trunk, the front hood. Through the side window, Rudy could see a dark wave of rodents retreating off toward the grasses and others up on their hindquarters, paws dangling, doing really good impressions of deer caught in the glow of oncoming headlights. The sky was a stormcloud of fowl, thousands of sparrows and swallows and various other winter birds swooping down in dark waves, driving torrents that speared rats who were scattering all along the asphalt, across the concrete divider, and into the meadow-weeds.

The onslaught continued for about forty-five seconds, and Rudy didn't remember ever seeing so much relative gore even in the movies; pierced underbellies, exploding innards, smashed eggshell craniums, blood-darkened fur. The street was slick with it, the top of the car littered, nine or ten pinned to the hood, four lying along the base of the windshield—paws up, soulless black eyes staring open as if they had X's drawn through them. The birds were dead too, most of them buried neck-deep inside their victims, the others who missed their marks making wet spots on the asphalt.

The invasion within the underside of the vehicle had ceased, it seemed, or at least it had paused, and Rudy opened the driver's side door. Three brown rat pups that had been trying to worm through the recesses fell into the cab space, two of them running across Rudy's thighs, the other squirming in behind his back. He jumped out of the vehicle, clapping and brushing himself off, stamping and cursing, teeth clenched. A small dark blur soared in from the front side and swooped down into the cab. There was a squeal, and the baby rodent that had wormed in behind Rudy was pressed against the seat cushion, pierced straight through the belly, rubbing its tiny paws along the face of his assassin in a manner that would have seemed loving in any other circumstance. Then it went limp. The black bird shook off its prey and stood there on the car seat, looking at Rudy sideways with that dead glassball stare.

"Thanks," Rudy mumbled.

It jerked its head in stutters, pooped on the seat, and flitted off looking for stragglers. From under the vehicle Rudy could hear things dropping to the blacktop, and he stepped away cautiously. But they didn't form up, make a pack, organize a charge. Like drops of oil in water they spread from under the car in all directions, one of them scampering across the tip of Rudy's left dress shoe. Most of them made it to the edges: up or down the highway, straight ahead to the high bluff on the far border all brush and rockface, back to the guardrail, into the meadow grass. There were still birds knifing down out of the dark sky, but they were spot-shotters, the last of a drizzle. The curve in the highway was littered with roadkill, and Rudy started to make his way through it. At first he was careful, stepping between the bodies to avoid the old squelch and burst from under his shoes, but when an awful sort of dawning realization began forming in his mind, he started to jog, to trot, then to sprint.

Desperately now.

For these birds didn't show up just by chance. . . .

He tore down the road in the breakdown lane.

The math wasn't difficult. In fact, it wasn't math at all. This was an interlocking analogy, and it didn't take long to fill in the blanks: dog is to Rudy as rat is to Sullivan, and therefore rat is to Sullivan as bird is to Patricia. Yet that was the wrong order, now wasn't it? Rudy's ex-wife was the first to retain said power over a particular animal with her painted birdhouses and fishing-line tripwires. And considering the slaughter on the blacktop that Rudy had just witnessed, this was advantage Dark Guardian, certainly heads and shoulders above ratpacks and canines.

But why here and now? What purpose did it serve his ex-wife to save him out here in the semi-darkness? Rudy would have imagined she'd have been on Sullivan's side, partying with the bonfire crew in whatever given shape she had chosen, raising her beer can, cheering the mass crucifixion of witches. Were not her winged subjects the enemies of the recently buried prisoners, taunting them all these hundreds and thousands of years from between the flittering leaves of the prison stalks? And they'd killed Wolfie. Still, one could not ignore the fact that this particular action caused the mass emancipation of those long incarcerated. But on the other hand, one had to consider the idea that Wolfie's violent death also acted as a defense mechanism that protected men, the descendants of the fiends who had put the women under the dirt in the first place.

And so, after all the back and forth, who was Patricia finally siding with?

Scary version—no one. She was a free agent with no loyalties to bog her down, no fellow pioneers to dampen her purpose with compromise.

And what was that purpose exactly?

Unclear, yet only blurred if you included in the equation the fact that she'd just saved Rudy's life out here. Maybe the key word was "saved," a term that made perfect sense if offered in a different context. Rudy had done nothing to earn anything but wounded scorn and righteous rage from Patricia, and maybe she had *saved* him out here, yet just for *herself*, for the chance to concoct a direct confrontation that more fit her melodramatic vision of poetic justice.

She was here somewhere. Waiting.

Rudy raced toward the hill overlooking the battleground, the latter a dull vision off left and below, all smoke and dull light and silhouettes, most of them congregating back by the crosses that were currently half-relieved of their unwilling occupants. One strategy would have been for Rudy to have taken the straighter course back through the ice-coated meadow grass. But he was banking on the possibility that Patricia was not with him out here in the dark within a stone's throw, watching. No, she was blending in back at the campsite, ready to draw him into the dying firelight. The woman was a drama queen at heart and she was setting the stage, he could feel it. And Rudy didn't necessarily want to play into her little scene with a clumsy telegraphed entrance, thrashing through the weeds. Maybe he'd learn a bit by hiding in the wings for a hot minute. The hill was a perfect spy point. Duffey hadn't seen him arranging the dogs and their riders there at the back edge of the Franklin Heights football field because of the height of the rise. If he could scale it from the side here, he would be able to crawl to the front lip. Get a closer view. Check things out. Weigh his options and see if he could pick her out of the crowd by her mannerisms.

Of course, if she could sense his trouble out here on the highway, she'd know if he went back up to the high school the long way. Or would she? Many of the "powers" allotted to the players in this new state of being seemed incomplete. Wolfie was defeated. The rats had failed. Rudy had dogs, but they weren't magic nor omniscient. If they had been, he would have gotten a "giddyap" and gained the ability to run down Sullivan long before the bastard got into the concrete piping. Patricia could actually have sensed she was going to lose her face-to-face with Rudy unless she somehow intervened, all without a detailed vision of his peril. A blind intuition kind of thing.

Or not.

Either way, they both were getting what they wanted. She was going to be awarded her confrontation and he was going to enter the arena in his own way. And even if she "saw" him doing it, the very audacity of it had a chance of enraging her, making her more prone to folly.

Rudy made his way down and around the bend in the road and had to slow a bit, shimmying between vehicles that had finally cluttered the shoulder as well. They all had gone nowhere fast. Even though this particular stretch of highway was void of the treeline, down in the grove where the industrial green road signs had been catty-cornered, massive trees had toppled down making the forks and arteries for merging a clogged, scrambled mess. Rudy strode straight down for the signage area, worked his way through it, and vaulted a concrete culvert at the rear. The mountainous terrain ascending before him was quite steep, possibly forty-five degrees, but the timber lying across it made for a crude sort of graded stepladder, at least for most of the journey.

There was a bad moment when two trunks that seemed fairly stable shifted beneath him. They held for a moment, then gave. Rudy slid down for a few rough feet after them, rough dirt and embedded stone bunching his shirt up and scratching him pretty good up the belly and chest before his feet met any sort of support. He cursed lustily, holding there for a second plastered to the rise, arms spread, heart pounding. Wind blew hard across him, causing one of those breathless moments, and he looked up to measure his recent loss of progress.

There was only a matter of about fifteen feet separating him from the crest.

Slowly, he shucked over four steps to the right. It seemed to take weeks, but once there he came upon a combination of handholds and foot-stops above that made scaling the rest of the incline fairly elementary. No more slips down the cliff, but when he finally pulled himself over the top edge he was spent. He rolled away from the precipice to his back and lay still for a moment. The wide sky was poor company, black and heartless, and he turned a shoulder to get to his hands and knees amidst the clutter of downed border foliage.

Things rustled in the grass as he rose, a scattering nest of newts or salamanders or whatever you called those little flat-headed wood lizards. Ha. He didn't think anything creeping in the undergrowth would ever skeeve him again after what he had just seen out on the highway. He brushed off, started moving.

It was silvery and strange up here, the landscape washed pale in the residue of a cold moon. There at the base of a crude path cutting between clusters of fallen birches was a tangle of leafy brush, and Rudy prayed it wasn't poison ivy. He was limping and his chest was bleeding a little. Just ahead, there was a short dirt path to cut across, and beyond it a baseball field with splintered wooden benches and a wrestling mat tacked to the backstop so onlookers couldn't argue balls and strikes. Rudy shuffled across the batter's box area and made sure to step on home plate, an old habit like knocking wood or crossing fingers. "Ha," he said again, this time out loud. There was no such thing as luck or superstition, if there ever was to begin with. There was no fate or chaos either, no social sciences or psychology. Everything was just scatter-pattern now, land masses in the static that no one had quite figured out. He moved up the third base line and through a fenceless outfield that bled into a parking area. Beyond that to the left was the football field.

Rudy made his way toward it, straight for the goal posts. On the far side of the end zone behind the visitor's bench was the short walk through a long rectangular space they used for teeing up practice kicks and warming up the quarterbacks, and behind that was the fallen wooded area to navigate through. Then was the downhill run void of timber, leading to the campsite and the crosses. When Rudy was a kid, he and his friends used to sled down it after a good snow. They called it "Suicide Hill" of course, and one of the cancer patients had mentioned a similar memory. It had caused a moment of somber silence before the charge, and Rudy had wondered if they'd all be able to switch the light bulb back on, working up enough fire to execute an effective attack.

Oh, the light bulb had come back on, all right.

When the fireworks torched the sky and he'd cried, "Charge!" they'd gone mad with it, bodies taught with adrenaline, eyes rolling with bloodlust, all of them galloping down the bluff with their guns out and their hospital gowns furling up from behind as if they were warrior ghosts come straight from the depths of some Gothic nightmare. That Lifeblood was no joke, indeed.

Rudy passed across the gridiron, straddled the visitors' bench, and almost tripped over an old Coleman water cooler left lying on its side in the frozen grass. For the hundredth time that evening he was about to unload a string of curse words up at the sky, but he heard something.

Muted laughter.

Muffled, lunatic sniggering. Down twenty feet or so, coming from behind the Porta-Potty.

Rudy advanced cautiously, head cocked at a slight angle. This was advanced for Patricia. There was no audience present for her little revenge scenario here, just empty bleachers. What did it mean? Did each vacant space along the benches represent a day gone by that Rudy had been an empty participant in their marriage? Was the unlit scoreboard a reflection of their many disagreements, so worn and battered with the tally that the only markers remaining were the faded baseboard zeroes in the darkened arrangement of bulb lights?

Rudy moved closer, the portable bathroom unit before him now, leaning a bit to the right, black spray-painted letters slanted across the vent holes at the top in some tag of indiscernible graffiti. From behind it, the snickering had gained intensity—a wet, lunatic chuckling, stifled as if the individual having the fit were pressing both palms to the mouth area.

Rudy paused there by the unit's access door. The real question here wasn't "why" in terms of symbolism. That would come later if Rudy lived through it. The question was "what," actually. What was waiting for him on the other side of the Porta-Potty; what had Patricia turned herself into? She could shape-shift, but did that mean she had to have a live model to form herself after? Or could she invent things? What if the giggling thing behind this obstruction came from, say, some six-foot circus clown with razor teeth and alligator claws, a man-sized hyena walking on its hind legs holding a machete, a spider-giant with the painted face of a jester? Rudy wasn't armed.

Had she heard him coming?

Of course she had.

Enough. Rudy came around the corner of the unit, face steeled, fists clenched at his sides.

* * *

She was there facing away, shoulders shaking, and her body language gave every indication that she was fully prepared to turn and pounce. Rudy was going to reach for her shoulder, but didn't. For what it was worth, he put his hands in a defensive position in front of his face.

"Patricia," he said.

"No!" she exploded, turning suddenly.

Rudy fell back a pace. It was Caroline, dressed in the clothes she had evidently changed into before setting off the fireworks from the edge of the battlefield: pinstriped train engineer's hat, a three-quarter sleeve Tribal Love shirt with a wide neck and eagle insignia, and black stretch jeans. Even with her face soiled from crawling around and setting off the explosives, wet and smudged with grief, she looked good to him, stunning in fact. Rudy met her stare, but it wasn't easy. He had deluded her, cheated her in a manner that was irreconcilable.

"You son of a bitch," she spat. "My mother could have had fifteen more years, twenty even. She was a good woman, awaiting your arrival all her life and helping me prepare for it. And I just borrowed the shovels of monsters to bury her in a shallow grave."

Rudy's mouth opened, then slowly closed, a soft breath of forfeit coming through his nose.

She didn't wait long for the explanation that wasn't coming anyway. Rudy had used her and it was over. Period. She moved past him and walked off, making her way across the twenty-yard line, shoulders shaking with grief again, one arm swinging as she picked up speed in a manner so ultimately girlish that Rudy's heart broke.

He had sacrificed her mother and the other cancer patients for a greater good, true enough. But it was her mother and the standards of ethics didn't apply, not when it hit home like this. Rudy thought about going after her to apologize, to try to rationalize his actions, explain his logic, attempt to meet on some sort of common ground, but he didn't. It would have been pointless. He pretty much knew Caroline Schultz didn't care about the witches anymore, and both of them were totally alone now.

Something came from behind and whisked past Rudy, brushing his ankle. He almost shrieked in surprise, yet bit it down, shaking his head, smiling wryly. It was Killian, that goofy little spaniel, running for Caroline and then jumping at her heels, trying to get her attention. There on the far side of the field she made a halfhearted attempt at picking him up in stride, but he was playing hard to get now, darting away and then coming back, leading her slowly toward the alleyway between the two sets of home bleachers. Finally he broke away into a playful run.

"Killian . . ." Rudy heard her say faintly, making the grudging chase, following him into the darkness. Gone.

Rudy wanted to weep. Such loss on so many fronts here. He turned slowly, shoulders deflated, and walked to the edge of the slope to look down at the smoldering war zone. He had made his statement there and then promptly vanished. Time marched on, and he had that feeling of overwhelming insignificance return to him: speck on the road, dust on the hill, same difference. Even his troops were represented thinly at this point, as all the rider bearers had seemingly disappeared—no wolves, no shepherds, no Danes, no huskies. There were no living cancer patients mulling around either, and Rudy concluded that they had used their animals to gallop off to the fallen wood, far from the light of the fire so they could die with some sort of dignity in solitude. That, or they were presently heading back to the hospital. Rudy sighed. There was a medium-sized pooch, maybe a beagle, sniffing at the remains of a dead man in dress clothes face down at the front edge of the fire, and two corgis playing tug of war with one of the guy's shoes. There were a few dogs at the perimeter of the tent area, and two out in the meadow jumping in the high grass. Only the playful ones had remained for show in the wake of this brutal demonstration of blood and justice. They were his emblems. Absolute irony.

Like that loving spaniel showing up right at the moment he and Caroline had gone their separate ways, his little ears flopping all over the place, tail wagging like mad.

Rudy's breath caught in his throat.

Killian = Patricia.

Oh yes. It fit her like a glove, didn't it . . . turning herself into an entity that would avoid all suspicion, a cute little dog he'd let close to him. She'd been watching him from that intimate perspective, waiting patiently, nuzzling in his ear the moment before he made love to another woman, lying at his feet while he planned his campaign.

And she'd used his own strategy against him, hadn't she? While he'd occupied Caroline with setting up the fireworks, he'd been free to solicit her mother and the other patients. And while his biggest dogs had borne his soldiers, he'd left the basement unattended.

This was Patricia's chance to get Caroline alone there and kill her, slowly by torture most probably. Rudy would go down in history as the one to liberate the witches, but Patricia was to make sure he'd do it without the one who'd meant the most to him in the end, breakup or no.

Rudy looked around his feet and got incredibly lucky. One of the sick had dropped his holsters there in the grass, Gus Glick his name was, and he had insisted on wearing his pistols at the hip like the cowboys he'd idolized so much as a boy. Rudy had been fastening the buckles for him when the fireworks went off. Clearly, he'd failed to snap home the clasps properly, and the weapons had dropped, leaving Gus an unarmed rider. It hadn't mattered. Like Caroline's mother had done, Rudy recalled Gus Glick jumping off his mount mid-stride to fly into one of the Hell's Angels, rolling with him in the dirt and winding up in a top position, biting at his throat and ripping up strips of flesh.

"Thanks, Gus," Rudy muttered, slipping both pistols from their sheaths. Caroline and the mutt had a healthy head start, but he thought it was possible to avoid this tragedy if he pushed it.

He strode back to the edge of the football field.

Then he started to run.

He just couldn't catch up. The river behind Caroline's house was a mere quarter-mile away from the high school, at least when you avoided the jogs, U-turns, and detours you'd need to make if using a GPS. A straight beeline across the landscape made it a hop and a skip, but that only applied if you were limber enough to hop and skip, both of which Rudy was not. Out front past the high school and into the woods beyond he found he had to stop constantly to fight his way through patches of brushwork, nests of upturned roots, shanks, and trunks crossed up and splintered.

Just when he thought he'd found a lane it got blocked, and climbing over piles of logs was risky, the bases often shifting beneath him as they had on the cleft above the signage grove, making him pause and reroute. He finally made it up what had been a long slope with a gradual incline, which crested a valley of sorts. He leaned over, guns to his knees, breath heaving. Down the slope at the base of the gulley were the remains of a wooden fence that must have bordered an area back in the nineteenth century, and up the twin rise on the other side he thought he saw movement disappearing over the bluff. He had closed some of the distance, but not nearly enough. In the back of his mind he had entertained the dark possibility that Patricia would transform herself out here in the dark amidst the fallen wood, then turn and stick a shank of splintered oak through Caroline's chest—but that just wouldn't be "poetic" enough for someone like her, would it? No. Straight murder didn't have enough "craft" in it, and Patricia was not one to fall short on "message and delivery." It was clear now. She had been a secret witness to his and Caroline's affair, she had snuggled between them right up until the moment of consummation, and she was going to address this at the point of original sin.

He burst down the hill taking crazy chances, hurdling trunks, dancing between obstructions. At the bottom, he tripped over the broken base of a splintered fencepost and almost went into a headlong belly-flop, windmilling his arms, barely retaining his balance. The final incline was choppy, littered with rock and trunk and branch, each step a new jigsaw puzzle to navigate through like a cross-hatch of gargantuan pick-up sticks after a toss. He reached the top of the rise, face drenched with cold sweat, clothes sticking to him, his breath a sharp scissor in his side. There down the bluff was the river, the log bridge leading to the camouflaged tarp opening, and Caroline following Killian across it. Rudy took a deep breath to attempt a warning cry, but the dog put on a burst of new speed, disappearing through the cutout with Caroline following two steps behind.

Rudy shouted her name, but a second too late, the sound of the river drowning it to further insignificance.

He sidestepped down to the log bridge. It seemed to take forever, and Rudy was moaning now, muttering to himself, blood pounding in his temples. He almost slipped at the bottom edge on a dark swath of ice-covered pine needles, and even with cautious stepwork the log seemed more slippery and treacherous than earlier in the day. Arms out now, he became that idiot highwire guy working the slow drama of the pass.

Once he finally pushed through the cutout it was a sprint to the finish, and he tore down the tunnel with all that he had, breath rasping, arms pumping. Somewhere in the back of his mind he formulated the symbolic connection that this enclosure was vaginal, but going back in sure as hell didn't represent life or birth. Light poured out of the basement opening up ahead, and something ran suddenly over the lip. Rudy came to an abrupt halt, feet scratching in the dirt, and he raised both firearms.

It was Killian, scampering down the ramp.

Rudy almost shot the dog right there, but as it bolted past him yelping and yipping down the tunnel, he heard some kind of struggle ensuing up there in the room, grunts, short shouts, footwear scraping along the concrete.

Rudy ran up the ramp.

And there in the light cast by the bare bulb were two Carolines, both with identical three-quarter sleeve Tribal Love shirts and pinstriped train engineer hats, both of them bleeding, one from the left nostril, the other along the cheek in a dripping slash. They had fought their way over to the gun lockers and each had a pair of pistols they'd just aimed at each other. Rudy raised both his weapons and each of the girls aimed a weapon back at him, one with the left hand, the other the right, and there they all stood, breathing heavily, a six-gun triangle.

"Rudy!" the woman on the left said. "She can read biographies just as she can clone a set of jeans and a top. She knows everything I know."

"She was the English sheepdog with the sad face, Rudy," the other one said. "It was perfect cover, mothering the spaniel who got all the attention. She waited until you emptied the basement and waited here for you."

"No!" the first one cried. "She gives away information that seems important, but stands irrelevant now."

"Don't fall for it, Rudy. She's too perfect. I did just give useless information to you, and it's because I'm nervous as hell. She's playing the both of us to the tee, three moves ahead, and no one can think that well under pressure."

"Ignore that! She messed up and now she's covering."

Rudy fought to think of something personal that only Caroline would know.

"Why are you angry with me?" he said softly.

"Because you screwed me over!" both said, unfortunately. A pause. Then Rudy said, "Considering the paradigm I've been following throughout my career with my research and my writing, what do you think the title of my *next* article would be . . . the one I haven't even started brainstorming yet, quick, before Patricia can read the other's biography."

Both spat out a title, the one on the left—*"Word, An Aesthetic Function,"* and the one on the right—*"The Sacrifice of Syntax in Lyrical Modules."*

Rudy blinked and said, "Back your claim, quick now."

"Your work has always been a celebration of phonetics and the beauty of sound and inference in oral tradition. You never gave up on the poetry of it," said the woman on the left, followed directly by the one on the right who blurted, "It's a plea for grammatical precision even if the linguistic rhythm is compromised. Teacher first, artist later."

That got him. Patricia had always claimed with an absolute finality her intensive lack of interest in his writing, that it was too lofty for anyone to really enjoy. She'd never read a word. So he had thought. But here, there was no doubt his wife had secretly immersed herself in his work all these years. He'd never discussed it, but his writing had always reflected his personal battle between virtuoso freedom and mechanical discipline. He still didn't know which side of the fence he finally fell on, and the choice one way or the other was not in any biography, not Caroline's, not even his.

Both women were staring at each other in bald hatred, and the one on the left with the bleeding nostril suddenly surrendered to a look glazed over with realization.

"Rudy," she said. "The riddle can't be solved here like this, don't you see? Even the fear of guns is a shared aspect between us. We're so terrified to miss we can't take the initial shot. And we're dead equal in our passions for you, at the same time lost together in the darkness of your betrayals. We could go on like this forever. In effect, we're the same woman now."

She took the gun covering Rudy and brought it beneath her chin.

"I think I can conquer this fear of pulling the trigger, Rudy. And this way, I won't miss."

"No!" he shouted, and the report of the pistol cut his plea to the quick. The bullet burst through the back of Caroline's head in a red plume that spattered the gun lockers, and Rudy promptly fired at the woman on the right. It shattered her breastplate in a bloody implosion and she fell hard on her bottom, skidding from the weighty import, her face coming back to true form—blooming rounder and wider. By the time she banged against the steel doors she'd fully transformed back to Patricia, double chin, head lolling, eyes fluttering. Rudy stepped in and stood over her, guns aimed and ready. She focused on him then and managed,

"I always just wanted you to love me, Rudy."

Her lashes did their final flamenco, then fell wide open on eyes rolled back showing all their whites.

The Lord doth not kill directly. Unless he has to.

Rudy moved off. He wanted to cry, but couldn't. He wanted to shake with emotion, scream with it, but didn't. He was cold and dry and something looked odd, familiar, a blurred context from before brought to sudden perspective. It was a crack in the basement floor, a long one in a squiggle shape, the two women lying dead across the top side of it. He went over to Caroline's body and lifted her shirt, exposing the hip. There on her skin, the tattoo with the squiggled line was raised on her skin, highlighting the two dots above it. Slowly, they canceled each other out, fading, disappearing, this time for good.

Chapter 4
Wanderer

Citizens:

There is a man named Rudy Barnes who wanders by night in the company of wolves. He is wanted by the unified authorities, but has so far evaded capture. Some believe he has been given temporary shelter (and asylum) by renegade groups of Ancient Sisters, those who assimilated before the identification and tagging laws went into effect, and others insist that he lives in the wild. Regardless, there is no *other* malignant entity at work in the tri-state area, residing in the underground piping system, exercising some kind of hazardous control over rodents. It is believed by Washington experts and Harvard sociologists that this demon-myth was created by Professor Barnes as a way to rationalize his own actions through tainted comparison, therefore altering (and lowering) the standard of ethics formed in this great and powerful land. It is important for us to recognize such dangerous propaganda and to rest assured that there is no, repeat, no monster living in the sewers.

Professor Rudolph Benjamin Barnes, however, is a dangerous fugitive who wears a mask and cloak, and during this time of rebuilding he has been reported to have come upon groups of militia, ritualistic cults bent on the continued purification of the human bloodline. Similar to the Massacre at Runnemede Meadow, this criminal has met these extremists with deadly force. This coincides with a lethal wave of copycats, lone gunmen who have recently surfaced nationwide, claiming when incarcerated to be prophets following the path and word of the Fluttering Cross.

Please know that this brand of reciprocal violence is considered terroristic on both sides and will not be tolerated.

Please know that all temporary camps and mobile developments have been deemed humane by the U.S. Department of Housing, and all Ancient Sisters are hereby required by federal law to register at one such county facility by the end of the work week at midnight.

Please know that any natural-born citizen who escorts an Ancient Sister to one such facility will receive a three percent tax credit retroactive to this fiscal year. Any natural-born citizen who reports criminal activity in the form of communal gatherings of Ancient Sisters outside the boundaries of state-legislated space will receive a month's worth of food credits, and wood chipper vouchers.

Please know that any Ancient Sister masquerading as a natural-born citizen will be immediately arrested for treason.

Please know that even though there is anatomical evidence suggesting that the Ancient Sisters once possessed abnormally rapid birth cycles, we have determined that their abrupt divorce from the grain has triggered a sort of counter-evolutionary trait indicating a more standard nine-month gestation period. Nevertheless, physical contact between Ancient Sisters and natural-born citizens will be considered a felony (until our scientists have completed the above-mentioned studies), and all Ancient Sisters must undergo pregnancy tests on the third of each month. In conjunction with the former, all citizens must register according to Social Security number for a routine physical on the tenth of each month at appointed sites listed on our web page by state and township. For more details about various post-test treatments and patient rights, see section 49143 of the Federal Fertility Code, Hall of Records, Washington D.C., by appointment only.

Please know that in the time of this great crisis, cooperation, order, and subservience are of the utmost importance. After the winter, when the roads and properties have been cleared and the

damages assessed, financial recovery plans will be instituted and restitutions made. It is projected that by mid-May, funds allocated for national infrastructure will be freed up for the purpose of constructing a settlement province for the Ancient Sisters consisting of vast landscape areas in Wyoming, Montana, Idaho, and the Dakotas. Mandatory relocation will begin in the latter part of the summer.

In all, we wish to extend our appreciation in advance for your patience, your kindness, your willingness to sacrifice what had been your well-deserved and expected comforts, and especially your ability to remain calm and rational within a paradigm of national, patriotic obedience.

And finally, if you happen to see the man with his mask of gauze and cloak of canvas, please do not approach him. Immediately inform your nearest agency of law enforcement and rest assured that the authorities will prevail.

For Rudy Barnes is dangerous, but he is not any sort of a god.

And for all his guns and dogs and video clips, he's just a man in the end, bound to the night, and destined to walk at the fringe on his own.